Soul Survivor

Also by the Author

Out of Body, Into Mind

Beyond Skepticism,
All the Way to Enlightenment

Soul Survivor

by

Stephen Hawley Martin

RICHMOND, VIRGINIA

FIRST EDITION   ⁷/₀₁

First Printing, 1996

ISBN 0-9646601-8-0

About the Cover

The front cover photograph was taken by the author at twilight on a beach near Propriano, Corsica.

For Hilary

Being is spirit, and matter is only a manifestation of spirit,
and that which is manifested is never the entire truth of
that which supports it, but only one aspect, a side,
a perspective; and the spirit is always greater than matter,
animates it, gives it form, supports it."

U. S. Anderson
The Secret of Secrets

Prologue

The soul mate of Linda Cheswick and his companion angel, Otto, hovered on the astral plane in the apartment of Rick Henderson, advertising executive and crack head. They observed Rick, who sat on the sofa working with a butane burner and other apparatus. He held the blue flame beneath a worn metal tablespoon filled with white crystalline pebbles.

The soul mate communicated with his companion by means of telepathy. "I thought they sniffed the stuff, Otto. You know, up the nose, through a straw?"

"You're thinking of cocaine. Mild by comparison. This stuff's going to kill him."

"Good Lord, Otto, look at his aura. Brown as mud."

"Whoop, there he goes. His lungs are full. Won't be long now—may require a second hit."

Linda's soul mate noticed the dark force hovering near Rick. "Depressing. He's headed for total isolation. Lost. Not even a family member here to greet him."

Otto said, "It's a rather large understatement to say he hasn't made good choices in this lifetime."

"Isn't it time to get the girl to call, Otto? We've go to make sure the body gets revived."

"You're absolutely sure you want to go through with this?"

"We've discussed all that, Otto. I've got to."

"Remember—just don't create any negative karma, okay? That's the danger."

"Here he comes, Otto. Go to the girl. Quick."

Otto was gone the moment the spirit of Rick Henderson exited. The dark force engulfed it instantly. Linda Cheswick's soul mate cringed from the silent scream, so utterly helpless and forlorn, but wasted no time slipping into the lifeless body.

The soul mate's astral body was too big for Rick's physical form. He contracted, then expanded slightly, then found he was incorrectly aligned. He wiggled, squirmed to bring himself to the proper angle.

He could feel the body around him now. The flesh was heavy, cold. Rigor mortus already was setting in.

Concentrate on the heart. Think of it beating, pumping blood. Make the blood move. Think, think, think. Get the brain in place. Line it up. Think! Yes, that's it. Yes!

It beat once. Twice.

Keep it going. Yes, it was going. Faintly but going.

Now. The brain. Loaded with junk. Heavy. Spinning.

Concentrate. Remember.

Don't let the amnesia take over. Don't let it. Concentrate. Remember why you're doing this—remember. Remember why you're taking this incredible risk—remember. Why, why, why.

It's for her. You're doing it for her. Don't let that thought slip away.

What's that? A bell? Ringing?

He had not heard sound in so long that it hurt. Pain shot through his thoughts.

He had forgotten sound could hurt.

The body was so heavy. So cold. Chills. He must animate it. Shivering. Shivering. So cold.

Pump the heart. Pump it. Make it go. Elevate the blood pressure!

He must remember why he was here, why he was doing this. He must. For her, it was for her. He was doing it for her.

8

The ringing, incessant ringing. Why? Was that the telephone?

Otto, of course. He was doing this for Linda. Otto had gotten the girlfriend to call so that she would send an ambulance. He must answer the phone. He must do it for Linda or Linda's soul would be recycled.

How? How would he do it?

He must lift the arm, the arm of this lifeless body.

No, it wasn't lifeless. The heart was beating. Faintly. Make it beat.

He must at least knock the receiver off the cradle. Make the effort. More. More effort!

All you can muster!

Yes. Good. It was done.

"Rick? Is that you?"

Make a sound. Make the larynx vibrate. Force air through it. Do it now.

"Help. Meg. I need help." His voice was hoarse and soft.

"Rick? Are you all right?"

"Send help. Please. Help."

But each incarnation, you might say, has a potentiality,
and the mission of life is to live that potentiality.

Joseph Campbell
(1904-1987)

One

Linda Cheswick stepped between the French doors that opened onto the veranda and looked down upon the lawn shrouded in steamy mist rising with the sun. As always it seemed too luscious to be real. Her gaze skimmed the undulating turf that dipped and rolled three hundred yards on either side of the alley of trees to the brown ribbon in the distance, the James River making its way unhurriedly from the Blue Ridge Mountains to the Hampton Roads. Here and there beads of moisture sparkled. Vibrant shades of yellow and green poked through the haze. Soon the sky would be that bright, brilliant blue almost never seen in summer. The arrival of oppressive heat and humidity would be postponed for yet another day.

She leaned against the door jam, blew her nose, stared at the tissue, folded it. Absentmindedly, she stuffed it in a pocket. Tall, big boned, with auburn hair and freckles, she had the milky-white complexion of a redhead. A thousand years ago she might have been a Celtic huntress from the heart of Gaul or the highlands of Scotland. Strong, rugged, ready to raise her sword to slay a beast, or to strike the wicked Grendel down with an arm ripped from his own body. But the twenty-first century lay just ahead in this life. Rather than building muscle with a sword and an axe, she had done so with a hockey stick and a tennis racket. Now in the prime of life physically—twenty-five years old, soon to be twenty-six—she worked out on the Stair Master and the treadmill at the Club to keep herself in shape.

She breathed in cool morning air, wiped away a tear that trickled down her cheek. A voice from behind jolted her from reverie.

"It's your turn, Linda. Your turn to see her."

She turned. Dr. James stood there with his shoulders slumped. "You need to know—I'm afraid she doesn't have much time."

A nurse stood by, her eyes round and dark. She bowed her head as Linda gently pushed open the door.

Morning light poured in through the large bay window creating a checkerboard pattern on the white linen comforter cover. The old woman turned her head slowly, with effort, tethered by tubes that spouted from her nose and led to an oxygen tank. Recognition unfolded in her eyes as the muscles of her face relaxed.

"Linda. I knew you'd come."

"Oh, Minnie. You know I'd be here, no matter what."

"It won't be long, Linda. I won't be here . . . much longer."

"Don't say that, Minnie. Think positive, remember?"

"Am. . . . Won't need these tubes where I'm headed."

Linda searched her pocket for a clean tissue.

Minnie touched her hand. "I'm going to be with Robbie. He's waiting for me. I've seen him."

Linda wiped her eyes. "I'm gonna miss you, Minnie."

"Don't cry, Linda . . . promise me."

Linda leaned forward.

"Promise me, Linda, you'll make sure Live Oaks stays . . . stays the way it is. It's—it's the roots of the Cheswick family, your roots, Linda. . . . Keep it . . . keep it as it is. Pass it on. Pass it to your own children."

Linda touched her frail hand. "I don't understand, Minnie. Are you saying Live Oaks will come to me?"

Minnie looked past her. "Robbie?" She struggled to rise up, then fell back, her eyes closed.

Linda gasped as though a strap had been wrenched around her chest. She hurried from the room.

"Doctor James, come quickly."

12

"Yes," he said and darted past.

Linda followed. The doctor bent down and took Minnie's wrist, held it, looked up at Linda.

After a few seconds he said, "No. She's still with us."

Linda exhaled, turned, walked from the room. She placed one foot in front of the other and somehow managed to pass through the house to the veranda, all the while staring at the crumpled tissue. Then, as though Minnie were standing beside coaching her, she forced herself to throw back her shoulders and stand erect. Her gaze swept the lawn, paused for a moment at the gazebo on the knoll, stopped on the alley of huge live oaks that led to the landing on the river. The trees. They were so amazing, so lush. Like one living organism, the way the branches intertwined to form a tunnel—a canopy. Yes, many trees perhaps, but a single living organism.

She crossed the bricks to the entrance way, looked up at the gnarled old limbs. In her mind's eye flashed a procession of men and women moving toward her. She stepped aside and watched them pass, dressed in their eighteenth century garb. Ladies with parasols and broad hoop skirts. Men in knickers, felt top hats and frilly white collars. She remembered now. They lived here. In this place. This space between the trees. Just as they lived in the drawing room and the library and in the old warming pantry. When she had been a child, she had talked to them and they had talked to her. They had been as alive and real to her as her grandmother, as the servants, as her friends at school.

But that was impossible. Her imagination surely.

They were gone now. Yes. She must have imagined it. Imagined it now. Imagined it then. There was nothing in this alley of trees but squirrels and birds and chipmunks.

Linda had learned about the trees when still a rough and tumble tomboy. Her nanny had been more interested in Nancy Drew than in her and Linda had stolen away, shinnied up an oak and scooted out a limb. As she reached for a higher branch she'd dropped her doll.

"Hey, what are you doing up there?" a boy had said. He was older than she and tall for his age.

She looked past him to the ground. It suddenly seemed a long way down. The boy picked up the doll.

"Climbing," Linda said.

"I can see that." He squinted one eye. "Does your nanny know?"

"She's on the veranda."

"You better climb down—or she's gonna be mad."

"I don't care."

Linda felt a fluttery sensation in her abdomen. She hadn't realized how high she'd climbed. Perspiration was forming on her brow.

"You know, that limb might break if you don't come down off it. You don't want that limb to break, do you?"

Linda wrapped her arms around it. "No."

He shook his head. "Your great, great, great something grand daddy had those trees planted. They're old—real old. They're so old they're in the history books, and I'll tell you one thing that's certain—something that old might break."

Linda looked down and wished that fluttery feeling would go away.

"Hang down," he said. "I'll catch you. Drop your legs and hang."

"I don't want to."

"You don't want your nanny or your grandmother to see you up there, do you?"

"I don't wanna come down."

"Sure you do. All you have to do is hang down. I told you—I'll catch you."

It took more coaxing, but she finally did hang from the limb by her hands. The boy grabbed her feet and then her legs, and lowered her to the ground.

"What's your name?" she said.

"Charles. I know your name, Linda."

"How'd you know about my great-something grandfather and the trees?"

He sat on the ground and leaned against one of them. Linda took her doll and kneeled beside.

"I expect everyone around here knows about the trees. They're old, all right, real old. More than two hundred and fifty years, they say." He looked up. "Your great-something grand daddy had them planted before the main house was even finished because he wanted folks to have shade when they walked up to it from the river. Back in those days, the river was the highway—it's how folks got from one place to

14

another." He put his hands behind his head and gazed into the canopy. "I've been told it was *my* great-something grand daddy who planted them—since my ancestors were the ones who did all the work."

"Why'd they do all the work?"

"They had to—they didn't have a choice." He looked at her. "Your great-something grand daddy *owned* my great-something grand daddy."

Linda stopped walking and looked at the tree Charles had sat against that day. The two of them had become friends, had remained close while growing up. Since then they had gone separate ways. She missed him, but was happy for him, too. He was a resident in surgery at the Medical College of Virginia.

She turned and looked at the house through the tunnel of trees. A swelling sensation inflating her chest as she studied the details: The black slate roof, white-washed dental molding, massive chimneys, handmade red brick, stately Georgian design. The house had an indelible place in history enjoyed by only a handful of Colonial homes along the James: Shirley, Berkeley, Sherwood Forest, Westover, Carter's Grove . . . Live Oaks. How thrilling and how fitting that it would be hers. The house, the trees. In a way they were her family. Not the building itself, nor the individual trees, but the space inside the house and between the trees. It was where her ancestors lived. Or had lived. They were her family, the ghosts who had populated her youth.

Growing up, her classmates at St. Catherine's School had come home each day to their mothers and their sisters and their brothers. She had come home to Live Oaks and the ghosts. And in the mornings, her friends had been driven to school by their mothers in car pools, or by their fathers on the way to work.

Not Linda.

One day stuck in her mind. A teacher opened the back door of Minnie's black Cadillac station wagon and Linda stepped out with her book bag over her shoulder. She fell in step with two of her classmates.

"Is that a hearse?" Mary-Randolph Hinton had asked.

"What's a hearse?" Linda said.

Emily Miller said, "A hearse is a car that carries dead people. I got to ride in one when my grandmother died."

The two girls and Linda walked toward the front door of the lower school.

"No, that's not what it is, then," Linda said. "Henry calls it a station wagon."

"Who's Henry?" Mary-Randolph asked.

"He's the man who drives me here," Linda said.

"Why doesn't your mommy or daddy drive you to school?" Emily said.

Linda felt a hand clutch at her throat. "I don't have a mommy or daddy."

The three of them stopped inside the door.

Emily said, "Why not?"

Mary-Randolph pulled Emily toward the lockers. "Don't ask her that," she said in a whisper. "Don't you know her mommy and daddy are dead?"

Linda was aware now that children could be cruel to one another and not even realize it. But that didn't make the pain she'd felt back then any less.

She sighed and started toward the house. Live Oaks was proof she wasn't created out of whole cloth, that she had flesh and blood ancestors. It had never been more apparent to her than in the sixth grade, when her glass came here for a picnic and a tour.

"Wow, Linda," Emily Miller had said. "Mrs. Hinnley said your great-great-great grandfather was a colonel in the Revolutionary War, and that George Washington and Thomas Jefferson had dinner with him in your dining room."

Linda recalled how her lungs had filled. "They were on the way to Williamsburg."

She, Emily and Mary-Randolph had been walking toward the gazebo. Mary-Randolph had pointed to the field beyond it.

"Are those your horses, Linda?"

"Yes—that one's Millie and the other's Jacques."

"Do you ride them, Linda?" Emily asked.

"Oh, sure," Linda said. "But I like Travis-George the best. You can see him way down at the other end."

"Wow," both Emily and Mary-Randolph said at the same time.

Wow, thought Linda. That had been a long, long time ago. She gazed at the same field. Now the son of Travis-George was grazing

16

there.

Linda breathed in the odor of hay and manure, felt the warm sun on her cheeks. She'd assumed Live Oaks would pass to William, but from what Minnie had said that did not appear to be what was going to happen.

It was fitting that it should be put in her hands and if caring for a place, loving it, meant anything. William had always been so blasé about Live Oaks—had taken it for granted. Now, the deed would be recorded in her name, and she would be its owner and its keeper—a conduit for its safe passage to future descendants of Robert Cheswick. She would care for it and cherish it as much as the first owner had.

That evening, three places were set with the best family china and crystal in the main dining room. The glow of candles atop silver candle sticks reflected in the dark, polished wood of the Queen Anne table. Linda sat across from Dr. James. They both ate soup.

"Sorry Uncle William's stood us up. I don't know where he is."

"Don't worry about it, Linda. It's a treat to eat at this table—where the future of this nation was discussed and decided upon. I only wish this dinner were under happier circumstances."

"You're nice to stay. Poor Minnie."

A man's voice said, "So whatta ya think, Doctor? When's she gonna die?"

Linda looked up. It was Uncle William, obviously drunk. She watched him take a sip from a paper cup.

The doctor stood.

"Naw, don't get up." William patted the air as he moved unsteadily to the chair at the head of the table. He sat down, picked up the servant's bell, held it over his head and shook it. "Mosell! Soup for the lord of the manor."

"Looks like you're pretty far into your cups, Uncle William," Linda said.

"Got an excuse. Ma mother's dying."

"To answer your question, William, I'm afraid it would surprise me if your mother hung on for more than a day or so."

Mosell put a bowl of soup on William's plate.

"What's this?"

"Vichyssoise," Mosell said.

"Cold leek soup? Psst! How 'bout bringing me a ham sandwich?"

She frowned. "Whatever you say, Mr. William."

"Uncle William, this is only the first course," Linda said. "Mosell has a roast prepared."

A silly smile appeared on William's face. "A roast? Yeah, that sounds good. Potatoes, too, I imagine. What say I skip the cold soup and move on to that?"

Mosell left with a scowl.

William blinked. "You were saying, Doctor?"

He cleared his throat. "Technically, your mother has pneumonia. But it's really a side effect of emphysema."

William took a pack of Marlboros from his breast pocket, offered them around, stuck one in his mouth and searched in his pockets for a match.

"Her lungs are filling up with fluid. There really isn't anything we can do." Dr. James shook his head. "I'd take a lesson from her if I were you, William. Cigarettes did it."

"Ma mother's eighty-one, Doctor. I should live so long." He pulled one of the candles to him. The flame engulfed the end of the paper cylinder and turned the last few millimeters black.

"Really, Uncle William," Linda said. "If you must smoke, do you have to do it at the dinner table?"

"I can do what I want—s'my house."

Ah, but you're wrong, Linda thought.

William picked up the bell and rang it hard.

"Mosell, an ash tray. And some wine, a bottle of St. Emilion. That'll go nicely with a roast."

Linda was relieved when dinner was over and she could go upstairs. Uncle William was obnoxious and an embarrassment. She had never cared for him. He always had seemed to have a chip on his shoulder toward her. Toward everyone, for that matter. But he was Minnie's son, and with his mother on her death bed, Linda supposed his drunkenness could be excused. People handled grief in different ways.

She felt an enormous sense of loss, too. Or maybe what she felt was guilt. Guilt that she'd never really gotten close to Minnie. Oh, Linda respected her. Had learned from her. But affection for her was not something she honestly could say she'd ever felt.

Still, there was hollowness inside, and the tears kept welling up. Whatever caused them, she knew it would only add to her pain to try to fill the emptiness with alcohol.

She sat at her vanity and looked at herself in the mirror. A redness rimmed her hazel-green eyes, and her cheeks were flushed. Affection or no affection, the passing of her grandmother would be a loss. Other than Uncle William, Minnie was the only blood relative she knew.

Her father, Robert Hilliard Cheswick VI, had brought her to Live Oaks to live with Minnie a long, long time ago. Linda had not yet turned four, but she vividly recalled the sense of anticipation, and the anxiety she had felt on the drive along the dirt road from Route 5.

"Are we almost there, Daddy?" she'd asked.

"It's a mile and a half from the highway to the house, Lily," her Daddy said. "But yes—we're almost there."

Linda was afraid to meet her grandmother.

"Where's Mommy?" Linda asked.

Her Daddy didn't answer. He cut the wheel to dodge a goose.

"Where's Mommy, Daddy?"

He sighed. "I told you, Linda. I told you a hundred and fifty times. I don't know where she is. Wish I did. I know you miss her. I miss her, too."

They came around a curve and her Daddy pointed. "There it is, Linda."

Linda had never seen such a big house, red brick, black slate, white wood trim. It was flanked by huge trees with dark trunks, and surrounded by lush green lawn. The flagstone walkways were crisply edged. Tree wells brimmed with chocolate-colored mulch.

"Of course, this is the back," Daddy said. "The other side's the front. It faces the River." He looked at her, touched her hand. "There's something I want you to promise me, Linda. Will you do that?"

"What, Daddy?"

"Don't be asking your grandmother where your Mommy is, okay? She doesn't know, either, and it'll only make her angry."

Linda shook off the memory, picked up a brush, ran it through her hair. Not long after she had arrived at Live Oaks, Daddy had left her, too. When she'd learned he would be going away, she had cried and cried.

"Why do you have to leave, Daddy? Why?" She buried her face in his chest.

He folded his arms around her. "I'm in the Army, Linda. They tell me where I have to go. But I'll be back. I promise I'll be back. And maybe they'll send me someplace where you can come with me next time."

Linda brushed her hair harder. More tears welled at the memory of that day six months later. The wind had whipped up from the river in swirls and cut through her sweater and blouse as if all she wore were goose bumps. She'd gone to her room and occupied herself with a tea party for Raggedty Ann and Pooh. The Mad Hatter was her role and she was midway through pouring half a cup when a shrill sound brought her hand to a halt and sent a ripple cascading down her spine.

Her first reaction had been that it must be the ghost of the Confederate soldier, who like Ann Frank was said to have hidden in the attic. He must have been reliving his impalement by a Yankee's bayonet.

Then came another screech and a long, low moan.

Linda crept onto the gallery above the entrance foyer and listened. The sobbing came not from the attic but from somewhere on the first floor.

She descended the long curved staircase slowly, pausing halfway down. No doubt about it. Someone or something was in pain.

By the time she reached the black and white tiles there was no longer any doubt. The location was the ante room, Minnie's office, to the right of the enormous front door of polished walnut.

Cautiously, Linda peeked in. "Minnie?"

Minnie was flat on her back on the sofa. Her head rolled toward Linda to reveal swollen, red-rimmed eyes.

"Are you all right, Minnie?"

"Not now, Linda. Please leave me alone."

Minnie had never actually said it, but Linda had no doubt now that Minnie believed that Linda's mother was to blame for her father's death. She could almost hear the words that were never spoken. *If the tramp hadn't run off, Robbie would never have joined the Army.*

"It's your Daddy, Linda. He's, he's dead—gone forever. Killed in the war in Vietnam." Minnie took her in her arms. "I'm, I'm so, so sorry, Linda. This shouldn't happen to anyone—especially to a child. Oh Lord, Linda. I told him not to, I told him not to join the Army."

Linda put down the brush and wiped away the tears. She never would have known anything at all about her mother if it hadn't been for the letters she'd found when she was a teenager. She'd been searching Minnie's desk for a stamp, had felt a surge of joy when she recognized her Daddy's handwriting.

She was sitting on the floor reading them when Minnie came into the room.

"Linda, what are you doing?"

"Just reading some of Dad's old letters. What's wrong with that?"

"They aren't yours. They were written to me."

"He was *my* dad."

Minnie sat in a chair and let out a sigh. "Yes, I suppose. But it would have been nicer if you'd asked."

"Why didn't you ever tell me about my mother, Minnie?"

Minnie cut her eyes toward Linda. "My blood boils whenever I think about her. She was from the wrong side of the tracks, Linda, and she behaved that way, deserted you and Robbie. If you can't say something nice about someone, don't say anything, and that's precisely what I've done."

"These letters don't say she deserted us. Daddy said she disappeared. He had no idea what happened to her. Maybe she got amnesia or something."

Minnie shook her head. "Oh, Linda. Amnesia only happens in pulp novels and B movies. It's more likely your mother came down with a case of wanderlust and took off. That's what happens to people without a sense of family, or roots."

Linda screwed the lid on the jar of moisturizing cream. That had been almost ten years ago. She'd thought and wondered about her mother all her life. What did she look like? What had happened to her? Linda couldn't remember a thing. It were as though her memories began in the car with her Daddy as they drove to Live Oaks. She hadn't even known her mother's name until she found the letters. Now she knew her first name was Nina. From the return address on the envelopes she also knew the address in Baltimore where they had lived together as a family.

Her mother must be out there somewhere, though. For years Linda had hoped, prayed her mother would return and rescue her from being an orphan, rescue her from being different from her classmates. Now she felt a strange sense of ambivalence and resentment. After all, she'd abandoned Linda, hadn't she? Perhaps it was best if they never met. At least now Linda would have Live Oaks. That would be family enough.

Linda slid between crisp clean sheets and looked up at the four posts. Generations of Cheswicks had slept here in this room, many in this bed. She owed them everything: her character, her sense of history, her roots. She'd give back what she had been given. She'd deliver Live Oaks to future generations.

Linda drifted to sleep, but bolted up some hours later as though she'd been held under water by some ghoulish prankster and was suddenly set free. She gasped for air as she got her bearings. It was dark and the light from the moon cast shadows of mullions on the lightweight summer blanket.

She struggled to remember the dream she had just escaped. She'd been on the bank of the River. Yes. But the river bank had not been the same as it was now. The house hadn't yet been built. The bend in the River was the same, and she could imagine that the land undulated to the knoll where the house now stood, but there was no meadow, no alley of live oaks. Trees were all that she could see, a virgin forest of walnuts, hickory, oaks, and other hardwoods.

The River was its usual muddy self. That she remembered. And now she remembered what had startled her so. It had been a group of Indians in canoes, a hunting party. At first when they had paddled toward her she'd been amused, half expecting to see Chief Powhatan or Pocahontas, somehow knowing this was a dream. It had to be a dream. It was true that Pocahontas and Powhatan had lived nearby, but that was four hundred years ago.

They had seemed so severe when they stepped ashore.

"Get away from here. Go on," she'd shouted as if they'd been a pack of dogs. "This is my land, my house. You're trespassing."

22

"You cannot own the land," the leader of the group had said. "No one can own the land. The land, the earth, the sky owns you, not the other way around."

The next morning, a knock on the door awoke Linda.
She sat up, struggled to orient herself.
"Come in."
The door opened slowly. Dr. James looked at her with sadness in his eyes. "She's gone, Linda. Your grandmother is . . . dead."
Linda gasped. She had known this moment would arrive, but was unprepared for the sudden tightness in her chest.
"She died in her sleep, Linda. It was a peaceful death. As peaceful as death can be. A blessing, really."

It was sunny and breezy a few days later when Linda's grandmother was buried next to the grandfather Linda never knew in the plot on the hill that overlooked the bend in the river. Mourners walked back to the house in silence and clustered on the veranda where coffee and pastries awaited them. They sipped and munched, and after a few moments, spoke in subdued, hushed tones. Everyone except William. It seemed strange for a man who had just lost his mother to be so cheerful. He slapped a golfing buddy on the back and said he'd be back in a second, then reappeared with bottles in each hand and another under his arm.
"Brandy, anyone? Kalua? B and B? Schnapps? No sense in being morbid."
People turned and looked, eyebrows raised.
He tried to pour cognac in Linda's teacup. She covered it with her hand.
He shrugged and poured himself a healthy dose, tossed it down, poured another.
"I can see it now." His hand swept toward the river. "A road, bending that way. Four-hundred-thou—no, make that five-hundred-thousand dollar houses on each side. Quarter acre lots with no view that go for a hundred and fifty grand. A dock with motorboats tied up. A seafood restaurant with a fake lighthouse." He poured himself more cognac. "And next to it, where those damn oaks are, that's where I'm

gonna put the condos. Studios'll sell for over a hundred thou."

"What are you talking about, Uncle William?"

He took a swig; looked at her over the rim of his glass. "I'm talking about the exclusive and very, very expensive development I'm putting up right here." He sniffed, gazed toward the meadow. "I'm talking about an eighteen-hole championship golf course. I'm talking about how I'm gonna be a rich sonofabitch, that's what."

"What do you mean, putting up here? I thought—"

"What *did* you think, Linda dear?"

"Well, from what Minnie said, I thought Live Oaks would pass to me."

He stuck his nose in the brandy snifter and inhaled. "You'll get your inheritance. Robbie's share. But I get Live Oaks."

"But, then, why did she say?—"

"She did, did she? Who knows? She never did understand legal stuff—wills and trusts. Anyway, what do you care? I told you, you'll get yours."

"But Live Oaks? You can't turn it into a housing development."

"I can damn well do what I please. It's mine, or will be soon."

"But where you pointed—the trees. How can you put up condos?"

"Cut 'em down." He laughed. "Oh, I know what you're thinking—history, right? You and Minnie. You're more concerned about what was, than what is—like that good for nothing father of yours. She cared more about him when he was dead than she ever did for me alive. Well, don't you worry. I'll leave thirty yards or so up here near the house for show. It's called marketing." He pointed. "I plan to leave from here to there, where the drive will be. But there's no way the rest will stay. They obstruct the view, and views are worth a lot of money."

Uncle William drained his snifter, then reached for the cognac.

Linda stared at William as he poured a hefty refill. "And the house," she said softly. "What are your plans for the house?"

He took a sip, smacked his lips. "Oh, I couldn't possibly tear it down if that's what you're thinking. It's what makes the property so desirable. Creates historical value, makes this place so marketable." He nodded to himself. "It'll need a few minor alterations, of course. Move a wall here, add ventilation ducts there. Put in central air. It'll make a dandy restaurant, or a club house for the golf course, or maybe a conference center. I'll make the final decision when I'm further along."

I have said souls do have the freedom to choose when,
where, and who they want to be in their physical lives.
Certain souls spend less time in the spirit world in order
to accelerate development, while others are
very reluctant to leave.

Michael Newton, Ph.D.
Journey of Souls

Two

Rick Henderson opened his eyes and found he had to squint from the bright light. Actually, it wasn't Rick. It was the soul mate of Linda Cheswick who had awakened in Rick's body.

Poor bastard's in the black sphere now, the soul mate thought.

A woman who sat in a chair by his bed stood and rushed to his side. "Rick? Are you awake?"

He blinked. It had to be Meg Hargrave, the girlfriend of Rick Henderson. "Meg? Is that you?" His voice was hoarse, a whisper. It hurt to speak, and his throat—he could hardly swallow. "Oh, Meg. I feel awful."

She smiled. A tear rolled down her cheek. "You scared the shit out of me, Rick. When I think—if I hadn't had the sudden urge to call. It was like I *knew* something was wrong. Oh, Lord, Rick, we'd have lost you."

Good old Otto. "Thanks, Meg. Thanks for sending help."

"You know I'd do anything for you, Rick."

He was going to have to get used to that name. He also was going to have to find a way to separate himself from this woman. The trick

27

was to do it in a way that did not create negative karma. He'd have to ease out of it.

He had an incredible headache but forced himself to speak. "What happened, Meg?"

"The crack, Rick. You've got to cut it out. It almost killed you."

"How long have I been here?"

"You've been out, well, in and out—delirious—for twenty-four hours."

Rick did his best to look sincere. "I promise, Meg. I will never do the stuff again." He paused. "Do people at the office know?"

"God, Rick, it took everything I had to keep from spilling my guts to anyone who would listen. But I didn't. I knew if you did survive, you'd lose your job. So I told them you'd had an appendicitis."

He let out a sigh. "Thanks, Meg. You're an angel."

She regarded him. "Strange. You seem different, somehow."

"Yes, well. Wouldn't you? I almost died, Meg. I think it *will* change me."

"Don't tell me you had one of those out-of-body, near-death experiences."

Rick looked past her, as if remembering. "As a matter of fact—"

A doctor entered the room. "Ah, I see the patient is awake." He took the chart from the end of Rick's bed. "Good. Once you started babbling we thought you'd make it. For a while we weren't so sure."

"When can I get out of here, doc?"

He looked up from the chart, his eyes visible over half moons. "I'm afraid we're going to have to keep you here a couple of days. You almost died, you know."

Rick made himself frown, but inside he smiled. "Meg, would you do me a big favor? Would you bring me all my files and any information you can lay your hands on—stuff I've got going at the office? I need that job and I have a feeling I'm going to have to play catch up."

Her brow furrowed. "Sure, Rick. I'll be happy to."

Three

It was the day after Minnie's funeral. Linda Cheswick sat in a high-back leather wing chair in the walnut-paneled lobby of Carter Wells Randolph & Studwick. Her feet rested on a time-mellowed oriental rug, her eyes on an old engraving of two golfers on the moonscape surface of a Scottish moor.

A tall man with gray hair and an out-of-season suntan appeared. He clapped his hands in delight. "Linda Cheswick, is that you? The last time I saw you, you couldn't have been more than twelve." Linda stood. He took her hand, shook his head. "I can't get over how you've grown. Stylish, good-looking. I must be getting old. Where has the time gone?"

She gave him a firm shake. "I'd rather you were impressed with my newly minted MBA, than with the work of Estee Lauder and Ralph Lauren."

"Really? Darden?"

"Start work next week."

He gestured as he started along a hallway. "Last I heard you were women's singles champ at the Club. Not tempted to turn pro?"

"I'm not that good, Mr. Wells."

"Call me Rod." He stepped into a large office with floor to ceiling book shelves and dark stained wood paneling. "Please, have a seat."

He waited until she was situated before he sat. "This business with Live Oaks and your inheritance—apparently there's some confusion."

"Minnie indicated Live Oaks would come to me, but my uncle says the estate is his. I'm concerned because he's planning to develop the land."

"Uh-huh." He opened a folder. "Let me come to the heart of the matter. Let's see. Yes. Your grandfather died almost thirty years ago. According to the terms of his will, everything was left in a trust for your grandmother to use during her lifetime. Then the contents of the trust were to be divided evenly between your father and your uncle, or their wives if one or both sons were deceased. In this case, with both your parents gone, your father's share comes to you."

Linda nodded.

"The catcher is Live Oaks. It was to pass to your father, his oldest son, or to his wife if he were deceased, provided there were offspring of the marriage. The idea was for it to pass on down the line through the oldest son, which was your dad. Your grandfather was loyal to his English roots and that's the tradition in England. Live Oaks has passed in the same manner from one generation to the next since the first Robert Cheswick died back in Colonial times. The way the document is worded, though, with both your father and mother gone, Live Oaks goes to William, and the fair market value of it will be included as part of his fifty percent share."

"I see," Linda said. "Let me be sure I heard you correctly. You said it was to go to my mother if my father were dead."

"Right."

"But suppose she isn't? In fact, I've always assumed she's still alive."

Wells lifted his hand. "No one has heard from your mother in twenty years. In anticipation of the complications her disappearance was sure to cause because of the terms of this will, the papers needed to have her declared legally dead were filed a long time ago." He opened a brief. "Yes, almost seven years ago—the waiting period is almost up."

"But what if she isn't? What if I can find her?"

Wells peered at Linda over half-moons. "Live Oaks would go to her, and so would the rest of what's now coming to you."

"How much would you estimate that to be?"

"Quite a tidy little sum. Your share will be something over five million dollars, after estate taxes are paid."

Linda took a breath. "Five million."

"Five, five and a half. Most of it's in stocks and bonds. It fluctuates."

"How much is Live Oaks worth? I mean, couldn't I just buy it from Uncle William?"

"You could if he'd sell it. According to the appraisal, it's worth about two and a half million—as a residence."

"How much if he develops it?"

"Oh, well." His eyes searched the ceiling. "A lot more. Maybe as much as ten million, considering the location. If he plans to develop it, your uncle won't sell it for less, I guarantee."

Linda suddenly felt nauseous. "How long do I have?"

"How long before what?"

"To find my mother. "

"Oh, I see. Uh, William will be pushing to get this resolved I know, so we'll probably be in court practically the day after the waiting period is up." He glanced at the document in his hand. "I'd say you've got until sometime in the first week of July."

"A month. That's not much time."

Rod Wells stared at her. "You haven't asked for my advice, but I am your family's lawyer so I'll give it to you anyway. I can't imagine why you'd want to find a mother who, there's no delicate way to put this, a mother who abandoned you as a child, and then turn over a five million dollar inheritance to her." He shook his head. "What makes you think she wouldn't turn around and develop the land herself? You'll be out five million and accomplish nothing."

Linda stared at the hands in her lap. "Good question, Rod. Very good. I've got a lot of thinking to do before I answer it. For that matter, I've a lot of thinking before I decide what I'm doing with the rest of my life."

Linda soon realized she had no desire to become a lady of leisure at the age of twenty-five. What would she do? Play tennis in the mornings? Twiddle her thumbs in the afternoons? Go bar hopping every night? She'd worked hard for an MBA and now she was going to do something with it—start the job she'd accepted at the ad agency in Baltimore. So what if she didn't need the money? She wanted a career. Life was supposed to be an adventure and the time had come for it to begin.

Deciding whether to try to find her mother so Live Oaks would stay out of the hands of Uncle William was not as easy. She spent two sleepless nights thinking about it. She thought about it as she packed. She thought about it as she drove to Baltimore.

The tires thumped rhythmically on cracks between ancient slabs of concrete on the Baltimore-Washington Parkway, and she thought about it.

She saw a couple of sea gulls soaring in the distance and the downtown skyline came into view. The tall building with mirrored windows was where her office would be, overlooking Harbor Place. The image flashed in her mind of tall masts and sailing ships, and she could almost smell the scent of salt water.

She was still trying to decide.

She asked herself if it was irony or a subconscious urge that had led her to chose Baltimore after graduation. This was, after all, the city where she had been born, the city where she'd lived the first three years of life. If there was a purpose behind it all, if each individual came to earth with a mission, there must have been a good reason she was born here. And there had to be a reason she was born to her particular set of parents.

On the other hand, her college professors were probably right. People who believed that sort of thing were soft in the head. It was New Age nonsense. Wishful thinking. If the truth was that there was no rhyme or reason, our minds manufactured them anyway.

She maneuvered in stop-and-go traffic through the business district, then turned onto Mt. Royal and headed toward Bolton Hill.

How to find out about her mother was the question that plagued her. She braked for a light. It must be a subconscious longing to know. That's what drew her here. She might as well face it, she couldn't rest until she found her mother, it was that simple. Once she did, she'd decide whether to risk letting her know about the inheritance.

The light turned green.

Who knew? Maybe she could strike a deal with her mother to keep Live Oaks intact and pass it on to Linda's children, assuming Linda had children. She'd gladly give up five million dollars to keep Live Oaks out of Uncle William's hands. Live Oaks was so much more important to her than money.

It seemed doubtful, of course, such an agreement could be made legally binding, but it was worth a try. If it were apparent her mother couldn't be trusted, if she were a down and out heroine addict, for instance, Linda simply would not tell her about the inheritance. Even so, she might be able to use the fact her mother was alive and stood to inherit the estate as leverage to persuade William to cut back his plans—at least to force him to spare the trees and the house.

Linda turned one corner after another, checked street signs and noted numbers on houses. Once she was satisfied she was close enough, she backed into a space and turned off the engine.

What if her mother were a heroin addict? Could she walk away and leave her in a flop house, or a gutter?

Linda closed the car door and looked around. The foliage of the tall trees that lined the street formed a canopy that reminded her of the magnificent oaks Uncle William planned to topple. Even beyond that, the street, this scene, seemed oddly familiar. The nineteenth-century townhouses on each side had no yards in front. White marble steps jutted out from porticoes to arrive abruptly on the sidewalk.

When had she been here? Certainly not since she was small.

She walked for half a block or so, noting the numbers. Her pulse quickened: 1308, 1310, 1312. She stopped. Was this it? The other houses were red brick. This one was stone. Cold, gray stone.

She took the envelope from her handbag and looked at the return address. The ink was faded, smudged, but there was no mistake.

What did you know? A sign in a first floor window advertised an apartment for rent. She climbed the steps and rang the bell.

After a few moments the door opened six inches. An elderly man peered at her from the shadows.

"The apartment, is it still for rent?"

"Yes, yes." He opened the door. "My wife usually shows it, but she's out just now."

Linda stepped in and looked at a crystal chandelier. Her eyes shifted to the cobwebs in the corners of the high ceiling.

Déjá vu.

"The one for rent's on the second floor in back." The old man turned toward the stairs. "Under the steps is the door to the cellar. I point that out because there's a washer and dryer down there that the tenants can use."

Linda looked at the cellar door and felt a sense of cold breath on her neck.

Déjá vu.

"Two apartments up here." He climbed slowly, lifting each foot deliberately. "One takes up the second and third floors in back and the other takes up both floors in front."

"Are both for rent?"

"No, no. Our son lives in the one in front. Back's for rent."

The old man found a key on a ring attached to his belt.

"This front room here's got a fireplace," he said as they walked in. "Works, too."

The fireplace and the passageways on each side matched a pattern buried in Linda's memory. Her pulse began to thump. This must be it, the apartment where she had lived.

She took a couple of breaths to calm herself.

"Has your son lived in the other apartment long?"

"Twenty years—more, except when he was in the service. Can't rent you that one. Down here's the kitchen." He moved through the passageway on the right. "That is, if you're interested."

"I'm interested."

He pointed up stairs. "That's how you get to the bedrooms. There's two of them."

"Mind if I have a look?"

"Help yourself. I'll wait here if you don't mind."

The first was a good size with a big window. She gave it only a glance and moved to the next.

It was oddly familiar but seemed smaller than it should have been. She turned slowly. The color . . . gray wasn't right. She stepped to the bay window, sat on the window seat. That feeling again. This was it. This was her room.

34

She turned and looked at the walled garden three floors below. The view matched one buried in her mind. She shivered, stood, rubbed her arms.

The old man was Mr. Pritchard, and there would be a Mrs. Pritchard. The letters from her father had mentioned them. He had been suspicious of the Pritchards, had felt they may have been involved with Maman's disappearance.

Maman?

French for Mommy. Odd. Had she called her mother Maman?

Linda descended the stairs and found the old man in the kitchen.

"What'd you think?"

"I like the little bedroom in back."

"Ah. Most use that as a spare. Other's bigger."

"It would make a nice nursery," she said. "Of course, it would have to be painted something besides gray."

"Reckon it has been used that way. You'll want your husband to see the apartment then."

"No, that won't be necessary. I'm not married."

He cut his eyes toward her.

"Oh, I see. No, no children, either."

The old man scratched his head.

A woman's voice called out, "Harold! Harold! You in there?"

"That'll be my wife," the old man said. "In here, dear!"

A woman with a smooth, dark complexion and silver hair tied in a bun came down the steps, an aging beauty of Mediterranean descent—high cheek bones, jet black eyes.

"This is Mrs. Pritchard," the old man said. "Sorry, don't think I caught your name."

"Linda Cheswick. Happy to meet you, Mrs. Pritchard."

Mrs. Pritchard's eyes grew narrow.

"Miss Cheswick's thinking of renting the apartment."

Mrs. Pritchard waved away the idea. "No, Harold. I do not think so."

"Why do you say that, dear? I think she is."

She flashed a look at him that said to hold his tongue. "We do not want young people living above, Harold. You are aware. Parties, music."

Mrs. Pritchard had accent. But what? *Italian?*

"Excuse me, Mrs. Pritchard," Linda said. "I don't like loud music either, and I don't know anyone in Baltimore. So, I can't invite them to a party."

"Your roommate will know others." She shook her head. "No, I will not have it."

"I'm not going to have a roommate. I don't want one. I like my peace and quiet much too much."

Mr. Pritchard nodded and smiled. "Did you hear that, dear?"

Mrs. Pritchard glared at him. "I will not tolerate loud parties, and that is that." She walked from the room.

Mr. Pritchard shook his head. "Sometimes I just don't understand that woman, even after forty-five years. What's got into her? There's no reason you shouldn't have this apartment. A nice young lady like you."

"Hope I haven't caused a problem for you, Mr. Pritchard."

He smiled and shrugged. "She's like that sometimes, but she always gets over it. I'm in charge of the renting and the upkeep. Anyway, it's my building. Belonged to my father before me. I can decide who we rent this apartment to. You take it, if you want."

It wasn't long before Linda had moved in and was busy painting the little bedroom in the back. That hideous gray had to go. Yellow was her choice.

She surveyed the job she'd done on the woodwork. Nothing had been left uncovered. But she hadn't gotten to the inside of the cupboard beneath the window seat. No thorough painter would leave that undone.

She put her brush on the paint tray next to the roller, kneeled, and pulled on the knob. The door wouldn't budge.

She scraped firmly all the way around with a trowel and tried again. It gave a little.

She used the trowel again.

It popped loose.

Yellow?

The inside of the cupboard was yellow—almost exactly the same shade. Somehow, she had known it should be.

And this? The pudgy, rounded leg of a doll—and a toy block.

A time capsule.

Linda tried to visualize the rest of the doll . . . but no luck.

Too bad. Anyway, it was time for a break.

She went down the stairs, looked at the dingy kitchen. More work. Getting this place in shape would take awhile. Finger print smudges everywhere, a layer of crud incrusted on the top of the back splash that rimmed the counter. It had probably been thirty years since these cabinets had seen the wet end of a brush.

And there, the basket of clothes waiting to be washed. Why was she putting off the trip to the basement?

She moved to the back door, looked out. Bright, glorious sunshine—not a day to be inside, much less in a basement. The trip to the moldy bowels could wait.

She stepped onto the second-floor back porch, looked up at blue sky. Bright sun made her squint. Below, the garden was green and lush and the rhododendron were in bloom, a creamy shade of violet.

Mr. Pritchard reclined in a lawn chair.

"Beautiful day, isn't it, Mr. Pritchard?"

He looked up, waved. "What have you been painting?"

Linda touched her painter's cap. "The room in back." She descended the steps. "I've just discovered that it was the same color once, and that a little girl used to live there."

"Really? How so?"

"The closet under the window seat was painted shut," she said. "A doll's leg and some blocks were inside."

Mr. Pritchard's nose twitched. "Must have been some time ago." He closed his eyes.

Linda strolled along a walkway, stared at weeds that grew in cracks between bricks.

Careful, Linda, she told herself. "When do you suppose it was?"

"Wha-what's that?"

"When do you suppose a little girl lived there?"

His brow furrowed.

"Can't remember offhand. No, wait." His nose twitched again. "Have to be twenty years, more."

"Did they live here long?"

"Who?" He blinked. "Oh, yes, the child and her family. Lemme see. Don't think she was even born when they moved in. Lived here till she was three or so, then the mother disappeared. Poor fellow couldn't believe she'd walk out on him like that. What were their names?" Mr. Pritchard's eyes opened wide as though something had occurred to him. He stared skyward.

"Harold, are you there?" It was Mrs. Pritchard's voice.

"Here, dear."

The back door flung wide. "You said you'd fix the faucet."

Linda cleared her throat. "I'll just be leaving now."

"Oh. It's you," Mrs. Pritchard said.

"Excuse me, chores to finish. Good to see you."

Linda hurried up the steps and did not exhale until the door was closed.

Surely Mrs. Pritchard knew who Linda was. That must have something to do with it. But why didn't she say so?

"Recognized your name. You lived here with your mother and father when you were little."

Maybe she was just naturally unpleasant. Or could there be more to it?

More to it. More to it. Maybe. But what?

She thought of Mr. Pritchard on the day she had rented this place.

"Just like that, sometimes."

Maybe so. At least Linda hoped that was the case.

The next day, Sunday afternoon, Linda decided she had stalled long enough. She took the basket of dirty laundry, opened the door and started down the stairs, straining to see her feet because the clothes were in the way. She placed each foot carefully.

Soon she stood in front of the cellar door. *Cold breath.* And an odor. Foul.

What was it? Something in the basement?

No. The door wasn't even open. What had she been thinking? There was no odor. She must have imagined it.

Was something wrong with her? What could possibly be down there? Some creepie-crawlies? Big deal.

She pushed the door open, found the light switch. That odor again, only this time she wasn't imagining. There was a dampness about it, mildew mixed with something rancid.

She felt weak, wiped perspiration from her forehead.

There's nothing to be afraid of. Move, Linda.

The bricks . . . something was strange about them. They oozed.

Bricks don't ooze and there's no such thing as ghosts.

Why'd she think of ghosts?

One step at a time. Take them one at a time and soon you'll reach the bottom.

At last she stepped onto the concrete floor and stood directly beneath a bare, twenty-five watt bulb. A bead of perspiration slid down her temple.

Light from the naked bulb disappeared into darkness. She closed her eyes to force them to adjust. She opened them and saw the cellar for the first time in twenty years: A washer and dryer, pipes overhead, a furnace, rafters, wires, and crawl space above the bricks. She felt a shock of panic, the impulse to run as the image of a dark, hulking figure rushed forward to engulf her. She screamed and jumped backward, swooned, dropped the basket, fell against the wall, and slid into a crouching position, trembling, the world spinning out of control, darkness closing in.

Her heart seemed to have stopped and in an instant she was viewing her body from a vantage point outside herself. A demon bent over her lifeless form. He thrust a pitchfork into her chest and split it open to reveal a bloody mass of organs. The demon turned and smiled, acknowledging her presence where she hovered, then reached inside her chest cavity and ripped out her heart. He held it for Linda to see, blood pouring from the severed arteries.

Oh, God, this can't be happening.

Then the apparition was gone and she was back inside her body. Her heart was beating again.

She drew in air, exhaled, forced herself to focus on her breathing. She must not think of that horrible image. She must shut it from her mind. It had only been something she had imagined, she told herself. It hadn't really happened.

After ten breaths she began to get her bearings. What was buried in her subconscious that had caused her to react this way? Did it have to do with her mother? Had they come here to do the laundry and something terrible had happened?

Why had she imagined a fiend ripping out her heart?

She struggled to her feet. Her knees wobbled.

The horrible vision flashed in her mind again.

Why? Why? What did it mean?

Then it occurred to her. What she had seen had indeed happened. It was not something she'd imagined. The disappearance of her mother had been the same as having her heart ripped out, just as surely as if a demon like the one she'd imagined had done it.

A creaking noise. She jumped. Her heart pounded.

It's only a pipe expanding, silly. There's no such thing as ghosts.

Unless buried memories were ghosts. Yes, like the demon. He had been lurking in the shadows ready to pounce.

Where there others?

Ghost or no ghost, demon or no demon, nothing would stand in her way. She would find Maman and persuade her to sign over Live Oaks in exchange for her inheritance—no matter what it took. She wanted Live Oaks for herself, for her children, for the sense of permanence and for the pleasure it would bring. Nothing could keep her from having it.

Again the vision flashed. Again she pushed it from her mind.

It would not stop her. Nothing would.

Not a ghost, not a demon. Nothing.

Four

The morning sun was at their backs, just over the horizon, but high enough to light up the royal blue Corsican sky. On both sides of the road the maquis was lush and green, peppered with wild flowers. Pedru Ghjuvanni inhaled deeply. The maquis smelled honey sweet—the wet, perfumed odor of the final weeks of spring. By July when the tourists came in their campers it would be dry as tinder. The hordes of scum from the continent would litter it with their droppings and set it ablaze with their camp fires. But today it was pure, virginal, primal, unspoiled, the way the Corsica of Pedru Ghjuvanni's ancestors was meant to be. And it would be so again, would be for all time, when the National Front for the Liberation of Corsica finally won the long and difficult struggle.

Ah, but today his business was not to further the cause of liberation from the oppressive boot of French colonialism. Family came first. Country second. Today, his duty was to uphold the honor of the Ghjuvanni clan, a matter of supreme importance that took precedence even over the defense and deliverance of his native land.

Pedru felt a lift in his stomach when the car shot over the crest of the hill and started down into the hairpin turns between Ponte-Leccia and Belgodere. The squeal of tires reverberated in his ears. He thought fleetingly about using the safety belt, but safety belts were for old woman and children. His cousin, Santu, was driving hard and wore no belt. Pedru would not open himself to the certainty of ridicule. Instead, he grabbed the strap that hung on the post between the front and back seats of the sleek Jaguar sedan.

"Do not worry, my cousin," Santu said. "I will not allow us to miss your flight. Grandfather has instructed me so." Santu spoke to Pedru in the native tongue of Corsica.

Pedru closed his eyes as they slammed into the curve on the left side of the road and thought, *We will make the flight if we live, you fool.*

"It is now less than forty-five kilometers, Santu. Perhaps you can slow down. These curves—they are very difficult on the car."

"Do not worry for the car, Pedru. The wishes of our Grandfather are of greater significance."

It was true that one must never go against the wishes of a grandfather, particularly when that grandfather was patriarch of the entire Ghjuvanni clan—one of the most powerful in all of Corsica. It was a fact of which Pedru Ghjuvanni was most proud. Indeed, his grandfather could count on Pedru for utmost and unquestioning obedience. Someday, the Virgin Mary willing, he might also sit in the place of power that his grandfather now occupied.

They skidded into the next turn, also on the left. Pedru held tight to the strap to keep from being flung against Santu. He felt beads of perspiration forming on his forehead.

"How does it feel, Pedru, to be the chosen one? Grandfather has recognized that you are quick with a knife and brave. You must be proud."

It was true that he liked the knife. It gave him a feeling of power in a way the revolver never did. The revolver was a necessary weapon, of course, in the event one was out-numbered or needed to defend himself from formidable opposition. Yes. His weapons gave him a sense of security and control. But not from every hazard. If he had ever before been on an airplane, perhaps he would not now be so frightened. Perhaps it would also help if Santu would slow down.

"I do my duty, Santu. We each must do our part. Absolute loyalty to the Family is essential."

Santu glanced at him with reverence. "Would that my knife were as quick as yours."

They skidded around a left hand curve and Santu was almost thrown from behind the wheel.

Would that you would slow down, you idiot.

"Would that my knife had been quick enough to save my brothers from the Vezzani scourge," Pedru said. "To save our little cousin, Alena. The scum will pay for that."

"What will you do, Pedru? What is your plan to avenge her?"

Pedru thought of his little Alena and his heart ached. Eighteen. Untouched and sweet as the highland maquis in spring. He could see her in his mind, braiding a chain of anis flowers. Untouched, that is, until the blackguards got a hold of her.

"I will seek out the youngest granddaughter of Tino Vezzani."

Santu chuckled. "And you will make her beg?"

"She will grovel at my feet."

"And you will make her perform?"

"Like a virtuoso, blowing a flute." Pedru chuckled in spite of his fear.

"You will cut her throat?"

"I will make sure a full-length mirror is available so that she can watch herself bleed to death."

"Oh, how I wish I could be there," Santu said.

Pedru wiped his forehead with a handkerchief, and felt a sense of relief as the sign for Belgodere came into view. The young fool would have to slow down for a town.

They overtook an old man leading a donkey heavily laden with olive oil. Santu pounded the horn.

"Santu, did you not see the sign for Belgodere? Why do continue at this pace?"

"I do not wish to miss your flight. We have already discussed the urgency of this mission."

"If a gendarme is in the town, he will stop us. If we are stopped, he will force you to blow up a balloon. He may search the car. This will take time. We will miss my flight. If we miss my flight, Grandfather will have you strung up by the balls."

Santu took his foot off of the gas. Pedru breathed a sigh.

A half hour later they reached the strip along the beach by the airport. Pedru looked at his watch. As he had anticipated, there was time to spare.

They passed the pastel-painted cinder block hotels and gaudy signs advertising rooms with kitchenettes which had been newly erected since his last visit to Calvi. The hair stood on his neck. Anger welled within him. It was too bad he did not have time to plant some bombs. The colonists were bad enough and deserved to die, but the so-called Corsicans who pandered to the foreign rabble were far worse. Death was too good for these traitors to their land. They had a lesson coming.

Next trip perhaps.

Santu drove the car up the access road to the front door of the one-story white airport terminal. A porter with a hand truck appeared. Pedru waved him away as he and Santu stepped from the Jaguar into the bright sunshine.

"Shall I come inside with you, my cousin?"

"That will not be necessary. Your mission is complete. You have delivered me to my plane—on time."

Santu embraced Pedru and kissed him on both cheeks. "Good hunting." He continued to hold him by the shoulders, looked him in the eye. A corner of his mouth turned up. "Slowly, cousin. Do it slowly. The quality of the revenge is proportional to the suffering."

Pedru took his bag from the back seat of the car and went inside. He saw several ticket counters for charter airlines that catered to the scum of northern Europe but recalled that his flight was on Air Inter. He found it easily, and checked his bag. The attendant directed him to the gate.

Merde.

The gendarmes of the fascist colonists were searching people with a metal detector. He had supposed, of course, that the baggage would be x-rayed because of the havoc the brave and valiant leader of Libya had visited upon the world. Pedru's .45 automatic was safely inside a lead-lined container shaped like a silver tray with handles. But he had not anticipated this.

He quickly ducked into a restroom. It was a shame to part with a pearl-handled stiletto such as the one he carried in the holster in his boot. Uncle Ghjesu had given it to him for his sixteenth birthday.

And to go unarmed. He would feel naked.

But his mission was clear: Go to the United States. Avenge the rape of Alena. Carry out the vendetta. Duty first to family.

He held the stiletto, turned it.

The handle was worn. His hands, his fingers had done this. A thousand, a million caresses. The hundreds of times he had held it tight, had pressed the flat side of the blade against a throat.

How it sparkled. So sharp it could split a hair in two.

But, no use. He would look a fool to all if he did not make it off the soil of Corsica.

He could buy another in the American city of Baltimore. The Americans were well known for making weapons available of every description to anyone with a need.

Even so, it was with the heavy heart of grieving for the loss of an old friend that he dropped it in the waste paper container.

He looked in the mirror and straightened his black tie. Along with his charcoal-colored suit, it was usually reserved for funerals. But today he was going to a foreign land. People would be impressed with his businesslike appearance.

He squeezed a dab of hair cream from the miniature tube he kept in his pocket, rubbed it between his palms, spread it on. He rinsed his pocket comb under water from the sink and ran it through his jet black hair, pushing it with his free hand to get some lift.

How nicely it shined today, and the consistency—it was perfect—every strand in place.

He leaned close to the mirror and inspected his chin. He had shaved only two hours before and already the stubble showed. By the holy Virgin, what was the use?

More to the point, what did it matter? He was handsome. Women loved him. Even foreign women. *Especially* foreign woman. All of them. They loved him, craved him. So what if his nose had been flattened in a fight when he was sixteen? It was his badge of courage. Women swooned over men of courage. That is why they always swooned when they saw him. Always.

The plane was only half full. It was not yet the season, as the pigs who engaged in tourist trade referred to it. Still, there were several rather succulent, buxom Parisiennes on board who caused the loins to stir. Their behavior was disgusting. They were the same *putains* who flaunted their bosoms on the beach. They would bare every inch of their bodies to arouse. They lacked any sense of modesty—any sense of decency, propriety, or dignity. They needed a man, a real man to teach them these qualities. With a whip, if necessary. Not some prissy Parisian.

The plane was rolling now and the woman in uniform was speaking of safety belts and smoking, of oxygen masks falling from compartments in the ceiling and a life vest under the seat.

By the Holy Mother, would a life vest be needed? Would they crash into the sea? And oxygen? Why would oxygen be needed?

Now what tongue was this? English? Yes, English. Those few years in school were enough to know what language she was speaking. And he had diligently been practicing sentences from the phrase book in preparation for this trip. But this? Who would have expected this? A French airline, a French *putain* in uniform. She was speaking English.

How did she expect him to understand?

He rose from his seat and looked fore and aft. All on board were either French or Corsican. How did she expect anyone to understand?

A uniformed *putain* rushed to him. "Your seat belt, Monsieur. You are required to have it fastened." She reached down and buckled it around him.

Pedru was about to grab the French bitch by the throat and shake her well. What did a grown man need of a safety belt? But she left as quickly as she came.

The airplane turned and started to roll faster, faster. Pedru was pushed back in his seat. The idiots. They were headed directly into the side of the mountain. Did they not see it? What manner of insanity was this?

Pedru felt an uncomfortable lift in his stomach and grabbed the armrest of the seat. He looked out of the window. By the mother of God, they were free of the ground.

The plane tilted. He tightened his grip. His fingers and his knuckles were white. He needed air. He must breathe. His brow was covered with sweat, his underarms dripping wet.

He forced himself to look out the window. Below was the sea, white caps frozen on waves that did not move. In the distance the tallest mountains pushed through white, smoke-like clouds.

He settled into his seat. He was headed on the biggest, the most important mission of his life, and already he felt an empty place within his heart, a void that would always be reserved for the home of his ancestors, that most habitable of all islands, the land of those chosen by God to live in beauty: his native Corsica.

Life is difficult.

M. Scott Peck, M.D.
The   Road   Less   Traveled

Five

Rick Henderson walked past Linda's cubicle.

"Good morning," he said without breaking stride.

"Good morning," she replied.

He stopped at his secretary's desk and exchanged a few words, then continued into his office.

She smiled as she straightened the pile of papers she was working on, thinking she could have done a lot worse out of grad school than J. P. Morton Advertising. The atmosphere was good and she liked her boss. He knew his stuff and he'd already turned over a good deal of responsibility.

Then there was the kicker. He was handsome.

Not that it mattered, really. She didn't have time to get involved. And one thing was certain. If she did, it wouldn't be with her boss. It didn't take a genius to see the problems that could cause.

Funny. When she was little she was more interested in being a boy than being a boy's girlfriend. Then when she became interested in boys as members of the opposite sex, they were no longer interested in her. Minnie said it was because she was tall. Maybe she'd been right. It had never been more apparent than in middle school. She cringed when she remembered Mrs. Abercrombie's Cotillion.

A picture of Mrs. Abercrombie popped into her mind whenever she thought back. Tall, gray hair in ringlets, no waist. She stood on the stage of the Woman's Club ballroom, a four-piece band behind her, speaking into the microphone.

"Let's have the girls on this side—my left, your right. Okay, girls—this way. Boys on this side, to my right, your left." She clapped her hands. "Let's go boys."

Linda shuffled in the direction she'd been told.

"What do you suppose is going on?" she asked Mary-Randolph Hinton.

"She's trying to teach these stupid boys some manners," Mary-Randolph said. "Fat chance."

"Spread out, girls," Mrs. Abercrombie said.

"Come on, Linda," Mary-Randolph said. "Let's stand up here on the front row. You want to be chosen, don't you?"

Linda stood beside her, the boys ten feet away, bunched together. They looked at their feet, glanced toward the girls from the corners of their eyes.

"Okay, boys," Mrs. Abercrombie said. "I want each of you to walk up to one of the girls, extend your hand like this. Bow slightly from the waist. Then say, 'May I have this dance?'"

A groan arose from the boys' side of the room.

"Come on, boys. You can do it. Girls, you know what to do." She turned to the band leader. "George, let's have a waltz."

The band played "Casey Would Waltz with the Strawberry Blond."

The boys held back.

"Get moving, boys," Mrs. Abercrombie said over the microphone. It squawked.

Haltingly, the boys started forward. Two broke from the pack and walked straight toward Mary-Randolph. One put it in passing gear, almost knocking the other down. The loser scooted past Linda and took the hand of a girl in a flowered dress.

Linda felt her pulse begin to race, her chances slipping, as the pairing off gathered momentum.

She decided to make an effort to catch the eye of one of these fourteen year old midgets before it was to late. She plastered on a smile and looked from one to the next. The pairing continued. Each time a boy's glance stopped on her, he quickly looked away.

Finally all the girls were chosen except Linda and two others. These started dancing with each other, leaving Linda alone. She headed for the wall. The meaning of the term, wall-flower, had been made painfully clear.

She was rescued from total humiliation by one of the monitors, a boy two or three years older who was employed by Mrs. Abercrombie to insure the midgets did what they were told.

He ended up dancing with Linda several times that night.

Linda shoved her pencil into an electric sharpener. It whirred. She pulled the pencil out, blew off the excess graphite and opened a folder.

At least by the time she got to college *some* boys were taller. The basketball team, the football team, even a few gawky ones. One or two from each category actually seemed interested in her. And, oh yes, there had been one in particular who had been very interested. Brad James. She'd met him in the library at VCU when she was home from Charlottesville for Thanksgiving. She'd gone there to research a paper and was at the card catalog with a drawer out, searching, when she looked up and saw him staring at her.

He was good-looking in a rough-hewn sort of way. Piercing blue eyes, black hair. The Robert De Niro type who had a five o'clock shadow even if he'd just put down the razor.

"You don't go to VCU, do you?"

"No, I don't. Why?"

"If you did, I'd have seen you before. And if I'd seen you before, I'd remember."

A tingly sensation had taken her by surprise. It had started in her toes, run up the backs of her legs, then up her spine. Perhaps it was the way he looked at her as though he couldn't tear his eyes away. She could almost feel hers dilate as though he had hypnotized her.

She went out with him three nights in a row, convinced she'd found true love. She wanted to carry his water, chop wood, darn his socks, hike across the blazing desert, build a log cabin on a mountaintop, go with him to the remotest part of Alaska and sleep outside in 70 below temperatures. It didn't matter. Not as long as they were together. Until that Sunday, a day she wished she could wipe from her memory. He was on the back porch of a house in the Fan District, a rickety back porch made of wood that had been painted pea green over a layer of white. Linda was sure because the green paint was chipped. Inside was the apartment that he shared with another guy. Between his index finger and his thumb he held a hand-rolled cigarette. Smoke from it curled skyward.

"Stuff's a hundred-twenty bucks an ounce." He squinted, sucked in a lung full, held his breath. "Colombian gold. All you need is two good hits." He wrinkled his nose, offered her the joint.

She hesitated. It smelled so pungent that it took her breath away. She looked at the burning ash, drooping. The bulging, wrinkled paper. The business end, twisted. Wet.

"Go ahead," he said. "Before the damn thing goes out."

She loved him. What was she to do?

She sucked in a mouthful and inhaled. To her surprise, it did not burn. "That's not so bad." She laughed. A puff of smoke exited. She coughed.

"Here, let me have another hit." He took the joint and sucked hard. The end flared redish-orange.

He passed it back and she did the same.

"Two hits of this weed is all you need." Brad burst out laughing.

This also struck Linda as hilarious. She joined him in laughter. Between guffaws they smoked the joint to a nub.

Brad used his thumb and forefinger to snuff out the spark, popped the roach into his mouth, swallowed it.

He put his arms around her. She felt drawn into those baby blues. Her body melted into his.

He kissed her. His lips were so incredibly soft. She'd never felt anything quite so soft. Yet they were fiery, inciting primal urges. A stirring. The tingly rush from her toes up the backs of her legs.

"Inside the house," he said with a nod and a Cheshire grin.

They seemed to float through the door two feet off the ground. They floated along the hall, past the kitchen, a closed doorway. She hadn't realized the hall was so long as they continued to float.

The back porch seemed far, far away. They were standing by a bed.

"Your clothes—off," Brad said.

"No, Brad, I'm not . . . we're not."

He pulled her to him, kissed her, rubbed her body with his palms. She squirmed, made a half-hearted attempt to pull away but it was difficult to resist that warm tingling the rubbing and the kisses sent all over her.

Maybe if they kept it like this—petting, necking . . . it was really fairly harmless, and it felt so, so . . . sensual. Yes, that was how it felt, sensual. Parts of her she didn't know existed were expanding, filling out, pushing against those palms, his hands, the rubbing . . .

Almost before she realized it, he'd unbuttoned her blouse and pulled it out of her jeans.

"No Brad, we can't."

He unhooked her bra. In an instant she was naked from the waist up. He kissed her and licked her and she felt an incredible fluttering sensation. She was going to explode.

"Stop, Brad, stop." She needed air. Her heart was pounding. "No, stop, Brad, no, don't, I shouldn't, we shouldn't." Damn that wonderful, warm tingle and the longing, the incredible longing to go wherever this was leading.

He pushed her on the bed, pulled down her jeans, lowered his face. All she could see was the top of his head. What was he doing? Oh, God, he was licking her. His tongue was encircling . . . Oh, God, it was like nothing she'd ever experienced. Her insides were welling up. Welling, welling, ready to explode. She moved her hips in a circular motion and pushed against him. Don't stop. Don't stop. Please, don't stop now.

He lunged forward, spread her legs with muscular arms. She twisted, turned, tried to wiggle free. He pinned her.

No, no, don't, please.

The pleasure turned to pain. "No, Brad, stop, please! Stop!" His rough cheek scratched her. His animal panting reverberated in her ear. He arched his back, cried out.

At first she had felt shame and disgust. Putrid disgust. Then anger. Then she had plunged into a deep depression, worried sick that she was pregnant.

She never saw him again. Oh, he called—left messages on her

answering machine. He actually acted surprised that she was angry and refused to speak.

She had not been interested in men since that day. Didn't care if every single one of them dropped off the face of the earth. She avoided them; turned them down whenever they asked her out.

It didn't look as though being asked out was going to be a problem anytime soon. She had a job in a new city, didn't know anyone. She also had to track down her mother, which would occupy every spare moment.

But she did have a good-looking boss: Rick Henderson.

It seemed as though he might be different, too, than most men. Although what was different was hard to put her finger on. Maybe it was how he made her feel.

Safe? Respected?

She'd better get these thoughts out of her head. She'd better direct her attention to this report. She wanted to review it with him before lunch. If she could get it done by then, she'd be ahead of schedule. She'd rack up brownie points.

She wanted brownie points.

So work was good. But what about the other part of her life? What about finding her mother?

She hadn't slept most of last night because of the incident in the basement. Seeing that place again had brought back the shadow of a memory and that horrible, ghoulish mental metaphor of a demon ripping out her heart. Yes. And with all that the fear. Terror. Unequivocal terror. Something hidden deep inside. It was there, all right, waiting to reveal itself. Like yellow paint inside the cupboard. And all the while time ticked away. Precious time.

Two hours later she stood at the doorway to Rick Henderson's corner office with the report in her hand gazing through floor to ceiling windows. What a view. The harbor stretched toward the Chesapeake Bay until it dropped off the edge of the earth.

Sandy blond hair fell across his forehead as he looked up at her. She felt a knot form in her abdomen. Perhaps his eyes caused it. One was blue and the other, hazel-green. The man with kaleidoscope eyes was how she thought of him.

"Come in. Have a seat."

"I think the Watsford Distillery report is almost ready. I'd like to go over it."

"Great. Ahead of schedule. Maybe I can cover it with them when I'm down there tomorrow."

"It's what you thought. Bourbon and scotch, all the browns except Canadian in a nose dive. Vodka and light rum holding their own."

Rick took the report, leafed through it. "Right, right. You've summed it up succinctly. Vodka's what they should get into. Good job, Linda."

She felt a warm rush.

Rick's eyes moved from her and stopped at a point above her left shoulder. "Hi, Meg."

Linda turned and saw Meg Hargrave in the doorway.

"Lunch?" Meg said, ignoring Linda.

"Sure," Rick said. "Linda and I are almost finished."

"See you in the lobby," Meg said.

Rick stood. "Good job, Linda. So good in fact, I think you ought to come with me and help explain it to the client."

"Really?"

"We'll have to put it in finished form this afternoon—may run into this evening—and decide how we're going to present it. We'll fly out in the morning and be back tomorrow afternoon." He gave her a little wave and was out the door.

Darn. What was the hurry?

Admit it. Meg Hargrave was an attractive woman and a full account executive. Why shouldn't he go to lunch with her?

She had to stop thinking this way. It was none of her business who he went to lunch with. No way was she going to get involved with someone at the office. Especially her boss.

Linda and Rick worked together into the evening, summarized information and put it into quickly-readable charts. They edited much of the text down to bullet points, organized everything into a logical flow that built a strong, air-tight case for the recommendation they'd make.

"Vodka really does look like a good bet, doesn't it?" Rick stood and put his hands flat on the table. He leaned toward Linda, his body a silhouette surrounded by an incredible view: dark water forming a razor-sharp horizon, the lights of a ship over his left shoulder. His face radiated an inner light. "The client desperately needs to get sales turned around, and this can do it. Plus, the billings generated for the agency will be enormous. Tell you one thing, this won't hurt your career—or mine either."

"I wouldn't have thought it was that big a deal" Linda said. "We had case studies in grad school like this one every day."

Rick's kaleidoscope eyes sparkled. "This ain't grad school, Linda. This is life—a helluva lot more exciting, I think. The difference between playing poker for match sticks, and playing for keeps." He looked at his watch. "Look at the time. What say we order a pizza?"

She watched him press numbers into the keypad of a telephone.

"Doesn't it concern you that we're working on a plan for the distribution and consumption of alcohol?"

He glanced at her. "You mean, we're like drug dealers, only legal?"

"Right. For example, how many destructive acts will we be responsible for, indirectly, if we're successful?"

"You don't think people are going to drink the same amount of alcohol whether it's our brand or someone else's?"

"Maybe so. It's just, I don't know. . . . My grandmother died of emphysema. My family's grown tobacco for 250 years. There's irony in that."

"Sort of like, what you give out comes back? Karma?"

"What's karma?" Linda said.

He ordered the pizza; put the phone down. "We haven't time to get into that tonight. But look at it this way. If your family grew potatoes instead, do you think it would have made any difference?"

"No. But at least we wouldn't be contributing to the problem."

He nodded. "In which case you'd have no blood on your hands. You do believe in karma."

"You're going to tell me what karma is, right?"

"I'd like very much to discuss it sometime, but not tonight. Look, I wouldn't feel right about pushing cigarettes. In fact, I'd quit my job before I'd take on that assignment. But man's been drinking alcohol since before the time of Christ. Christ himself turned water into wine because they ran out of joy juice at a wedding feast. There's even evidence moderate drinking may be beneficial. Look at all the wine the French drink, and there's a much lower incidence of heart disease. People who abuse alcohol are creating their own karma. We're not doing it. I agree that those who market cigarettes eventually will have to answer for it, but not alcohol. Not if it's done responsibly."

"I can't wait to find out what karma is."

"Sorry we don't have time now to discuss it. I will say this. We each have our roles to play in the scheme of life. Sometimes we don't know why we're led to do what we're led to do at a given point. But we won't go wrong if we follow what the still small voice inside is telling us. We just need to stay alert." He glanced at his watch. "Right now mine is telling me this marketing proposal for a new brand of vodka is what I should be doing."

It was almost midnight before Linda left the building, but she had hardly noticed the time passing. It was one of the most exhilarating evenings she'd spent in a long, long time.

Before she dropped into bed, she looked up karma in her American Heritage Dictionary: "*Hinduism & Buddhism.* The sum and the consequences of a person's actions during the successive phases of his existence, regarded as determining his destiny."

Successive phases of a person's existence? What did that mean?

Rick Henderson was a strange one, all right. A girl had to wonder all what was going on inside that handsome head of his.

She pulled up the covers and turned out the light. It would be interesting to find out, though, wouldn't it?

Too bad he was her boss.

The next morning Linda found herself in a small, twin-engine plane for the first time in her life. Although she was an experienced traveler, she'd always flown commercially before.

It was not particularly warm inside the cabin, but she felt perspiration form on her upper lip as she watched the pilot's hand push the throttles forward. The engines roared. Butterflies that recently had inhabited her stomach took flight, and all of them—Rick, the pilot, Linda, the butterflies, shot down the runway, lifted off and banked away from the morning sun. The thunder of the engines receded to a steady drone, the plane leveled off, and all but one or two of the most nervous of those abdominal denizens found a perch and settled down.

Linda shifted in her seat and straightened the jacket of her olive-colored linen suit. She'd chosen it and her bright, butterscotch-yellow blouse because the suit made her look professional and the spice tones complemented her auburn hair and creamy complexion. She touched her handbag, secure in the knowledge she'd brought an extra pair of panty hose, just in case disaster struck in the form of a run.

Rick sat facing her, his back to the front of the plane. He finished leafing through the inch-thick document they'd prepared together, put it on the table top between them; tapped it with a finger. "Thought out, organized, difficult to argue with. Haven't even spotted the inevitable typo. Darn good work."

"Thanks to you," Linda said.

"No, no. It's ninety percent your effort."

For the next half hour they discussed the recommendation they would make, thought of every possible objection which might be raised. At last, when Rick appeared satisfied they'd covered every detail, he settled back into his seat and stared at the ceiling of the plane, apparently lost in thought.

Or was he meditating? Wasn't that what Buddhists did?

Linda gazed out the window—far down to the white fences and rolling hills of horse country. Blue grass, they called it. Before long they'd land in the heart of Kentucky.

But her mind did not remain on horse country and Kentucky, or meditating or Buddhism or even Rick Henderson. It shifted instead to the need to find her mother and to the incident in the cellar. The latter had not left her mind except when she and Rick had been absorbed in work.

What did it mean? What could possibly have caused her to have such a violent reaction? If only she could remember.

She wanted desperately to talk about it with someone. She wanted an objective opinion. She wanted someone to help her get it straightened out in her mind. Maybe if she could talk about it the memory would surface. Whatever had happened could very well have something to do with her mother's disappearance.

Was it possible her father had been right? Did Mrs. Pritchard know something she wasn't saying? Maybe she'd seen what had happened in the basement.

Should Linda confront her?

Perhaps her mother hadn't abandoned her—maybe Minnie was wrong. After all, Minnie had never even met her mother. What could she possibly have known that made her so sure Nina had walked away from a small child, a child who needed her desperately?

Linda had friends she could talk to about such things, but none in Baltimore. They lived in Richmond, Atlanta, New York. And this wasn't something she could chat about over the phone.

She looked at Rick. He was a heck of a nice guy. A bit strange, perhaps, but nice. Maybe she could talk to him. She didn't know him well, but aside from that karma weirdness, he seemed level-headed and understanding. He was certainly intelligent.

Would he think she was crazy?

The pilot leaned between the seats and asked them to check their seat belts. They'd be landing shortly.

The plane touched down on a grass strip and taxied to a small building. A tall man in a plaid fishing hat and checkered shirt greeted them. Rick sat next to him in the front seat of the big Oldsmobile. Linda sat in the back.

They meandered through beautiful, rolling Kentucky countryside with green meadows. Horses and cattle grazed. Linda knew they had almost arrived when they passed over the top of a hill. She looked down and saw a cluster of dingy, weathered buildings beside a small river. A tall brick smokestack stood among them, steam rising from it.

When she opened the car door, the heavy-sweet odor of corn mash cooking met her. They entered a building through a screen door with "Office" lettered on it, and a receptionist behind a wooden desk asked if she could be of service.

A few minutes later a young man with wavy blond hair and a dimpled, aristocratic chin came to meet them. Decked out in a blue blazer, a knit tie and khaki slacks, he appeared to be about Linda's age.

Rick introduced them. The young man's name was E. F. Watsford, III. He rolled his eyes and smiled at Linda. "But you can call me Frank."

"At your suggestion," Rick began as he took a seat in Frank's office, "we've been taking a look at other markets E. F. Watsford Distillery might consider entering."

Frank nodded.

"This is a study of the liquor industry, along with our observations and recommendations," Rick said.

Frank leafed through it as Rick summarized the situation the distillery faced. Bourbon and scotch sales were way off; beer, wine and clear liquors holding their own.

At the predetermined time Linda said, "The problem is, people don't go in for the heavier drinks the way their parents and grandparents did. They like beer and wine instead, and clear spirits mixed with fruit juice and such."

"Screwed by the screwdriver," Frank said.

Rick said, "There's another fact that's key to our recommendation. Nowadays, people are into regional pride and pride in things made in America."

They covered statistics to support this hypothesis, pointed to the findings of several national studies including the Yankelovich Monitor and a panel study by Opinion USA.

"So what we want to suggest to you today," Linda said, "is that Watsford come out with an entirely new product, Kentucky vodka."

Frank wrinkled his nose. *"Kentucky* vodka. You're kidding."

"Not at all," Rick said. "Most brands of vodka are made in Illinois or New Jersey, anyway. They're not even made of potatoes—they're made of home-grown U. S. corn. Yet they have foreign names no red-blooded American can pronounce."

Rick and Linda talked about the implications of taking what was now thought of as a foreign drink and making it uniquely American.

"Kentucky is the heartland of this country," Rick said. "People can relate to that—the Kentucky Derby, Church Hill Downs. There's a certain pride connected with it."

"Right," Linda said, her enthusiasm building. "It's time somebody capitalized on the situation. Kentucky's known for being a place that produces quality distilled spirits. It makes a lot of sense when you think about it, and Watsford can be the first."

"Kentucky *vodka.* I like it," Frank said.

Linda could sense that they were on the verge of a victory, and that it was time to move in for the kill.

"Tell you what," Rick said. "All we need from you today is to commit to a relatively modest budget we can use to develop our ideas further and to conduct some concept testing."

"We've prepared an estimate for you to sign." Linda knew this was the big moment, the close of the sale. She put the paper in front of Frank and handed him a pen. "Just initial it. Then, we'll be back in a few weeks to show you what we've come up with."

Frank's brow furrowed as he studied the figures. Linda held her breath. She felt her heart go ker-plunkety-plunk when he finally initialed the paper and handed it back to her.

How sweet was the taste of victory.

They had lunch at the Watsford family estate which was located a few miles from the distillery. Frank parked the car and led them through the house and onto the terrace in the back, which overlooked rolling Kentucky hills with white fences, horses and stables. They took seats and a man dressed in a white jacket and black bow tie appeared.

"Bourbon all around, please, Charles," Frank said.

Frank looked at Linda—who had to struggle not to gasp outloud.

"If you're going to work on the account," he said, "you've got to get to know the product."

It was a darn shame they didn't have a white wine account, instead, Linda thought.

Charles returned with three glasses of bourbon on the rocks, a peel of lemon floating on top of each.

"You ruin it when you put water in it," Frank said. He raised his glass. "Here's to Kentucky vodka."

They clicked glasses. Linda looked at it before she took a sip. There had to be four ounces of bourbon in that glass.

They had wine with lunch, a deep purple merlot that slid down as smoothly as glycerin between finger tips. No doubt the bourbon had paved the way.

An hour later Linda wobbled along the aisle of the plane and sank into a plush leather seat. A warm rush started somewhere between her sinuses and her frontal lobes and climbed straight to the top of her head.

"Tell me something." She groped for the safety belt. "Does Frank sample the product like that every day?"

Rick plopped in the seat facing her. "You were great, Linda, really great. It's like you've been at this all your life."

"Really?"

"I'm not kidding, partner. You're gonna go far in this business."

Linda felt her face flush. A tingle lingered. "What's the story on Frank? Is he always so hospitable?"

"He let his hair down for us. I suspect he was also showing off a bit."

"Why's that?"

"His grandfather really runs the place. Frank's a nice guy, but basically a go-fer. Believe me, Frank stays buttoned up when the old man is around."

The engines roared and the plane started rolling.

"His grandfather. . . . Does he have other family?"

"Sure. A mother and father—younger siblings. His father declined to go into the family business. He's a prominent lawyer in Lexington."

"The only parent I know is my grandmother." Linda realized the liquor had loosened her tongue, but she plunged ahead, anyway. She and Rick now were comrades in arms. "She raised me. My grandfather's been dead a long time. My father died in Vietnam."

"What about the other side of your family?"

"My mother disappeared when I was young. Only thing I know about her is her first name. Nina. I don't know anything about her family. Not even her maiden name."

"Disappeared?"

"My grandmother never wanted to talk about her. It was like she never existed. My mother apparently walked out on my father and me. Guess my grandmother never forgave her."

The engines revved. Then the plane shot down the runway and lifted off.

A few minutes later, when they had reached cruising altitude, the roar settled into a steady drone and they could talk again.

Rick said, "Why did you say 'apparently' walked out? You must have doubts."

"I was pretty sure my grandmother—I called her Minnie—was right, that my mother had abandoned me. Now I'm not so sure. You see, something happened the other night that ties in with some letters my father wrote to Minnie. Dad couldn't believe my mother left of her own free will. He hinted something else might have happened to her. I'd like to find out."

Should she also tell Rick about Live Oaks? Her inheritance?

No . . . she'd better think about the ramifications before doing that.

She opened her handbag and took out the letter, the paper yellow with age. "Have a look at this."

Rick carefully unfolded it; read it aloud.

> Dear Mother,
> Nina has disappeared. I realize you do
> not approve of our marriage, so I suppose this
> puts you in the position of being able to say,
> "I told you so."
> I can't believe she would walk out on
> Little Lily and me. It just doesn't make sense.
> Everything has been going fine between us, and
> she loves her daughter. I know she does.
> I've asked everyone I know if they've seen
> her or if they have heard anything about why she
> might have left or where she might have gone, but
> I haven't gotten any answers. I wonder if there's
> something they're not telling me. Especially Mrs.
> Pritchard. She and her husband own the building
> where we live. Their apartment is downstairs.
> Mrs. Pritchard is the nosy type. If anyone
> knows, I'll bet she does.
> She claims she doesn't, though.
> I just can't believe Nina would take off. I hope
> nothing has happened to her.

"That's about it," Linda said. The rest of the letter talks about me. 'Little Lily' is what my father called me. Apparently, I was restless and upset and I cried a lot after my mother left."

Rick handed back the letter. "Her trail must be pretty cold by now."

"Even so, I've started down it. I now live in the same apartment where we lived when I was a child. The same people own the building, too. They still live on the first floor."

"Whoa. Talk about destiny and what goes around coming around. Have they given you any leads?"

"Haven't told them who I am. Not yet. I thought I might learn more if they didn't know."

"Don't see why," Rick said. "Things don't usually fall in place like they seem to be falling in place for you. Not unless some higher power is at work. In which case, why not go all out? Why not ask them? Looks to me as though you're supposed to find your mother, experience living where she lived, where she lived with your father and with you. There must be something going on like that."

"I'm not sure I understand. What higher power?"

The skin of Rick's forehead wrinkled. "Fate, I guess. Sometimes it seems as though things are just *supposed* to happen. Even when you try to prevent it, you can't."

"Sorry, but I don't believe in predestination. Minnie's family are all Presbyterians, but she converted to Episcopalian because of my grandfather. That's where I went to church. When I went, which wasn't often if I could help it. Anyway, what if my father was right? I have this feeling he was. Suppose someone around there, the landlady, suppose she did something to my mother? Threatened her, or worse? Suppose that's why she went away?"

"Now I see. You're the one who's tapping into the still small voice. Any hard evidence foul play might have been involved?"

"No, but you're right about this, this *still small voice*. Only, I call it intuition. I do think the landlady had something to do with her disappearance. Actually, it's more than a small voice—or a feeling. I haven't told a soul because there's no one I feel close enough to. You won't think I'm crazy?"

"Of course not."

"The house. I constantly have this feeling of déjá vu. It's very unpleasant, like cold, damp breath on the back of my neck. And sometimes I think I smell this rancid odor. Then it's gone."

"Promise not to think I'm the crazy one?"

Linda nodded.

"The presence of evil sometimes manifests like that."

"Evil? You mean, like Satan?"

"If you think of Satan as evil personified. Something's coming through to you from another dimension. Psychics for example can feel where evil is or has been. I've heard it described the way you just described it—cold breath, an odor sometimes."

She told him about the trip to the basement. "There's no reason I should have been afraid, but I was. I forced myself to go on, and when I got all the way down and my eyes adjusted, this terrible feeling—this incredible fear—it overcame me." she shuddered, gave herself a little shake to push away the feeling. "I almost fainted."

"But you've no evidence that whatever may have happened long ago to cause this reaction had anything to do with your mother or her disappearance."

"You mean, maybe I saw a rat or something?"

Rick's face showed concern. "A rat or something else. I believe in a lot that science discounts, but even so I try not to jump to conclusions. You need to keep an open mind. Explore the possibilities. Eliminate them one at a time."

Linda searched his eyes. "I'm sure you're right. But tell me, how much stock do you put in intuition?"

"When the feeling is strong, it's almost always dead on," Rick said.

"Well, this feeling is strong, and it's telling me that whatever caused me to react the way I did had to do with my mother. And that Mrs. Pritchard was involved." She exhaled. "If only I could remember."

Rick sat back and closed his eyes.

A moment later he leaned toward her. "Listen, Linda, I want you to know I'll help you anyway I can. And the first thing I'd like to do is give you a piece of advice."

"Shoot."

"If foul play was involved and the person responsible finds out who you are and that you've been snooping around—you'll be in danger."

"I've thought of that."

"My advice is to turn it over to the police."

"What are they going to do after twenty years? I haven't a shred of evidence. They're the ones who will think I'm crazy."

Rick looked thoughtful, then nodded. "I guess you're right. You know, there's evidence that everything that's ever happened to you is buried in your subconscious mind. Everything in this life. Everything in past lives, too."

"Past lives? Please."

"I guess Episcopalians don't believe in past lives, right?"

"Nor do Presbyterians. But I do believe that whatever happened in this one is in there somewhere."

"So what you need is a way to pull it out," Rick said.

"Any suggestions?"

"You might try regression therapy," he said. "I know of someone who does that sort of thing. Of course, you ought to be aware, they say you experience whatever happened as though it were the first time."

Linda felt a fluttering sensation in her stomach. "I'm not sure that I believe it would really work."

"No harm in trying."

She shook her head. "No harm? What if it did work? Okay, the truth is, I don't think I'm ready to go through what I'd experience. I want to know. Of course I want to know. But you can't imagine how terrifying the glimpse of that memory was." She shook her head. "I guess I'll have to think about it."

An hour later, Linda backed her car into the only spot she could find within three blocks of her apartment. Parking was scarce this time of day. She supposed most people were home from work and had not yet gone for the evening.

She walked toward the small grocery on the corner. The air felt charged with a subtle energy and she noticed that the sky was darker than usual for the hour. Birds chirped frantically in trees along the street.

Linda passed through the open doorway, exchanged smiles with an Asian woman who sat on a stool behind the checkout counter, picked up a shopping basket and started down the produce aisle. She stopped in front of the artichokes, inspected one, and placed it in her basket. After that big lunch, an artichoke and a salad would be enough for dinner.

She selected a head of Boston lettuce, turned down the aisle toward the cash register and the words written in reverse on the store window at the front of the little grocery came into view.

Wu's Grocery. Established 1965.

Linda smiled at the woman as she placed the basket on the counter. "You've been in the neighborhood a long time," she said, nodding toward the window

"Thirty years. No, more now." She rang up the artichoke and the lettuce. "You're new, aren't you?"

"Moved in a couple of weeks ago. Just up the street. You know, I once had an uncle who lived around here. Maybe you'd remember him."

"His name?"

"Robert Cheswick," Linda said. "Would have been twenty or so years ago."

"Twenty years is long time." She cocked her head to one side. "Robert Cheswick . . . Robert . . . Robbie Cheswick." Her face lit up. "I remember Robbie Cheswick. Handsome man."

"He had a wife then, too, didn't he?"

"Oh yes, I remember. Nina . . . pretty." She handed Linda the bag. "They were handsome couple, and their little girl." The woman leaned forward as if sharing a secret. "She was precious. Used to play here while Nina shopped. Always wanted cookie."

An image of a little girl tugging at a woman's hand flashed in Linda's mind. It was a gentle hand. The little girl pointed to a box of cookies.

"I heard that she, that Nina, left them," Linda said. "Is it true?"

The lady frowned. "I suppose. Very sad." She shook her head. "People in this neighborhood used to come and go a lot."

A voice from behind said, "Although a lot of us have been around for years."

Linda turned to saw a woman with long, dark hair streaked with white, and large, round eyeglasses.

She smiled and extended her hand. "Gloria Barker."

Linda took it, thinking fast. Should she make up a false name? Should she lie—start weaving a web?

"Linda Cheswick," she said.

"Linda Cheswick? Not Little Lily?"

"No, no. As I was telling this lady, Robert Cheswick was my uncle. I'm Lily's cousin. People often mix us up because our names are so close."

"I see." Gloria chewed her lower lip. "I knew your uncle quite well. Whatever became of him?"

"He died in Vietnam."

Gloria brought a hand to her mouth. "I didn't know. I'm so sorry to hear that."

"Don't suppose you know what happened to Lily's mother."

Gloria's brow furrowed. "There were rumors . . . "

"Another man?" Linda said.

Gloria nodded. "People thought she ran off with Greg Hamilton. But he showed up about three years later claiming he hadn't laid eyes on her."

The lady behind the counter nodded. "That's what everybody said."

"Does, uh, Greg Hamilton still live in the neighborhood?"

"Yes. He's a lawyer now . . . married. Just left one day, about the same time Nina did." Gloria shrugged. "Everybody knew they'd been seeing each other before Nina and your uncle were married and that he was crazy about her, so people assumed—" She looked at Linda with an eyebrow cocked. "Should I be telling you this?"

"When he got back, where did he say he'd been?"

"He said he'd taken off to Europe for six months. Then down to law school in Virginia."

"And he didn't say anything to anyone before he left?"

"No. That's why everyone put two and two together. Of course, according to him we were all wet."

Lightning lit the store. A clap of thunder rattled the plate glass; the lights dimmed. Outside, leaves rustled and branches swayed. A gust swished through the doorway.

"Bad storm is coming." Mrs. Wu rushed to close the door.

There was another flash followed by another clap. Rain began pounding the pavement and streaming down the plate glass.

"Live far?" Gloria said.

"Next block. My apartment's in the Pritchards'."

Her eyebrows lifted. "That's where your uncle lived. Same apartment?"

"I believe it is. Second floor in back."

"Hal Junior live across the hall in front?"

"Right. I haven't met him, though."

Gloria put her hand on her hip and gazed at the rain. "Poor Hal. He was a law student at Baltimore University when I met him, but he dropped out. Then he got drafted. Never could get it together, especially after he came back from Vietnam. Now he's a bartender at the Rathskeller."

"Did he live there when my uncle and Nina did?"

"Oh yes, I'm sure, although I don't remember exactly when he went into the service."

The rain wasn't as heavy now. Time was running out. "Is anyone else still around from back then?"

"Well, let's see. There's Brenda. She married Greg."

"Greg Hamilton?"

Gloria nodded. "And I suppose there are others." She leaned toward the window. "The rain is dying down. We should make a dash for it."

"Which way are you headed?" Linda said.

"A block farther than you. Got an umbrella?" Gloria held up hers.

"Afraid I don't."

"We'll share," Gloria said. "Good night, Mrs. Wu."

Linda said good night, and the two of them stepped outside. Gloria opened the umbrella and made room.

"I love this old neighborhood." Gloria sighed. "You must meet more of your new neighbors. Once you do, I guarantee it will start to grow on you, too."

"I'd like that very much."

They walked together under the umbrella in the rain, not speaking, past wrought fences and gates, white stone steps and window boxes filled with geraniums and impatiens. The rain had settled into a drizzle. The look and the feel of vintage houses made Linda think of Mayfair or Bloomsbury in London.

Gloria broke the silence. "You should come to the Rathskeller.

That's where you'll meet everyone. The big day is Friday, beginning after work."

"Does Greg Hamilton go there?"

"Often," Gloria said. "I'll be happy to introduce you."

Gloria stopped in front of the Pritchards'.

"I know this house well." Gloria chuckled. "Especially the basement."

"The basement?"

"Before the laundromat was built, the Pritchards were the only people who had a washer and a dryer. They used to let people use them for a few dollars a week."

"Anyone could just walk in off the street?"

"There was a list of people who . . . subscribed, so to speak. You got a key to the front door. The apartments each have their own separate locks, of course."

"That's interesting." Linda looked her in the eye. "Nice to meet you, Gloria." She bounded up the steps and turned when she was under the doorway overhang. "See you at the Rathskeller."

Gloria smiled and waved. Then her face disappeared and the umbrella bobbed away.

Linda slipped her key into the lock. She paused by the cellar door before starting up the steps. If only it could speak. Well, now she knew someone who could. His name was Greg Hamilton.

Six

Rick's legs ached, especially the tops of his thighs. Even so, he pushed harder on the pedals of the stationary bike. The readout on the screen said he was now on the uphill stretch. More effort was needed to maintain speed.

It was best to put one's mind in another place when the going got tough, and this evening—thanks to Linda Cheswick—he was not having a bit of trouble in this regard. He could see her in his mind's eye, auburn hair cropped close, tossed casually across her forehead. The wisp of freckles across her nose. That smile. Her smile. How would he put it into words? It wasn't so much the straight, white teeth in contrast to creamy skin that made it special. It was more the way her mouth curved on one side setting her face askew. It gave her face character. Made her alive. Incredibly alive. Everything about her was. Her eyes. Green this time. The same light shone from them that had now for a millennium.

Funny how eyes were a window on the soul. Of course, he knew that hers was old, very old. As old as his. He also knew that hers was troubled. And not just because he could see it in her eyes.

The task in front of him wasn't going to be easy. Her case was proof of the axiom, "If it can go wrong, it will."

He had thought she was ready to move on. The whole group had. Okay, so she was a little slower than the rest. One last life, that's all she needed. He'd go with her. The others would sit this one out. Meditate. She'd get it right this time. Then they'd all move to the fourth degree. It was a great group of souls. No sense breaking it up.

But no. Events and her reaction to them had caused her to backslide. Instead of one last life on earth, another had been required.

The others had become impatient and moved on. But he couldn't do that. Even so, he had decided against joining her in life this time around. Of course he'd been skittish. There was danger in incarnating if one had no further lessons to learn. Because of the amnesia the possibility existed of creating karma that would draw you back again and again. This had very nearly been what happen to him last time. Better to wait.

Then complications had developed in the path they'd laid down so carefully for her, and he'd volunteered to enter Rick Henderson's lifeless body to try to get her back on track. What choice had there been? He didn't want to lose her, and if all went well, they could still rejoin the others.

If only she would have regression therapy done. That might make things easy.

Doggone it. He shouldn't have suggested it so soon. He'd played that card too quickly. Now he'd gone as far as he could. For now at least.

You can't interfere with free will!

Right, Otto.

His legs were churning and he was puffing but it was still a way to the top of the hill. Then he'd be able to coast.

Coast? On this bike, maybe, but not with her. Nothing was ever easy in these matters.

What in the world had happened in the basement? Why had the mother disappeared? Where was she?

Linda's upbringing was such that now she was oblivious. Blind. Without a clue. She had no inkling why she was here. All he could do was suggest. Hint. His hands were tied.

Nina and Robbie Cheswick had fit the requirements perfectly, had been sure to create optimum circumstances. The thing had looked like a piece of cake, to use a tired cliche. Then Nina had disappeared and Linda had gotten shuffled off to grandma's.

What had Linda said? Oh yes. Minnie had been a Presbyterian, then an Episcopalian. Brother.

A lot Linda could learn from her.

For the greatest of these is love, remember?

Easy to say where you are, Otto. Know something? I learned it again today. It's easy to make mistakes when you're looking for solutions and running out of time. Panic sets in.

It's unfortunate for Linda that the end of the cycle is bearing down.

Where is the mother, Otto? If Linda finds her, maybe it'll set her back on track.

You know as well as I do that I can't tell you, Rick. Free will. You and Linda will have to find her without my help.

If Linda will even allow me to help.

Be yourself.

Sounds like the Genie in Aladdin. Buzz, Buzz, *bee* yourself!

Still not bad advice.

The grandmother, Otto. Why did Linda have to be brought up by the grandmother?

The best laid plans . . .

But an Episcopalian?

Charity, Rick. Charity.

Uh-huh.

You'll bring Linda around, Rick. Talk to her. She'll listen to you.

You know the rules as well as I.

So there are some things you can't tell her. Things she has to find out on her own. That's the point of life.

Such a gift you have for the obvious.

Point her in the right direction. Talk theoretically.

What if she doesn't ask? Worse, what if she doesn't listen? Suppose she goes out of her way to make sure she never lets me in a position where I can talk to her about something other than advertising and vodka?

Stay centered. It'll work out.

There's no guarantee. I could lose her, Otto. She could get recycled.

That's a chance you and she agreed to take.

As if there had been a choice.

Rick focused on the control panel. There was nothing he could do but play the game. Except that it wasn't a game. This was the real thing. Her last chance. He almost could hear what the others would say if he failed. If *she* failed.

Came right to the edge, she did. The cusp. Messed up in her last two lives. Big time. But it happens. The free will. The amnesia. But, as long as you're in the third degree, you've got to have it. Everyone has to play by the same rules. A real shame in her case, though. She came so close. Had to repeat, to start all over. Recycled her to New Earth. Hunter-gatherer society, you know. Of course, she wasn't the only one who came close. Shame, though, she and Rick had to be separated. He had to advance with the rest of their group. It's extremely doubtful she'll ever catch up. But, let's hope. It could happen. Eternity is a long, long time. Anything can happen.

The pedals suddenly spun effortlessly. Rick felt the muscles in his thighs go limp.

After a short cool-down period, he stepped off the bike, put on his white terry-cloth bathrobe and walked out the door to the elevator.

So there were obstacles. What else was new? Life was full of obstacles, one right after the other. And he had volunteered.

He stepped aboard the elevator and pushed the button.

At least now she was here and they were back together even if Linda didn't recognize him. He'd just have to *bee* himself.

Now, if he could only extricate himself from Meg. He'd already come a long way in accomplishing this. Meg had said he wasn't the same man she'd known before his "near death" experience. How little did she know how accurate she was.

At least she was cognizant of the fact the situation between them had changed dramatically. They had not had sex since the "accident." The romantic spark was gone. It was time now to make their new status as friends instead of lovers official. He would be gentle, understanding. He sincerely liked and respected her. More important than anything, their relationship had the potential to create karma that would hold *him* back. Yes, he would be gentle.

Imagine the irony.

Did you hear? As it turns out, Linda made it and Rick's the one who got recycled. And all along we were worried about the wrong half of that pair.

Rick opened the door to his apartment, went to the telephone and dialed.

"Meg?"

"Oh, hi Rick. What's up?"

"Meg, would you be terribly upset if I canceled for Saturday?"

There was a pause. "No, I guess not. Is something wrong?"

"Something has come up. In a way it's something good. At least I hope you'll think so, too. What say we go for a drink after work on Monday? I'd like to tell you about it."

"I'd love to Rick, but I've got focus groups on Monday and Tuesday nights."

"Lunch?"

"You wouldn't believe what a bear next week is shaping up to be, and I'm on vacation the following week. I'm gonna have reports to write so I'm planning to eat in."

"How about a quick drink on Wednesday? It'll only take a few minutes."

"Sounds important. Not ominous, I hope?"

"I'd rather we talked about it then."

"Okay, Rick. We'll talk about it then. Wednesday, after work. Brass Rail?"

"Meet you in the lobby."

Seven

Linda looked up to see Rick in the doorway of her cubicle, straightening his tie. It was strange how his presence made that knot form in her stomach. It was getting so she looked forward to it being there. Or, was it that she actually looked forward to seeing *him?* She mustn't allow that to happen. She'd have to keep up her guard.

"It's Friday," Rick said. "What say we go for a drink?"

She put down her pencil. "Quitting time already?"

Rick checked his watch. "Five on the nose, and it's my treat."

"I'm honored." Linda opened a drawer and took out her handbag.

Rick said, "Any suggestions where?"

Twenty minutes later she and Rick walked into the Rathskeller and it occurred to Linda that it still may have been light outside, but no one would have known it. There were no windows. The room was lit by a few small bulbs behind the bar and candles in jars on wooden tables. A juke box on the far wall gave off some light but its multi-colored glow was dimmed by a cloud of smoke that floated against the molded tin ceiling.

"That must be the landlady's son," Linda said softly.

Rick leaned against the bar. Linda hoisted herself onto one of the high stools and watched Hal Junior fix a drink. He had long hair, sixties style, and an overgrown mustache. She wondered what he'd done with his peace medal.

He stepped in front of her. "Hello, neighbor. What's your poison?"

"Neighbor?"

"You're Little Lily. My mother told me." He held out his hand. "Call me Hal Junior. Everybody does."

"What'll it be, Linda?" Rick said.

"White wine."

"Light beer for me—draft," Rick said.

Hal Junior left.

"Did you hear that? People called me Little Lily when I was a child. Do you think he knows?"

"Play it straight and see."

A minute later Hal Junior arrived with their drinks.

"Linda's just learned that her uncle used to live in her apartment," Rick said. "That's a coincidence, isn't it?"

"*N'est pas?*" he said. "Sorry to hear he was killed in Nam. Put time in there myself. A real hell hole."

"Did you know him well?" Linda said.

"Better than you did, judging from your age."

"It is a small world, isn't it?" Rick said. "Imagine. You were knocking around in this neighborhood with Gloria and Linda's uncle, Robbie, and that whole crew—right?"

"I said so, didn't I?"

"Guess you also knew Nina, then," Rick said. "That was her name, wasn't it? I'm talking about Robbie's wife."

"Nina, right."

"Whatever happened to her?" Rick said.

"She left."

"Like that?" Rick snapped his fingers.

"Yep," Hal Junior said. "Excuse me. I got a customer."

"Big help," Rick said when he was out of earshot.

"At least he bought that I'm Robbie Cheswick's niece."

"Maybe. He's thought about it, or he's good at arithmetic to figure out how old you were back then. He doesn't look good at arithmetic."

Gloria Barker came through the door. Linda squeezed Rick's arm. "Casually look to your right. That's Gloria. The one with the long hair and glasses."

Gloria and another woman of about forty scanned the room. Gloria's eyes came to rest on Linda. She nudged her companion.

They started over.

"You kept your promise," she said. "How delightful."

"Thought it would be fun to meet some neighbors. This is Rick Henderson—Gloria Barker."

"And this is Brenda Hamilton," Gloria said.

"You must be Greg's wife," Linda said.

Brenda's eyes narrowed. "How do you know Greg?"

"I don't. It's just that Gloria said he knew my uncle."

"You two from around here?" Rick said.

"Grew up together in the neighborhood." Gloria cocked a thumb toward Linda. "Both had a crush on her uncle at the same time. There was nothing more exciting than a hunk who went to Johns Hopkins. We'd wait hours hoping he'd come in here."

"Why don't we just forget the old days?" Brenda said.

"But I'm interested to hear about my uncle," Linda said. "Hardly knew him. He went overseas when I was three or four and never came back."

Brenda's eyes grew narrow again. "You must be about the same age as Little Lily."

"Funny we got practically the same name, isn't it? You see, our grandmother's name was Linda and her nickname was Lily."

Hal Junior arrived. "The usual, Ladies?"

"I couldn't help noticing you didn't ask them if they wanted poison," Rick said.

"Poison's reserved for newcomers, like yourself." Hal Junior turned and left.

"Such a pleasant fellow," Rick said. "Has he always been this charming?"

"He was strung out on drugs for years, as I recall," Gloria said.

Brenda said, "If you can't say something nice, Gloria . . . "

"What about Lily's mother," Linda said. "What was she like?"

Gloria cut her eyes toward Brenda. "Some people were jealous of her."

"That wasn't necessary, either," Brenda said.

"True, though." Gloria shrugged. "And what do you expect when practically every male in the neighborhood was crazy about her."

"Must have been special," Rick said.

"Have to admit—she was a beauty," Gloria said.

Hal Junior reappeared and arranged their drinks on the bar. "You should have seen her in a miniskirt."

Gloria picked up a martini, sipped it, smacked her lips. "Brenda's problem with Nina was that Greg was hot for her."

"Gloria!"

"It's ancient history now," Gloria said. "What does it matter?" She downed the martini in two pulls.

"Anybody want another drink?" Hal Junior said. "I got another customer."

"Bring me another 'tini, H. J.," Gloria said. "That was the size of the last one. Teeny."

Rick said, "Aside from causing the male population of the neighborhood to take several cold showers a day, whatever happened to Nina?"

"Most still wonder if she didn't really run off with Greg," Gloria said.

"Can we talk about something else?" Brenda said.

Gloria said, "Probably claims he didn't so Brenda will let him live in peace."

"I know for a fact he didn't run off with her, or anyone," Brenda said.

"How so?" Rick said.

Brenda bit her lower lip. "It's just that he . . . he told me what he did and why he left, and Nina wasn't part of it. That's all."

"Boy, that's convincing, Brenda" Gloria picked up a fresh martini and sipped.

"I just know she wasn't with him—understand?"

Gloria raised her glass and looked over the rim at Brenda as she sucked in gin. "You haven't said anything that would lead me to believe Greg Hamilton didn't run off with Nina Vezzani."

Vezzani? Her mother was Italian?

Brenda's face turned red. "I don't have to take this from you or anyone. I'm not on trial here and neither is Greg." She slammed down her drink and walked out.

"Touchy, isn't she?" Gloria said.

Eight

The landing in Paris was both fascinating and harrowing. Pedru had never seen such tall buildings, nor so many of any height concentrated in an area so broad. Nor had he ever been subjected to the nauseating and fear-inducing effects of jostling, dipping, turning, banking and braking—a totally unexpected experience over which he had no control. The sudden, inexplicable noises alone were enough to drive a grown man into frantic and solemn prayer to the Virgin Mary.

The blessed Virgin deserved thanks also that he was able to find his way and make the transfer to the Air France flight bound for Washington. The terminal building was utter chaos, the crowds suffocating, and once again he was forced to pass through metal detectors, the paranoia of the fascist swine was so intense.

When he finally had located the correct gate, and he and the other passengers had been herded like goats on board, the inside of the airplane had inspired awe. Incredibly, the size of it was like the ferryboat to Genoa. He had had his doubts that anything so large could fly, but fly it did, and did, and did. The flight across the Atlantic had been interminable. Were it not for the American *putain* in the seat next to him, whose long legs and large breasts made him ache with longing, he might have lost patience. She attempted to speak to him and he with her, but without success. He could tell that she wanted him, wanted him badly. He was certain that she would join him in the lavatory for a tryst if only he could communicate the notion. Perhaps when they arrived in Washington, after they disembarked, there would be somewhere the two of them could be alone.

After what had seemed an eternity, the woman in uniform announced that the plane was on its final approach into Washington. Would this plane never come to Washington again? A bell rang and the light flashed showing a safety belt being fastened.

Moments later the airplane struck the ground with great force. The passengers applauded.

Were they happy to have landed, or was striking the ground hard an unusual accomplishment?

The plane rolled and turned for what seemed an extended period. The cabin was stuffy. Pedru felt perspiration form on his upper lip.

The buxom American seemed calm. Serene. Her eyes were half closed. It simply would not do to vomit in her lap. To vomit was unmanly. No, he must hold back.

Would that this plane would stop.

A jerk. The movement ceased. The engines wound down, diminishing in speed.

All hail the blessed Virgin!

A bell sounded twice. The passengers stood and gathered packages and luggage from under seats and the compartments above. Pedru kept his eyes on the buxom American. She squeezed past him into the aisle.

Oddly, she returned his wink with a look of questioning. He certainly would not let her out of his sight now that they would soon be able to bring to fruition what she must now be aching for. What he, too, was aching for.

He stayed close behind as they and the other passengers were herded once again like goats out the door of the airplane and directly onto an unusual kind of bus. He hung onto to a poll and stood over her as she took a seat.

Her eyes darted at him from time to time. She wanted him, there could be no doubt. He stared at her, mentally communicating that he wanted her, too.

Her eyes darted at him, darted away. She turned her body, showing him her backside, arched like the female orangutan he had seen in a nature film on television. Yes. He would relish playing the role of dominant male. Too bad they were in a crowded bus.

He smiled. Women found him irresistible. It never failed.

The bus jerked and began to lower like the car elevator on the *Comte de Nice*. Then it started rolling.

After a few minutes, the strange vehicle came to a stop and the doors opened at the opposite end from where they all had entered.

The buxom American jumped up and pushed her way though the mass of people in her haste to find a place where they could be alone. He found it difficult to keep up as she descended a carpeted ramp, weaving though the crowd.

A sign on the wall bid welcome to the United States in French and in many other languages. Another pointed one way for U. S. citizens and another for those with foreign passports. He followed her down the ramp for U. S. citizens and was stopped by a fat Moor in uniform.

"Excuse me, sir, may I see your passport?" the fat Moor said.

"I do not speak English." Pedru lifted the Moor's hand from his shoulder and dropped it.

"Passport. Passport." The fat Moor held out his hand.

Pedru pulled his passport from his jacket pocket. This jackass was going to cause him to lose the orangutan.

"I'm sorry, sir, this is the wrong way."

"I do not speak English."

"*Autre direction, Autre direction.*" The fat Moor pointed in the direction from which Pedru had just come.

Pedru eyed the man's night stick and revolver and wished he had not left the stiletto in the waste paper container in Calvi. He would like to let the air out of this one. He shrugged and trudged back up the ramp. No doubt the young woman would be waiting for him after they passed through immigration. That is, if her passion for him did not too rapidly cool down. He had rarely seen one so aroused in public.

He looked in both directions when he came through the swinging doors that led from the baggage claim and customs area into the main terminal of Dulles International. Many faces peered at him from the opposite side of the barricade. People were lined up several deep, straining on tiptoes to see who was coming through the doors. She was not among them. He had begun to suspect this would be the case when he did not find her at the baggage carousel. Her loins had cooled. American *putains* no doubt were as fickle as their counterparts from France. It was disgusting. They were animals. No wonder none were native to Corsica, where those of the fair sex tended to be steadfast in their affections. In Corsica, it was the way for women to keep their bodies covered in honor of their fathers and their brothers.

Pedru pushed through the mass of people into the main terminal, thinking that on the one hand it was good that women of his country respected the Corsican way but on the other it did not seem fair that the men of America and France had to themselves so many young women looking for quick and easy sex.

Yes, it was indeed a shame. He would like very much to have mounted that one.

Pedru stopped. Car rental counters stretched as far as he could see. Avis and Hertz he recognized. He had never before heard of Budget, Dollar, Alamo.

He would go to Hertz. They had an office in the center of Calvi. He knew well two people who were employed there during the season. Perhaps the workers at this Hertz counter would know them, too.

He walked to the counter, took his wallet from his pocket, removed his driver's license and Visa card and handed them to the clerk.

"How you doing today?" she said.

"I do not speak English."

"Uh, oh. We're gonna have ourselves a little problem, aren't we?"

"Can you please give me directions to the city of Baltimore?" Pedru said in French.

"Anybody around here speak this man's language? What is it, honey, French?"

"Yes, I speak French," Pedru said in English. He smiled. "I am please to make you acquaintance."

"Perhaps I can help," said a voice from behind.

Pedru spun around to see a young man wearing a cotton shirt with lettering on it, carrying a knapsack and a tennis racket.

The young man held his hand out to Pedru. "Jean-Paul DuPont."

Pedru took it. "Pedru Ghjuvanni."

"I see. You are from Corsica—the isle of beauty, isn't it?"

"Indeed," Pedru said. "You have been to Corsica?"

"Never, but perhaps one day I will be lucky enough."

The Hertz clerk said, "Okay fellas, we're in business. Thank for helping. I need to know what kind of car he wants, how long he wants it, and where he wants to go."

The questions and answers passed back and forth with Jean-Paul as the intermediary. They finished with the Hertz clerk tracing the route to Baltimore on a map, Jean-Paul translating word for word.

"But wait," Jean-Paul said. "I was planning to go to Baltimore on the bus. I could ride with you and help you find the way."

"It would be useful to have along someone who is familiar with the language."

Jean-Paul was competent in his interpretation of the map as well as precise and clear in the directions that he gave, although the tangled web of signs and roads made their exit from the airport difficult. Indeed, such large roads were absolutely incredible, as were so many cars together in one place. It was like a Saturday in August in Calvi, multiplied by ten. But this was not all that was amazing. The dimensions of automobiles were enormous.

"The Americans," Pedru said. "I have heard of course that they are known for doing everything on a grand scale, unparalleled in Europe. I believed these claims were gross exaggeration, but now I see that they are true."

"Big," Jean-Paul said. "The Americans think big is better."

"And you, for what purpose are you traveling to Baltimore?" Pedru glanced at him. "You need not answer if confidentiality is of importance to your mission."

"I attend Johns Hopkins University. I am returning for the summer session. And you. What brings you here?"

What difference would it make if he told part of the answer? The young man might even have useful information. "I seek out a family with roots in and close ties to Corsica. The Vezzani family."

"Vezzani? Vezzani Glass? Small world. I know them. They are friends of friends whom I have come to know in Baltimore." The young man was silent. Then, "You see, in an American city, people who speak French often form a network, and come to know each other."

It was with sadness and a heavy heart that Pedru extracted every bit of information about the Vezzani clan that could be gleaned from this sincere and genuinely likable young man. It was not the first time Pedru had found himself in the unfortunate position that now confronted him, and for this reason it was unnecessary to consider alternatives. He knew instantly and categorically what must be done at the moment of Jean-Paul's admission that he was acquainted with the Vezzani family. The only question that remained was when and where should be performed the unpleasant task that must be undertaken.

Nine

It was Monday afternoon. Linda gazed into Rick's office, past the ficus tree in the corner, out the windows and across the harbor. The building cast a shadow on the gray-blue water. Farther out, the haze of summer blurred the horizon. She could just barely make out a ship, probably a freighter bringing automobiles from Japan.

Once again that knot had formed. She wished it would leave. The scuttlebutt said Rick and Meg Hargrave were an item. She would not attempt to come between them. Even if Rick were free of romantic involvement, she wasn't interested in him as a member of the opposite sex. He was her boss.

Her boss!

She must keep that in mind. Of course, he also was the only person near her age she knew in Baltimore. An occasional drink with him after work was okay. Harmless, really. He had no interest in her. She none in him. It was convenience. Circumstance. They were business colleagues.

Rick's nose was buried in the *Baltimore Sun*.

"Don't you know that's old news by now?" Linda said. "It's five-thirty. At least two murders, three rapes and a couple of major bankruptcies have occurred since that was printed at one o'clock this morning."

Rick looked up. "You're right. But senseless killings like this poor kid from France who was a student at Johns Hopkins—it makes you wonder how anyone from another country would have the courage to visit."

"No kidding?"

"Yeah, a bullet through the back of his head, execution style. Left him in a drainage ditch along the Cold Spring Parkway." Rick folded the newspaper and dropped it in the waste paper basket. "Where are you headed? Still on your mother's trail?"

"I'm working on it. Haven't connected with Greg Hamilton yet. Thought I'd try the Rathskeller. Want to come?"

It was as dark and smoky as last time when they walked in. Hal Junior looked up from a glass, a dish cloth in his hand.

"Let me see," he said. "White wine and a light beer on tap."

Rick lifted his foot and rested it on the rail. "The man's mind is a ragged edge. Say, Hal, tell me, does Greg Hamilton ever come in here?"

Hal's eyes narrowed. "What if he does?"

"Understand he knew my uncle. I'd like to meet him," Linda said.

Hal said, "So he can tell you whether or not he really took off with Nina Cheswick? Don't count on it."

"What makes you so sure?" Rick said.

"He's gonna tell you he didn't, whether he did or not."

"Because he's got a jealous wife?" Rick said.

"Because he's got a jealous wife."

"But you think they did take off together," Linda said.

"No," Hal said. "She de-materialized all by herself." He nodded toward the end of the bar. "Anyway, that's him down there. Go ahead, ask him."

Hal started working on their drinks.

Linda looked out of the corner of her eye. A middle-aged, balding man with a pot belly leaned against the bar, a glass of ice and clear liquid in his hand. He swirled the ice, took a sip.

"Not exactly Don Juan," Linda said softly.

"Who knows what he might have looked like twenty years ago," Rick said.

Hal Junior stopped in front of Hamilton, said a few words and nodded to Linda and Rick.

Hamilton looked at them and took a sip.

Hal Junior returned with their drinks. "Go have at him. He's all yours," he said and left.

Linda stepped to Hamilton and introduced herself.

"Hal told you I'm Nina Cheswick's niece?"

"He said you *claim* to be her niece." Hamilton gave her the up and down. "Funny, you could be her daughter from your looks. Her complexion was darker and she wasn't as tall. What I don't get is, you have the same last name as Robbie. Her maiden name was Vezzani. My powers of deduction tell me that should mean you're not related to her. Not by blood. So how come you look alike?"

Linda glanced at Hal Junior. He was now talking to a customer. She stepped close to Hamilton. "I'm going to tell you something no one else knows, Mr. Hamilton. I'd appreciate it if you'd keep it to yourself. I am her daughter, as you suspect. I've got to find her. It's extremely important. So far, you're the only person I've found who might be able to help."

Hamilton looked into his martini and swirled the ice. He took a sip and placed the glass on the bar.

"Listen, young lady, this is against my better judgment, but I'll keep your secret if you keep mine. I didn't run off with your mother. I ran off to avoid the draft. It was right in the middle of Vietnam, and frankly, I didn't think that plot of real estate was worth me getting killed." He looked her straight in the eye. "When I got my greetings from Uncle Sam, I headed for Canada, non-stop and alone." He picked up his glass, looked in. "I'm not proud of it. Probably wouldn't help my law practice if it got out. Of course, we elected a guy president who did virtually the same thing. Anyway, keep it to yourself, okay?"

"Of course—you can count on it. I really appreciate you leveling with me." She paused. "What do you suppose happened to her?"

"I have no idea. Doesn't your grandfather know?"

"Grandfather? I didn't know I had one. You know him?"

"Tino Vezzani? Sure, I know *of* him." He looked her way and his brow furrowed. "No. I guess you don't exactly fit the mold of a Tino Vezzani granddaughter."

"Because I don't look Italian?"

"Italian? Not Italian. Corsican."

Corsican?

"Where can I find him?"

Hamilton looked into his glass. Two hunks of ice remained. He gave them a shake, popped them in his mouth, put the glass down. "Don't tell him *I* told you, okay? You never know what a guy like that is going to do."

"This conversation never took place."

Hamilton nodded. "He runs a glass shop near Sparrow's Point. You'll find it in the Yellow Pages. Vezzani's Glass." A wry smile appeared. "The phone company loves your grandpa because of the number of phone lines coming into the place."

"Thank you, Mr. Hamilton. Thank you very much. You can't know what a help you've been."

Linda turned. Hamilton touched her arm.

"There's something else. There were plenty of women in the neighborhood who were jealous of your mother. Her problem was, she was a looker. But she wasn't the type to run around. She and your father were devoted to each other."

Linda took his hand, squeezed it. Then she turned away.

She reached her place next to Rick and exhaled.

"So?" Rick said.

"Brenda knew what she was talking about. Excuse me, Rick, I've got to check the Yellow Pages."

Ten minutes later they were in Rick's car, headed for Sparrow's Point.

Rick glanced at Linda from behind the wheel. "You sure this place is open?"

"The ad said twenty-four hours. Of course, who knows if he'll be there. Imagine. Tino Vezzani. With a first name like Nina I'd always thought my mother's origin was Spanish."

"Italian?"

"Corsican. Where is Corsica, anyway?"

"Let me think. Corsica. An island in the Mediterranean. West of Italy, south of France. Napoleon was born there. It's part of France now. One of the French kings who predates Napoleon bought it. Before that it was the property of one of the Italian city states. Genoa? Yeah, Genoa is across a strait—not all that far. Fifty miles, maybe."

"How'd you know all that?"

"A past life."

"Come on. Really?"

"Oh, I guess I know a lot of history. Good memory."

"I guess I'd better learn as much as I can about Corsica since half my ancestors came from there."

Rick slowed for a light. "There's a James Bond book, may have been a movie, too, where the heroine was from Corsica. Her father was a Corsican don—head of a world-wide family network like the Mafia. They call it the Union Corse."

"The Union Corse?"

"Apparently it does exist—could be as strong as the Mafia. It hasn't gotten as much publicity, that's all."

"I wonder what Hamilton meant by the phone company liking my grandfather so much because of all the lines going into his business?"

The light turned. Rick pressed the accelerator. "Sounds like a bookie operation. Bookies need lots of telephone lines to take all the bets."

"Oh, brother."

Rick chuckled. "Should be interesting. A princess of yuppie-dom walking into a bookie joint and asking to meet her grandfather."

"No wonder my grandmother didn't approve."

"Your mother and father were from different cultures. Totally different. That's something you ought to spend some time thinking about."

"I'll say. My father's side is a bunch of Anglophiles. Ride to the hounds, that sort of thing. It's not easy to face, but I've always had the vague feeling my grandmother thought I was inferior because of my mother."

"It would be interesting to consider how the opposite sides of your family viewed one another. To get both perspectives. Yes, very interesting, don't you think?"

"I do want to find out about my mother and her background. I've been wondering all my life."

"You'll want to get her family's view of your father's side, too, don't you think? It might give you an important insight."

"I'm sure they view them as a bunch of up-tight, stuffed-shirt upper-crusts who look down long noses at the hoi polloi."

Rick frowned. "I wouldn't be so sure."

"Well, if they did think so, it would be the truth."

Linda thought she saw Rick shake his head. Odd. Her attention was drawn to street lamps flashing on.

"I know a terrific little restaurant in this part of town," Rick said. "Maybe we can have dinner there. That is, if you like Italian."

"Italian is good, although I'm not sure about my appetite right now."

"There it is," Rick said. "It's not going to be easy to find a parking place around here."

"Why would there be so many cars? It's the only store on the street that's open." She read a back-lit sign above large plate glass windows. "'Vezzani Glass, Twenty-four Hour Service. We Never Close.'"

Rick stepped on the brake and put on the blinker. A car was leaving. "Either it's the only glass shop in Baltimore and there's an army of kids out there with rocks, or they do something besides replace windows. I think I'd better come in with you."

"I appreciate the thought, Rick. But this is complicated enough already."

He shrugged. "Okay. Have it your way."

Rick backed into the spot. Linda got out and looked through the store window. A counter with clerks behind cash registers faced the front. Lines of men waited at each.

A man in a European-cut charcoal gray suit held the door. He had black, greasy hair, a flattened nose and a gamy odor. He regarded Linda with hungry eyes which gave her a sudden chill.

Everyone stopped talking, and turned.

She walked to the nearest register. "Is Mr. Vezzani in? I'm his granddaughter."

A quizzical look. "He's in back. I'll get him for you."

Less than five minutes later Linda found herself inside a walnut paneled office, sitting in front of a large, antique desk. She guessed the man on the other side was in his late sixties. He was handsome in a rugged sort of way, with gray hair and olive skin.

"So, you're Vanina's child. Yes, I can see the resemblance. You're the image of her, and here I thought I knew all my grand kids. Most are boys—men now. Guess you're the youngest granddaughter." He laughed. "Of course, you can never be absolutely sure. Seems like I've been surprised by kids all my life. Got ten of them." He counted on his fingers. "And you make twenty-seven grandchildren. Of course, there are a bunch of great-grandchildren already." Another laugh. "Wait until Maria hears about this." His brow furrowed. "No, wait, Vanina wasn't Maria's child, she was Columba's."

A sober expression appeared on his face.

"What happened to Columba?" Linda said.

"Dead." He shook his head. "Killed in the shoot out over Mario's bakery. I told her to keep her head down. What a waste."

"When was that?"

"Back in fifty-three. Hell, we was just kids, getting started. Coletti thought we was moving in on his territory. He was right, too. I tell you, those were the days."

He waved his hands in front of him, dismissing the subject. "Enough about the past. Tell me about your mother. How is she?"

Linda blinked. "I was hoping you could tell me. I haven't seen her since I was three. I didn't even know about you until an hour ago, or I'd have been here sooner."

"Hell, I can't keep track of all those kids. Vanina always did have a mind of her own, and she didn't care for her step-mother, either. She just took off one day, and I'll tell you, it broke my heart, but Maria, she said, 'Don't let it get to you Antoine. Kids got to go off on their own sometimes. Let her go,' she said." He turned his hands to the air as if he were releasing a bird.

"And you haven't heard from her since?"

"Not a word. When I saw all that stuff on television about Haight Ashbury, I figured that's where she was, dancing around with flowers in her hair. But hey, I didn't spend too much time thinking about it, not with nine kids left at home. Twin boys still in diapers."

"She never got in touch? Not even once?"

"She always was just like her mother."

"I don't understand," Linda said.

"Columba left home the way she did, when she was seventeen or eighteen. We got married, Vanina was born. Columba never went back." He shrugged. "She didn't like her step-mother either."

"But Columba was killed in 1953."

"Yeah, Vanina was still a baby when her mother died."

Linda said, "Don't you think Columba would have gone back to see her father, or at least have written him a postcard from somewhere eventually if she hadn't been killed?"

Her grandfather looked at her with a blank stare. "You mean, you think something may have happened to Vanina?"

"Don't you?"

"You haven't heard from her either?"

Linda shook her head.

Her grandfather remained quiet for a moment. "I don't know if she would ever have come back here. She and Maria didn't get along. But it's not like a mother to leave her child and never look her up."

"I've got to find her, but I don't know where to look. I was so hoping you could help."

"What can I do? Do you need something?" He opened a desk drawer. "Money?" He showed her a thick stack of bills with a rubber band around them. "Money's one thing I've got plenty of." He dropped the wad on the desk in front of her.

Linda shook her head and stood. "No, no. I don't need it. I appreciate the thought, but it's time for me to leave."

Ten

Linda found it difficult to pull her eyes from Rick. Perhaps it was the candlelight. She couldn't stop herself from studying the chiseled features of his face. He was handsome, but there was something else. He seemed so familiar, as though she'd known him somewhere. But that was impossible.

She forced herself to look away.

The man with a flattened nose in a nearby booth—where had she seen him? The five o'clock shadow, the greasy hair? His eyes met hers and he quickly raised a menu in front of his face.

"At least you met your grandfather. That must have been an experience."

Linda looked away from the dark stranger and back to Rick. She pushed her fork into a piece of veal. "I'm almost convinced now that I saw my mother murdered in the cellar."

Rick flinched. "You really think? But who could have done it?"

"Anyone who had access to the basement. Brenda, Gloria, Hal Junior, Greg Hamilton, Mr. Pritchard, Mrs. Pritchard, half a dozen or so others whose names we don't know."

"Your father thought Mrs. Pritchard was holding back."

"How can we get her to talk?" Linda said.

"We can't."

Linda shook her head. "I don't know what to think, anymore. I've got to get a grip. Life was simple when I thought my mother had abandoned me. It was easy to hate her. Now, I don't know what to think, or feel. What if she was murdered?"

"I'm sure she loved you." He put down his fork. "I know this is difficult, but it seems to me the only way to get this behind you is to find out what happened. You know, this isn't pleasant to think about, but if a murder was committed, there has to be a body."

Linda pushed the veal. "That's right. And so far, one hasn't turned up. If it had, my grandfather would have been notified."

"Right."

"Bodies in woods and alleys and the harbor turn up eventually," Linda said. "Bodies buried in gardens can stay there for a long time."

"You mean the Pritchards' garden?"

"Gives me the creeps," she said.

"I'm a believer in intuition, as you know. It'd be worth checking out. What we also need is a list of people who had access to the basement. They're our prime suspects."

"Maybe Gloria Barker could remember."

"I have a feeling it might be a mistake to ask her. She's still a suspect."

"How about coming with me after work tomorrow and let's take a look around the garden while it's still light," Linda said. "Then maybe we can check out the Rathskeller. We might run in to Gloria."

"Okay. I'm game."

Mr. Pritchard was sweeping the front steps when Linda and Rick arrived.

"Pollen all over the place," he said. "Mrs. Pritchard said the exercise would do me good."

"Mr. Pritchard, this is Rick Henderson, a friend of mine. Mind if we sit in the garden for a awhile?"

He wiped his brow. "Help yourself. Still a little warm, though."

In less than a minute they were inside Linda's apartment.

Rick said, "Strange little man, isn't he? Bet he's henpecked."

"His whole body is an open wound." Linda pushed open the back door and stepped outside. "This is the garden. When I look from here, I feel fine." She pointed to the window of her bedroom. "But when I look from up there, I get the strangest feeling."

"How so?"

"Cold breath on my neck."

"No specific memories?"

"None. Let's have a look around."

Rick paused at the bottom of the stairs. "Where does that door lead?"

"To the Pritchard's apartment. They live on the first floor."

"No outside door to the basement?"

"You mean, how'd they bring her out, if they did it in the basement?" Linda shivered. "This is giving me the willies."

"It isn't easy, but let's try to think. She'd have to have been brought through the Pritchard's place."

"Maybe there's a door around here." Linda started toward an iron gate on the right side of the house and stopped abruptly. Rick bumped into her. Mrs. Pritchard stood in the passageway.

"Can I help you with something?"

"Just showing my friend the garden. Rick, let me introduce you to Mrs. Pritchard."

Mrs. Pritchard's eyes contracted.

Linda spun on her heels. "The rhododendron I was telling you about is over here, Rick."

He followed her along the brick path to the farthest point in the garden.

"Ice water," Rick said.

"Do you suppose she heard us?"

"About bringing her out? Maybe."

"We'd better watch what we say," Linda said.

"I think you're right," Rick said softly. "She knows something and she certainly isn't going to tell us what." He surveyed the garden, shook his head. "The bushes and foliage are so overgrown that it's impossible to know where to dig. These azaleas could easily have gotten this big in twenty years. I doubt they've ever been cut."

Linda glanced toward the house. Mrs. Pritchard was watching.

"Let's go back inside," Linda said.

They climbed the steps.

Once inside the kitchen, Rick said, "I'd like to have a look from your bedroom window."

He followed her to her room. They stood in front of the window.

"Any place in particular that gives you more cold breath than another?"

Linda pointed. "Those azaleas. The ones you said could easily have grown that big in twenty years."

Rick nodded. "Let's take a trip to the cellar."

The thought of the basement gave her butterflies. "Why do we need to go down there?"

"To see how you get from the cellar to the garden."

Reluctantly, Linda nodded. "I've got a basket of dirty clothes. It can be our cover. Why don't you just happen to come along while I put them in the washer."

Rick opened the cellar door. Linda followed. Once again she felt weak in the knees when the smell of mildew reached her. Perspiration broke on the surface of her skin.

"That's the washer and dryer," she said. "Why don't you have a look around while I put the clothes in?"

Rick strolled in toward the furnace.

"There's an old coal chute over here," he said softly. "Of course, the furnace is oil now."

Linda heard a creaking noise, spun around.

Rick continued. "There's crawl space over here behind the coal bin. Dirt back there."

She closed the lid on the washer and moved toward Rick.

"You know," he said, "if I had to stash a body, I might dig a hole right there."

Linda stood on tip-toes. "Ugh."

"Under the azaleas would also be a good spot." Rick walked toward the back of the house. "Hey, look. There's a small staircase here. Wonder where it leads."

"Maybe this was a root cellar," Linda said. "Maybe it leads to the kitchen."

"Can't be sure it doesn't go outside unless we check it out."

"Harold! Is that you back there?"

Linda jumped.

Rick said, "Now does not appear to be the time, however."

Mrs. Pritchard's head appeared around the corner.

Linda forced herself to smile. "Hello, again."

"What are you doing here?"

"Just seeing if there's a place to keep a bicycle," Rick said.

"You will have much trouble getting one up and down the steps."

"It would be a little difficult because of the turn," Rick said. "But we noticed some steps back here. They'd work fine if they lead outside."

Mrs. Pritchard folded her arms. "I do not wish to have bicycles here. I will not allow the clutter. Renting an apartment does not give one the right to take up space in the basement."

Linda walked past her to the washer and flipped it on. "Let's go to the Rathskeller, Rick. Good evening, Mrs. Pritchard."

Linda leaned against the bar. Rick rested a foot on the rail. A man in a white shirt and dark jacket stepped up to them. He wore a name badge that said, "Hello, I'm Fred."

"Howdy, Fred," Rick said. "Where's Hal?"

"Night off. What'll it be?"

"White wine and a light beer on tap."

A minute later Fred returned with their order.

Rick said, "What does Hal do with his time off? Has he got a girlfriend?"

"Are you kidding? Hal likes girls, but I don't know that the feeling has ever been reciprocated. Closest he gets is an occasional x-rated flick."

"Charming," Linda said.

"Have you known him long?" Rick said.

"Since we both went to Baltimore University."

"Never was a hit with the ladies?" Rick said.

"Oh, he used to chase them. Never caught any. Probably chased too hard."

"You've known him a long time," Linda said. "Did you know

Nina Vezzani, too?"

Fred nodded. "Dark hair, eyes. A looker."

"Whatever happened to her?" Rick said.

Fred scratched his head. "Lemme see. Ran off with Greg Hamilton, right?"

"That's not what he says," Rick said.

"No?" Fred shrugged. "Guess I don't know, then."

Linda said, "You don't suppose someone might have harmed her?"

"Harmed her?" His eyes darted from Linda to Rick. "What's going on here, anyway? You two sound like a couple of cops on a third-rate television show."

"Don't know why I said that," Linda said. "You see, I'm her niece, and nobody's heard from her in all these years."

"Oh, I get it. Okay, I'll play along." Fred looked up at the ceiling. "If someone did her in, who would it have been? Not her husband. They were lovie-dovie. Greg had the hots for her, but then so did a lot of guys—including me . . . " He scratched his head. "But I didn't kill her. Not that I remember. Who else? Brenda and Gloria were jealous of her, but so were a lot of women." He shook his head. "Can't see that anyone had a particularly good reason to do her in."

"What about Mrs. Pritchard?" Linda said.

Fred's eyebrows lifted. "Hal's mom? That's a thought. Sure wouldn't have occurred to me. Why would she? Look, Miss. Your Aunt Nina probably took off for San Francisco and ended in a ditch. Or maybe she popped some LSD and landed on the moon. Back then people did, you know."

"With a baby at home?" Linda said.

"You got me, Miss Vezzani."

"Name's Cheswick," Linda said.

Fred rubbed his chin. "Sorry, but you look an awful lot like her. Maybe all that pot from the seventies has caught up with me. Didn't you say you were her niece?"

Rick said, "Probably a flashback, Fred. By the way, can we get something to eat?"

"Sure. Grab a booth. You'll find a menu stuck in the napkin holder."

Linda headed to one in back. Rick slid in across from her. His face was lit by candlelight. His mismatched eyes sparkled.

"Won't be long before the whole gang knows you think Nina was murdered," he said.

"I know," Linda said. "But how am I going to find out anything if I don't ask questions?"

Rick opened a menu. "Bet this place sells instant indigestion."

Linda looked up. "Hal Junior just walked in. He's shaking hands with Fred. Talking. Fred's nodding to our booth. Uh-oh. Hal Junior does not look happy."

"The word is out," Rick said. "I wonder if the bacon cheeseburger is good."

"How can you think of food?"

"We can't walk out now. Besides, lunch was hours ago."

Linda opened a menu, tried to study it, but her eyes were drawn to the door. "Oh Lord, here's Gloria. And Brenda and Greg. They're saying hello to Fred and Hal."

A waitress appeared with pad in hand.

"Crab cakes and more white wine," Linda said. "Oh, and could I have coleslaw instead of fries? And, uh, make that a half carafe of wine."

"Bacon cheeseburger—medium rare. Fries. Beer," Rick said.

The waitress left.

"Bacon cheeseburger? Fries? You look so trim," Linda said.

"There's a health club in my building."

"Uh-oh," Linda said. "They're talking and glancing in our direction."

"Can't wait to eat," Rick said.

Hal Junior was the first to leave. Then Greg and Brenda. The last to go was Gloria, two hours after Linda and Rick sat down.

"Another beer and I'll explode." Rick looked at his watch. "Ten o'clock and a big day tomorrow. Let's go."

Linda downed the last of the wine. Rick took the check, stepped to the bar and handed it and a credit card to Fred. "You guys figure out who did it?"

Fred ran the card through a machine. "No, but we had a good laugh. Came to the conclusion your friend is suffering from paranoia."

"Some people just can't take a joke," Linda said.

Outside, the asphalt was orange with the glow of sodium vapor lamps. The air was warm and muggy and alive with sound: a distant siren, horns honking, the humming of car engines, the rumbling of a truck. Air brakes of a bus screeched in the distance.

"I guess we can't dig in the basement tonight," Linda said. "No shovel."

"I'd say it's time to get some sleep."

They stepped off the curb. Linda heard the squeal of tires. She turned. Headlights came straight at her. She tried to move but her legs would not obey. She lifted her arms to brace herself. Images flashed of Rick's face, the doll in the cupboard, the box of cookies, a struggle in the basement, her father on the way to Live Oaks, Minnie on her death bed, Rick's eyes. She was off the ground, soaring. A wheel of the car popped over the curb. A crash. Glass sprayed, tinkled. She struck the ground. Air swished from her. She saw stars, felt pain—a throbbing sensation below her knee.

She sucked in air, opened her eyes to see Rick's face.

"Excuse me," he said. "I'm not being fresh, really."

"What happened?" Linda could feel his warmth.

"I pushed you and we fell." He pulled away, got to his feet.

She looked down and saw that her skirt was hiked up. She pulled at it, took Rick's hand.

"Are you okay?"

Up she came, took a step and limped. She slid her hand below her knee.

Blood.

Rick kneeled. "You skinned your knee. Ripped your hose, too."

Linda began to hyperventilate. "Did you get the license number?"

"The light was out. On purpose, no doubt."

Rick took her arm. They started to walk. She could hardly breathe. Her insides were all aflutter. She heard an engine, looked behind, felt a pain in her hip.

"Someone just tried to kill us," she said.

"Almost succeeded, too. Here's my car."

Ten minutes later Linda and Rick sat at a desk across from Sergeant Rhinebeck of the twenty-third precinct.

"Let's see if I've got this straight," the sergeant said. "You think you may have seen a murder when you were three years old."

"Three and a half," Linda said.

"But there was never any murder reported. No complaints were filed."

"No body ever found, either. I know what you're thinking, sergeant," Rick said. "But that doesn't change the fact that somebody tried to run over us—after people, one of whom may very well be the killer, found out we may be onto them."

"But you don't know the license number," the sergeant said. "What kind of car was it?"

"As I told you, I don't know," Rick said. "The headlights were on high and it was headed for us at full throttle. I didn't have time to notice."

"I always thought these things happened in slow motion," Sergeant Rhinebeck said.

"Isn't there something you can do?" Linda said. "Someone just tried to kill us. They very nearly succeeded."

"I would if I could, Miss. But who should I arrest? You said yourself you don't know who was in the car."

"Can't you at least put someone on it? Someone to investigate?" Linda said. "A murder was committed."

"A murder was committed, maybe. Twenty-two years ago, maybe. No corpse. No one filed a complaint. Not even a missing person report. Nothing." The sergeant shook his head. "I'm sorry, Miss, but you've been watching too much television."

Rick stood. "Let's go, Linda."

"I can't believe it," Linda said, shaking her head.

In the car, Rick said, "He's right, you know. What can he do?"

"What am I going to do, Rick? I can't go back to my apartment. The killer might be there waiting for me."

Rick turned the key. The engine came to life. "There's not much choice, is there? You're coming to my place."

"You're kidding."

"I've got a pull out sofa. A bit lumpy, perhaps, but it's all yours."

"I don't even have a tooth brush."

He pulled the shift lever, turned the wheel. "Where there's an all-night drug store, there's a toothbrush."

"I'll need clothes to go to work."

"Those will have to do for tomorrow morning. There are plenty of places you can buy clothes during lunch."

Minutes later Rick slid the key into the lock of his apartment. "We'll be safe in here. The outside doors to the building are locked. There's a guard. There's even a television monitor to see who's at the door."

"Nice place," Linda said.

Hand-rubbed antiques were interspersed with furniture made of glass and chrome. She noticed a Buddha on a sideboard and ebony and ceramic figurines that she supposed were gods and goddesses. Oriental rugs in different sizes and patterns were scattered on a dark-stained parquet floor.

"Here, let me open the drapes," Rick said.

They swung apart to reveal a panorama of buildings that seemed to form the walls of brightly lit canyons. Street lamps and neon signs sparkled as did lights from buses, cars and trucks.

"It's marvelous," Linda said.

"Sit down. Take it in. There's something magic about the juxtaposition of activity out there and peacefulness in here. Unlike most people I know, I meditate with the drapes open."

Linda sat and let out a slow sigh. "Talk about keyed up."

Rick kneeled at an antique buffet and took out a bottle of cognac and two snifters.

"Maybe a brandy will soothe our frazzled nerves. Want some?"

"Sure."

He stopped at a cabinet and flipped a switch. A moody song with a Brazilian beat emerged. He adjusted the volume down and turned another knob. The lights dimmed to the level of candles.

The knot formed.

It grew to the size of a grapefruit when he sat next to her. "My, my.

You certainly know how to create atmosphere," she said.

"What? Oh, yes. I see." He handed her the snifter. "Don't worry, Linda. I'm not going to try to take advantage of the situation."

She stared into the honey-colored liquid. She was attracted to him. No denying it. She felt as though she'd known him for a long, long time. Comfort was the word. Yet she had that knot. Strange.

She felt something coming from him toward her, too. It was eerie. And what about Meg?

Really. Meg and Rick weren't married. Not even engaged. She didn't even know for sure there was anything between them.

And what about Brad? What about sex? What about the hurt and pain of losing Rick if she ever did get him?

She looked his way. His mismatched eyes gazed into the brandy.

"Platonic?" She offered her hand. "Platonic, for the time being?"

He took it. "No sweat, Linda." He sipped his brandy and settled back. "Tomorrow, we'll go by the Pritchard's and get some of your things."

The knot was still there.

Rick backed the car into a space half a block from the Pritchard's house. Linda stepped out. Rick joined her on the sidewalk.

She touched his arm. "Mrs. Pritchard's on the front porch. She's talking with someone."

It was Gloria Barker.

"Hello, you two," Gloria said.

Linda waved.

"So nice to see you," Mrs. Pritchard said. "You've been so quiet."

"Busy," Linda said. "Very busy. Leaving early and coming home late."

When they were in her apartment and the door was shut, Linda said, "Am I dreaming or was Mrs. Pritchard actually pleasant?"

"You *weren't* dreaming," Rick said. "Interesting. Wonder what they were talking about?"

Fifteen minutes later Linda descended the steps from her bedroom, suitcase in hand. Rick followed her out the door and down the front steps to the entrance hall.

Mrs. Pritchard and Gloria were still on the porch talking.

Linda pushed through the door and nodded to her suitcase. "Taking a weekend trip."

Mrs. Pritchard smiled.

"Say, if you're headed downtown," Gloria said, "I could use a lift."

"Sure," Rick said. "Be happy to."

"Car trouble?" Rick said when they were underway.

"Yeah, doggone thing's got eighty-thousand miles on it. Time to trade."

"Where do you take your car?" Rick said.

"Call-Bill's-Garage near Mt. Royal."

"I think I know that place. They do body and fender work, too, don't they?"

"Indeed they do. I'm also having some of that as well"

They rode for a while in silence. Rick stopped the car for a light.

"You can let me off here," Gloria said. "I'm only two blocks from my office."

When she was gone Rick said, "I think a visit to Call-Bill's-Garage is in order."

Five minutes later they pulled into the lot.

"I'm thinking of having my car painted," Rick said to a man in a white coat. "Mind giving me an estimate?"

"No problem." The man adjusted some papers on his clip board. "I'll just start at the front and work my way around."

The man studied the car and scribbled on his pad.

"Neighbor of mine's having work done here," Linda said. "Gloria Barker."

"Yep," the man said.

"What kind of work's she having done?" Rick asked.

"Banged up right front fender. Broken headlight. Also needs a new muffler and exhaust pipe. Some other lights, too."

"Been that way for long—the fender?"

The man looked at Rick out of the corner of his eyes. "Don't think I saw any rust on it. Anyway, I wouldn't drive around with a broken headlight for very long. Would you?"

"How did it happen?" Linda said.

"Didn't say." He ripped off the top sheet. "Near as I can figure this job is going to run you twelve hundred bucks by the time we fix that little dent and the rust that's starting in the lower part of the left rear fender." He handed the paper to Rick.

"Rust?"

On the way downtown Rick said, "Don't tell me Gloria's smash up is a coincidence. Right front fender. Headlight?"

"I have a hard time picturing Gloria trying to run us down," Linda said.

"People can fool you. But I agree, there's more detective work to be done."

"Later, this evening," Linda said.

Rick looked at his watch. "Uh-oh. This is Wednesday, isn't it?"

"Right."

"I told Meg I'd see her after work," Rick said. "Her week's jammed up and she's leaving on vacation next week. It's the only time she's free."

"Of course," Linda said. "I certainly didn't mean to presume—"

"Don't be silly. Give me an hour and I'll join you."

"Sure, Rick. No problem."

This confirmed it. Rick and Meg did have something going on. He needed to explain to her what Linda was doing camped out in his apartment. Judging from Meg's schedule, though, it didn't look as though he'd be spending much time with her this week or next. That was something.

Cool it, Linda.

They rode in silence. At a stoplight, Linda had the strange feeling she was being watched. She turned and looked. The man in the car behind looked familiar. Where had she seen that flattened nose? And that five o'clock shadow and greasy hair? Whoever he was, wherever she'd seen him, the guy gave her a serious case of the creeps.

Eleven

Linda opened her eyes. Sunlight shone around the edges of the drapes. She reached for her watch.

Eight-thirty?!

Then she remembered. It was Saturday.

Saturday. Time was slipping away. The efforts of the past three evenings had been fruitless. She was no closer now to solving the mystery of the speeding car than she had been four days ago. And not an inch closer to finding out what had happened to her mother.

When Linda had been little she would lie in bed on Saturday mornings like this one and daydream about how her mother would come and take her away, rescue her from Minnie's stifling discipline, rescue her from the school where she felt different from her classmates. What would it be like, she had wondered, to have a mother with whom you could talk about things like boys? Boys who didn't ask you to dance. About the one boy who did.

Had that older boy asked her to dance because he was required to dance with the wallflowers? Or had he wanted her, wanted Linda, in his arms?

Linda had thought he was doing his job, what Mrs. Abercrombie had told him to do. But a mother, a mother would have said the boy most certainly wanted to dance with her. Of course he did, her mother would have said. She was pretty. She was tall and well-proportioned. It was ridiculous to put boys together with girls the same age. It took boys so much longer to develop. They didn't grow as fast, and they lagged years behind intellectually and socially.

At times she had thought she hated her mother. Hated her leaving, hated her because it was her fault she had to go to that snotty school, her fault Minnie was bringing her up, her fault there was no way out of a life Linda hated.

Then, a night would come when she would cry out in her sleep. *Maman! Maman!*

What happened to you, Maman? Did you leave because you wanted to? Or did someone steal you away?

Pots and pans clanked in the kitchen. Rick fixing breakfast.

Dear Rick. She'd dragged him into this before either of them had realized how serious it would turn out to be. Now, he had almost been run down by a speeding car, and she was camped out in his living room, wearing his pajamas, using his soap and shampoo. Rick hadn't breathed a word about the after-work date he'd had with Meg on Wednesday. But Linda suspected that Meg had thrown a fit.

Linda reached for her bathrobe. Actually, it was *his* bathrobe—dark burgundy with flashy gold lapels. It looked like something one might find in a Victoria's Secret catalog, except it had been cut for a man. Probably some girlfriend had given it to him.

Meg?

Anyway, it was not Linda's color or style but she was not in position to complain.

Sexy, though. Silky smooth. If she pulled her lapels apart she could display some rather deep and fetching cleavage.

Get real.

True, though, hypothetically. Under different circumstances, this live-in situation would be terribly cozy. And it all had come about so conveniently. Meet a guy you're attracted to. Go out a few times. A car tries to run you down—someone must be trying to kill you—so he says to stay at his place, or risk landing in the morgue. You get all caught up in the tension and the excitement of the moment. She'd read somewhere that coming close to death made you feel alive. It was true. So, next thing you know you tumble into bed and make mad, passionate love. The thought of it made her blood circulate and her heart thump.

A interesting fantasy, but not what had happened. Although, perhaps it might have happened, if she had let it. Now the tension of the moment had passed. The opportunity was lost.

Besides, Rick and Meg were . . .

Get real, Linda. The problem isn't Meg. The problem is you. You're chicken.

It was true.

Hurt me once, shame on you. Hurt me twice, shame on me.

When you put your trust in someone, you were asking for it. She'd been hurt enough.

A tap on the door. "Are you awake, Sleeping Beauty?"

Tell him no. Say a kiss is required.

She slipped into the bathrobe. "Best night's sleep I've had in a month."

Rick's head emerged, then the rest of him. He was wearing a white terry cloth robe tied around the waist. "Do you realize it's eight-thirty? I haven't slept this late in a long, long time. May even have been another lifetime." He stepped to the drapes and pulled the cord. The sun shot through. "Ah, summer in Baltimore. It's going be a hot one. Already hazy." His body was silhouetted against the glare. "Breakfast is ready. Coffee or tea?"

"Tea would be great."

Rick moved to the kitchen. "I've been thinking about Gloria and her car."

Linda followed. "Hope you've come up with more than I have."

He gestured to a chair. "I don't get it. If she tried to run us down, why would she tell us her car was in the shop? She may be kooky, but not dumb."

Linda spread margarine on toast. "Maybe it's a red herring."

"Why cast suspicion on yourself? Could she might be protecting someone?"

"We've got to find out if any of the others have banged up right front fenders. Then we'll know if her car was used."

Rick sipped tea. "Another thing I've been wondering, why was Mrs. Pritchard so friendly the other day?"

"You think she did it, don't you? Not run us down. You think she did in my mother?"

"Or is involved with whomever did."

"She and Gloria were talking intently, weren't they?"

Rick nodded.

Linda put down the knife. "Maybe they're together in some sort of conspiracy—although that doesn't feel right."

"I do have a feeling about Mrs. Pritchard, and Gloria. More is going on than we possibly can guess. What say we do some snooping? Saturday morning is a good time to find cars at home."

An hour later, Rick backed the sedan into a parking place near Wu's Grocery.

"So the story is," Rick said, "we're headed off on a picnic."

"But we have to get the car fixed, first."

They walked inside and started down an aisle. Linda picked up the makings of sandwiches. When they reached the checkout counter she introduced Rick to Mrs. Wu.

"Oh, by the way, Mrs. Wu, do you know where we could have some work done on Rick's car in a hurry?"

"I need a fan belt," Rick said.

"Try Call-Bill's-Garage. It's near Mt. Royal."

"I've heard of that," Linda said. "Do others in the neighborhood use it?"

"Most people, yes," Mrs. Wu said. "All the ones who have a car."

"Some don't?" Linda said.

"Lots. I don't, for example. What would I do with a car?"

"But Gloria has one, right? And Greg and Brenda Hamilton, and Hal Junior and the Pritchards?" Linda said.

"Gloria—sure," Mrs. Wu said. "Brenda and Greg, they got at least two. Hal and the Pritchards, they don't have one."

"Interesting," Linda said.

"Have a nice picnic," Mrs. Wu said.

Linda pulled the car door shut. "So, Hal and the Pritchards don't own a car. No banged up fenders in that household."

Rick slid the key into the ignition. "So it would seem. The Hamiltons—do you know where they live?"

"On Lanvale. Left at the next block."

Rick followed her directions.

"There's a place," Linda said. "Let's walk from here. We'll be on a Saturday morning stroll."

Linda could feel heat rising from the sidewalk and it was not yet much past ten.

"Whew," Rick said. "Maybe we really should go on a picnic. Unless they've put up a housing development, I know a place where there's a stream. Cool, clear, water."

She pointed. "There, that big, detached house."

"Try to be discreet," Rick said.

She turned toward Rick and he looked past, over her shoulder. "They're home," he said. "I can see them both in what is probably the living room. They're standing up, talking."

Linda looked at cars parked along the curb. "I wonder which are theirs?"

Rick stood on tiptoe. "There's a garage behind. I'll bet they keep their cars in it."

"Let's have a look." She led the way around the corner and down an alley.

"This must be it." Rick tried the door. "Locked."

Linda stepped back. "No windows." She moved to the gate on the side. "Here's a little walkway to the garden. Overgrown. Look at those vines."

Rick came beside her. "Shall I go in and have a look?"

Linda felt a fluttering. "Why don't we both go?" She flipped open the latch. Rick followed.

A spider web clung to her face. "Damn." She wiped it from her eyes.

"Shush," Rick said softly.

He moved in front of her when they reached the door, turned the knob and gently pushed.

"It's open. Come inside, quick."

Linda followed him and pushed the door shut. It was dark, but she could make out two cars, a Mercedes and a sports car convertible.

"Let's work our way around and have a look at those fenders," Rick said.

They squeezed in front of the Mercedes. Rick knelt. "No sign of damage." He scratched it with a fingernail. "Paint's hard as stone—couldn't have just been fixed."

"How about the convertible?"

"I'm sure it wasn't a sports car."

The door to the garden creaked. Rick grabbed Linda's arm and pulled her with him to the wall. They crouched. Linda held her breath, her heart pounding so hard she was afraid whoever it was would hear.

Seconds later, the door to the alley lifted and the engine of the sports car roared. The car pulled forward. In a moment the door dropped back in place.

Linda exhaled.

Rick shook his head. "Know what? Two weeks ago I'd have told anyone this was impossible. A grown man, more incarnations in this cycle than I dare to count, and I'm trapped in the middle of a Hardy Boys mystery."

Minutes later they were in Rick's car, headed north toward Greenspring Valley.

"I guess that settles it," Rick said. "Must have been Gloria."

"The question is, is she in it alone?"

"The feeling I have is stronger than ever," Rick said. "Mrs. Pritchard is in on it, too, somehow or other."

"It's still only a feeling," Linda said. "All we can be sure of is that Gloria is a definite. The Pritchards don't have a car. Brenda and Greg have two, but neither was used to try to run us down. Who else might it be?"

"The substitute bartender?" Rick said.

"Don't see how. He was still in the Rathskeller when we left." Linda snapped her fingers. "I know who we've overlooked, of course. Who definitely has a motive for not wanting me to find my mother?"

Rick glanced at her, then back at the road. "I give up."

"Uncle William."

"Uncle William?"

Whoops. Rick didn't know about her inheritance or of Uncle William's plans to turn Live Oaks into Levittown. "Oh, gosh, Rick, it's a little bit complicated. You see, my grandmother died recently and there's a will . . . " How much should she get into? What if he knew she stood to inherit five million dollars? Not that she thought he might want her for her money. But if he didn't know, it would never become an issue.

What was she thinking? He was her boss, for goodness sake.

"There's a will," Rick prompted.

"Yes, that's right. And if my mother is alive, Uncle William has to split his inheritance with her."

"Oh, I see," Rick said. "Is it enough to make it worth it to him to run you down?"

"Probably not. It was a dumb idea. Just struck me all of a sudden, that's all."

Rick drove in silence. At last he said, "I know a little place out here where we could have dinner. It's an old tavern that dates back more than two hundred years. First time I ate there George Washington was at the next table—stopped on his way to Mt. Vernon."

"Oh, Rick, you and your past lives! You just can't help making those jokes, can you? Anyway, I'd love to have dinner. Sounds lovely."

Fifteen minutes later, Rick slowed the car and pulled off the road. "A stream is down that path," he said. "If we're lucky, we'll have it to ourselves."

Linda pushed open the door. A hot, humid blast greeted her.

She met Rick at the trunk.

"Do you think we could go swimming?" she said.

"I didn't bring a bathing suit, did you? Of course, I suppose we could go skinny dipping if we have the place to ourselves."

Sure, right. Go skinny dipping is exactly what we'll do. She followed Rick down a bank.

Rick had a cooler in one hand and a blanket under his arm. "This way, there's a path. Careful, it's steep." He held branches for her as they made their way. "We'll be out of this thicket in a minute."

The ground leveled out and the path opened into a wood with tall trees. It almost felt cool in the shade. The air smelled fresh with the scent of pine. She'd forgotten how up-lifting it was to be out in nature, surrounded by it, as though woodland spirits and tiny creatures hidden in the foliage frolicked and danced.

Soon they came to a wide creek with large rocks and rapid water—white water in some places.

"Okay," Rick said. "This is where you prove you're not a sissy. We have to jump rocks to get to that big one in the middle."

"The number one tomboy in eastern Henrico County, a sissy? Rest assured that is not the case. But don't you think we'd be better off in the shade? I'll bet those rocks are hot."

"Not after we take our shoes off and dangle them in the water. Come on."

He skipped from one rock to another. Linda followed. When he reached the big one, he put down the cooler and spread out the blanket.

"You were right, Linda. It is hot." He put his hand in the water. "Water's cool, though. Feels good."

Linda sat on the blanket. "I'm going to put my feet in." She began untying her shoelaces.

Rick shaded his eyes and turned slowly in a circle. He paused. "For a second I thought I saw someone in the trees." He shook his head. "Guess not."

Linda lifted the lid of the cooler. "Beer?"

"Terrific. Hope you don't mind if I take off my shirt." He began to unbutton it.

Linda pulled the tab, handed him the can. She opened a Coke for herself, then took the sandwich fixings and went to work.

She glanced his way. His upper body was well-developed, his stomach flat. A tuft of sandy-blond hair sprouted from the middle of his chest. The right amount. A limited quantity of body hair was okay. Well, better than okay. If it was in the right places and in small amounts.

He took his shoes off and crouched at the edge of the rock.

Get a load of those buns!

He sat, put in his feet in the water up to his knees.

"Feels terrific. You ought to try it."

Linda squatted next to him, handed him a sandwich. She sat, pulled off her shoes, put her feet in. Cool water sent a refreshing chill over her.

She straightened her legs. The current pushed them downstream, causing her to brush against Rick.

Was he conscious of their bodies touching?

Of course he was. But he didn't pull away.

His skin felt smooth, firm. Yes . . . quite smooth . . . quite firm . . .

Wouldn't you know it? Wouldn't you know that damned knot would reappear?

She moved her legs, watched the water swirl around them, and tried to think of something else. Anything.

Should she have told him about the inheritance? What she had said was not precisely true, but it wasn't really a lie. Not exactly. Uncle William would not have to split his inheritance but the result would be the same. He would get less than he was counting on.

If the result was accurate, it wasn't a lie. Not really.

Or was it?

Perspiration formed on her forehead. The sun was hot. She could feel heat rising from the rock, even with her legs in water up to her knees.

Rick stood. "Don't know about you. But I'm going in."

"You're going in with your clothes on?"

"No, I'm taking them off. Turn around, if what I'm gonna do will embarrass you."

Linda fixed her eyes on the opposite bank. She heard a splash.

Rick's head popped out. He blew water from his eyes and tossed his hair back. "Come on in, the water's fine."

"I'd love to, but I can't take my clothes off here."

"Ah, come on. I won't look."

"You've got to be kidding."

Only his head was visible. Then his shoulders emerged and he turned a complete circle with his hand shading his eyes. "No one in sight. What's the big deal? You can trust me. I promise I won't look."

Don't be a dork, Linda.

"Turn the other way," she said.

Rick's head went under. When it popped out he was facing the

116

opposite way, his voice barely audible over the sound of gurgling water. "Scout's honor I won't turn around until you give the all-clear."

Linda stood and unbuttoned her blouse, let it fall, unhooked her bra. "Bet you never were a Boy Scout!"

"Oh yes I was. Made it all the way past tenderfoot to second class."

She unzipped her shorts and let them drop. "Prove it!" She slipped off her panties and tucked them inside a fold in her shorts.

"Let's see. I'm trustworthy, kind, obedient, reverent, helpful, courteous . . . "

Linda stood. A wild sense of exhilaration took hold of her. She was naked. Free, as though she could fly. "Boy Scout, my aunt! You don't even have them in the right order!" She jumped.

Cold, chilling water swept over her. She pushed off the bottom, let out a gasp as she broke the surface.

"Okay, okay! I told you I only made second class. Anyway, it was in the lifetime before this one. What do you expect? Perfect recall?"

She splashed water at him.

"Does that mean I can turn around now?"

Cool liquid covered every inch of her bare body. It was wonderful. Wonderful and naughty.

"Just don't look."

He turned around, not four feet away.

"Don't look? Don't look at what? Your face?"

"Am I blushing?"

He moved toward her. His brow furrowed. "I don't think I've ever seen you blush."

"Trustworthy, kind, obedient. . . . "

His expression turned from a grimace to a grin. He thrust his arms forward. A wall of water cascaded over her. She splashed water back at him.

They frolicked in the stream for more than an hour—until she was thoroughly exhausted. Rick looked the other way as she got out and put on her shorts and blouse. She fastened only two buttons in the middle and left her bra and panties for when she would be completely dry. Then she stretched out on the blanket face down, her eyes closed, to dry in the warm sun of late June.

Rick sat on the rock beside her. "Well, now, that was a welcome diversion from the humdrum world of tracking down whoever wants to kill us."

Linda rolled over, looked up at him and smiled. He gestured a toast with his beer, then took a sip.

"I'm having a good time, Rick. I haven't laughed this much in a month. Fact is, I haven't had my mind off my mother in all that time. Not since Minnie died."

"I take it the two of you were close."

"Minnie raised me, but she wasn't like my mother. I never thought of her that way. Something was missing. She was awfully strict, but it wasn't only that. There was a wall between us and the only explanation I can think of is, she disapproved of my mother. Vehemently. I don't remember my mother, of course, but Minnie's disapproval of her somehow made me feel that she disapproved of me, too."

"Makes sense. Why do you think your grandmother disapproved?"

"My mother was from the wrong side of the tracks. Or maybe it was because she was Latin—Mediterranean. Minnie, all my father's side of the family, you might say, they were Anglophiles."

"I see," Rick said. "Have you ever stopped to think about how your mother's side may have felt about your father's?"

"No. Why?"

"Perhaps they looked down their noses, too. Anglos don't have a monopoly on that. Your mother's folks may have been Mediterranean, but that doesn't mean they weren't proud. Quite to the contrary, I'll bet."

"I hadn't thought of that. Anyway, what possible difference could it make?"

"I believe we're each born into a particular family and situation for a reason. Usually, that reason is to learn something we need to understand in order to advance."

"Advance where?"

"In evolution. We come to earth in order to evolve, to round out and fill up our souls."

"Oh, right. Past lives. How could I forget?"

"It doesn't matter if you believe it. What counts is whether you learn the lessons you came to learn and conduct your life in a way that's true to yourself and others."

"You're a strange one, Rick Henderson."

"Perhaps. Anyway, so much for today's lecture. You need to find her, don't you? A parent is awfully special. When you're a child, you think they're gods. Then you grow to realize that it isn't true—but even so, they're still where you came from, the flesh and blood from which you sprang. I can understand your need to know."

"I used to dream my mother would come and rescue me."

"Rescue you?" Rick took another sip of beer. "Reminds me of the song from *Annie*, the one the orphans sang."

"I felt like an orphan. People at school used to whisper behind my back."

"I'll bet it was tough. You need to find her, all right. Maybe for more reasons than you realize. Or, if she's not alive, you need to find out what happened to her. I've a feeling something inside of you won't rest until you do."

"Yes. But it's more than that. More than curiosity. I came very close to lying to you a while ago in the car. Maybe I did tell a little lie. Anyway, it was a mistake. I want to set it right."

A wrinkle appeared in Rick's brow.

"I said my Uncle William would have to split his inheritance if I found my mother, and that isn't exactly true."

She launched into an explanation of the inheritance, her grandfather's will and Uncle William's plans to develop the estate.

"So you're willing to give up five million dollars to save the trees, and to keep the house in the family, the way it is," Rick said. "Must be pretty important to you."

She rolled onto her back, closed her eyes, tried to think of the best way to put it. "It's not easy to explain. It's not like Live Oaks is only a house and some trees. It's not even the historical significance—not really, although I guess that figures in. What Live Oaks is—is my family. People who came before me, who slept in the beds, gave birth in them, walked the alley from the river to the house, met their future husbands in the ballroom, were proposed to in the library. I never met them in the flesh, of course, but they are all my family. I feel their presence. I've spent countless moments with them, sharing important moments while I was growing up, climbing the trees with them, riding and feeding the horses with them, feeling them beside me when I explored the many nooks and crannies of the house. It's as though Live Oaks *is* my parents. I suppose it's because I didn't have a mother or father. Live Oaks gives me my sense of roots."

She opened her eyes.

He stared down at her. "A philosopher once said that something which gives great joy, will also bring great sorrow. Live Oaks has that potential."

"It will bring me sorrow if Uncle William has his way."

"You know, Linda, nobody, not one living soul, can really *own* anything. First that land belonged to the Indians. Except from the point of view of the Indians, the land *owned them*. They were part of it and it was part of them—one organism. Then the first settler from Europe came along and claimed it. He said *he* owned the land. Had a deed from the king of England to prove it. But eventually he died and he couldn't take it with him. So you see, he really didn't own it. Understand my point?"

Linda had the strangest feeling. "Funny you should mention the Indians. I had a dream about the Indians the night I thought I was going to inherit Live Oaks. They said the same thing. You can't own the land."

"My case rests. And I'm willing to bet it was no ordinary dream."

"Dream or no dream, that first settler was a grandfather of mine. He passed the land to the generation of Cheswicks that followed him, and they passed it down, and they passed it down, and so on. Now William wants to sell it off in lots. I'm not going to let him. It would be a betrayal of my ancestors to stand by and let it happen."

"I see how strongly you feel. You say there's a time limit?"

"They're going to court early in July—could be week after next."

"Guess we'd better get busy."

"I hope she's not dead," Linda said. "I hope she's not dead for Live Oaks, and I hope she's not dead for me. I want to meet her. I want to get to know her."

"She may disappoint you," Rick said.

"I know." Linda looked at the sky and didn't speak. Finally, she said, "What possible motive could Gloria have?"

120

"And why would she be in this with Mrs. Pritchard? Good questions."

"Gloria has lived in the neighborhood all her life. Mrs. Pritchard probably met her while she was still in a baby carriage."

Rick snapped his fingers. "Her parents must know the Pritchards."

"Right. They were probably the same age. Maybe they were close friends. Maybe Gloria killed my mother in some sort of fight. I may have witnessed it in the basement. Gloria really didn't mean to do it. Then Mrs. Pritchard came along, and because of her friendship with Gloria's parents, she agreed to help her hide the body."

"It's probably not what happened," Rick said. "But then again, it could have been something like that."

"The bottom line is, we need to do some digging in the backyard and maybe the basement, too."

"More Hardy Boys stuff? I'm not sure my ticker can take it."

Linda glanced his way. "You're right. This is not your problem. I shouldn't have assumed—"

"Now wait a minute. I've come this far. Listen. We'll do it tonight. We'll buy a shovel, we'll go to dinner at that place I told you about, then afterwards when it's really late and everyone's asleep—we'll dig."

"It's a deal," Linda said.

They bought a shovel at Southern States. Ate an excellent dinner. Linda had Maryland steamed crabs for the first time. Then they were on their way to Bolton Hill.

Was this insane? Was she crazy to dig up someone's azaleas in the middle of the night to try to find a body? Even if it was her mother's body?

An image came to her of what she might discover. She pushed it away. She had no choice. She must exhaust every possibility. She must push the ball forward inch by inch, until she got some sort of break. Time was running out. She couldn't afford to become frightened or emotional.

Rick turned a corner and nodded toward the Pritchards' house. "The porch light's on." He backed into a space.

Linda opened the car door. "I'll carry the shovel."

"I don't mind, really."

Linda inserted her key in the lock, gently pushed. The sound of a television came from the Pritchard's apartment.

"Doggone it," she said softly. "I had hoped they'd be asleep."

It was dark inside her apartment. The only light came from a street lamp in the alley. She turned one on over the stove, moved to the back door, peered through the glass.

"It's really, really dark down there," she said softly.

"Good. No one will see us."

"No one will see us. But how are we going to see to dig?"

"Guess we should have bought a flashlight."

"Except if we turned it on, the Pritchards would see. They're still awake."

Linda led the way down the steps. The garden wall blocked light from the street lamp. It became so black that she had to tap each foot before moving ahead.

"No light from the house, either," she said. "It's as dark as the bottom of a well, except for that one window. Must be the TV room."

At last she reached what seemed to be the right spot and stepped off the path. She held her hands in front of her—searching. "Here they are."

Rick came next to her. "We can't do anything now, Linda. I had no idea it would be this dark."

"Damn. I thought there would be some light at least.

"What do we do now?" Rick said.

She put the shovel in front of her, placed her foot on it. "Maybe our eyes will adjust."

A creaking noise startled Linda. Her stomach turned a flip, a flickering cascaded down her spine.

"Is someone there?" It was Mrs. Pritchard. "Felix?!"

Linda grabbed Rick's arm. His muscle flexed.

"Felix! Oh, Felix-x-x-x!"

Silence. Another call for Felix. Then the door shut.

Linda exhaled. "It's no use. There's no way we're going to accomplish anything tonight without some light."

She started along the path to the house.

"Careful with that shovel," Rick said softly as they climbed the steps. "Don't bump anything."

Linda held the screen door but Rick missed it. It slapped shut with a heart-stopping clap.

They hurried through the apartment, out the door and down the steps to the front. She pulled the big door open, slammed it shut when Rick was through, then scampered down the steps of the porch.

Rick shut the car door, turned the key. "The trip out was even more exhilarating than the trip in."

A dark cloud settle over Linda. "What a botch."

He pulled the gearshift. "You know, it is your apartment. Why did I feel like a thief fleeing from it?"

"What am I going to do, now, Rick? How am I ever going to find out what happened to her?"

Some who die as atheists, or those who have bonded
to the world through greed, bodily appetites, or other
earthly commitments find it difficult to move on,
and they become earth-bound. They often lack the
faith and power to reach for, or in some cases even
to recognize, the energy and light that
pulls us toward God.

Betty J. Eadie
Embraced By The Light

Twelve

Pedru Ghjuvanni looked up from his *Paris Match* and saw the granddaughter of Tino Vezzani with her American escort exit the incredibly tall building and walk west on Baltimore Street toward Eutaw. He waited for them to pass. Then he followed at a prudent distance of twenty-five to thirty meters as had been his custom for several days now.

The Vezzani granddaughter was unlike any Corsican woman he had ever seen. She was completely American in her appearance, and beautiful. Her legs stretched farther than the wake of the Corsica Ferry. She possessed a creamy white complexion and breasts the size of melons. She had large bones and was tall, strong and powerful for a woman. The only physical defect he could discern was freckled skin in places. Her mother had not told her about the medicinal value of buttermilk. Even so, she was so much more than he ever could have imagined. An exquisite creature. He was saddened, deeply saddened, that this magnificent flesh would have to die.

Nevertheless, the anticipation of it caused his pulse to race and his

125

skin to tingle. Twice in the past week he had awakened in the middle of the night from a dream. She was groveling at his feet, pleading with him. This dream had aroused him greatly, but it was best not to think about it. It was a distraction he could not afford.

The Vezzani woman and her escort waited for a traffic light. Pedru stared into a shop window, glancing at them from the corner of his eyes.

He must confess that her residence in the very tall building with a guard and television monitors had slowed the progress of his mission. She entered and exited only through the parking garage which required a plastic credit card device.

Ah, but she would let down her guard. It was inevitable. Time would be required, of course. Perseverance also would be required. Pedru Ghjuvanni was prepared. He could not return to his native land until his mission was complete. But when he did return it would be as an avenging angel. An angel not of mercy but of death. He would return to the glory and the adoration of the entire Ghjuvanni clan.

Thirteen

It was Wednesday. Linda and Rick had gone to the Rathskeller every evening and had questioned anyone who could remember anything about the neighborhood twenty years earlier. No luck. They had no more information now than they had had before.

As the days had slipped by an incessant queasiness had grown in her. She jumped at every sound. Her heart would race and she would stop whatever she was going to investigate. She knew that she must be cautious, extremely cautious, even though at times she felt like dashing ahead and to hell with the consequences. Often she felt outside herself, as if viewing action and events from a spot slightly above and behind her right shoulder. Time was running out. Perhaps as early as the middle of next week, Live Oaks would be delivered to Uncle William on a platter along with a carving knife and a whetstone. She must do something. Even doing something wrong was better than sitting and watching Live Oaks slip away. Soon there would be nothing to lose in confronting Gloria or Mrs. Pritchard head on.

Except perhaps her life.

She had not, however, tried to dig again in the basement or the backyard. The time had come. It seemed the only avenue available.

127

She came to this conclusion while she and Rick were in Kentucky making a presentation to E. F. Watsford, Sr., his CPA, and Frank. She was seated at a conference table, the three men across from her. Rick was standing with a projection screen behind him. He looked sharp in a dark gray suit, white shirt with red and blue striped tie.

"As you can see from this slide, gentlemen," Rick said, "bourbon sales have been declining from six to ten percent each year. During this time, Watsford's share has increased. But even with a bigger piece of the pie, sales volume is off."

The question on Linda's mind was, should she ask Rick to come with her, or should she work alone? His heart didn't seem to be in what he referred to as the Hardy Boys stuff.

"At our last meeting here with Frank, we recommended that the distillery introduce a brand of vodka, one of the few distilled spirits that has enjoyed even a modest increase in sales in the past few years."

She could sense that Rick wanted to be more than friends. She had not known him that long, really, but she could no longer deny she felt as though he had always been a part of her and she a part of him. A couple of times she even thought he might put his arms around her, pull her to him and kiss her.

What would she have done?

"This slide shows the history of vodka sales over the last ten years."

When she let herself think about it, when she looked at him like this, she felt as though she were right there on the edge. If he gave her a little shove she might just fall off.

But which way would she fall? If he shoved too hard, if he tried to force himself on her, she might find herself feeling repelled and repulsed the way she had with Brad. Things were bad enough. She was already practically a basket case. Throw a botched romance on top of everything?

It was better to keep Rick at arm's length.

What had he said? That which brings great joy will also bring great sorrow?

If she did not allow herself to experience the joy, she would never have to feel the sorrow.

Play it safe, at least in matters of love.

Was it fair of her to expect him to risk his neck digging under the azaleas and in the basement? For that matter, was it fair to continue living in his apartment? Wasn't she being what the girls in college called a tease? At best, a mooch?

Can you believe Linda? She's like a sponge—soaks up whatever she can from that poor Rick.

She'd been at Rick's more than a week. She should either return to her own apartment or find a new one.

"This minimal share goal, if achieved," Rick was saying, "will double the utilization of your bottling plant, absorbing the excess capacity you now have as a result of the decline in sales of bourbon.

"Now, my colleague—Linda Cheswick—will share our ideas on how to give this product a unique position in the marketplace, a position that will attract the customers we'll need."

Linda took Rick's place at the head of the table. She looked into the eyes of old E. F. and the CPA as she straightened her notes and gathered her thoughts. They both appeared as though they sampled the product regularly. Each had red-tinged bulbous noses and crusty-looking eyes.

"Let's cut to the chase, gentlemen," she said.

She pushed a button on the clicker and a slide of three bottles, each a different brand of vodka, appeared on the screen behind her.

"These are the top brands—the ones we'll be up against. As you can see, none is positioned as American. One has a Russian name, though it's made in Connecticut, one has an English name and feel. It's riding on the coattails of a sister brand, a leading gin. And the top-seller in the category is Scandinavian—Swedish to be exact."

She pressed the clicker and a mock-up of a full-page newspaper ad appeared. "In this concept we've called the brand 'Watsford's Kentucky Vodka.' The headline says, 'Announcing the First Vodka Made for Southerners by Southerners.' It would, of course, run south of the Mason-Dixon."

Linda leaned toward E. F. and spoke in a stage whisper. "We discarded our first headline because it had too hard an edge. It said, 'Announcing the First Vodka Not Made by Yankees or Other Foreigners.'"

E. F.'s face lit up and he struck the table with his fist. "Hey, I like that. 'The First Vodka Not Made by Yankees or Other Foreigners.' Sorta reaches out and grabs you. . . . Why'd you discard it? What's wrong with it?"

The CPA leaned toward E. F. "Damn Yankees might find it offensive. Gotta be politically correct, E. F."

E. F. said, "Politically correct? They're going to run the ad in the South. It's politically correct in the South. Damn right, it is."

Frank said, "E. F.'s right, Henry. Besides, it's tongue-in-cheek. Anyone can see that. Even damn Yankees can take a joke. Can't they?"

The debate continued and developed into a discussion, not only about the headline, but also about other ideas and ways to promote the product. Linda and Rick left with the charge to develop three or four different approaches and to return in August to review them all. By that time Frank would have completed a study on what would be needed to adapt the plant so that vodka could be made as well as bourbon. The tentative goal was to introduce the new brand sometime after the first of the year.

Linda climbed on board the plane and took her seat. Rick sat across from her.

"Once again, Linda, you were sensational. Are you sure you never worked in this business before?"

"Just doing what comes naturally."

"I thought I would die when they jumped on that throw-away headline, but you did the right thing, Let them talk about it and debate it among themselves. If a client has any sense, and those fellows have at least a little, they'll come to the right decision on their own."

First one engine then the other roared to life. The plane began to roll. Rick settled into his seat. "A presentation like that takes it out of you. Brother, what a grind. And I've got to go back to the office for a manager's meeting tonight at seven o'clock."

That settled it. Rick couldn't come with her even if she asked him to. She'd do her digging alone. The only question left was, should she move out of his place as well?

When they were airborne she said, "You know, I've been thinking, Rick. It's been over a week now since the attempted hit and run. Maybe it didn't have anything to do with the questions we were asking about my mother's disappearance. Maybe it was just some nut using us for target practice."

Rick shrugged. "Anything's possible, I guess. Kind of a big coincidence about Gloria's fender, though, wouldn't you say?"

"I suppose. But I've been thinking. They say house guests and fish start to smell after three days. I've been at your place more than a week."

He gave her a long look. "Let me assure you, Linda, you could live at my place a lot longer than a week and never start to smell."

She shifted her eyes to the hands in her lap. "That's kind of you. Still, I don't want to overstay my welcome. I think it's time I went home."

Rick frowned as though his feelings had been hurt. The drone of the engines filled the silence.

After a while he said, "You're a grown woman, Linda. Your will is your own. There isn't anything I can do to force you to stay. But I have to tell you, I'll be worried about you. I don't expect you to understand, but I feel responsible for you. More than responsible. It's, we're—I wish I could explain it all—everything—to you, but I can't. You're not ready. You're not ready to believe what I have to say and even if you were I'd be interfering. I can't do that."

"I appreciate your concern for me, Rick. I've got a key to your apartment. If it looks like there may be any kind of problem, I'll come back. What say we leave it like that?"

"Suit yourself," he said.

An hour later, Linda and Rick rode in the car from the airport to Baltimore. The buildings of downtown appeared on the horizon. A partly cloudy sky with streaks of sunlight provided the backdrop for the old Bromo-Seltzer tower and the mirrored glass of the World Trade Center.

Rick usually seemed calm, collected and sure of himself, but not at this moment. He fidgeted; tapped the steering wheel. Finally, he said, "I'm sorry I have this meeting, Linda. I wish we could talk. We need to discuss things. A conversation like the one we need to have takes two people. I just can't blurt stuff out."

"Just drop me off. I'll pick up a few things, and come back later for the rest."

He glanced at her, then back at the road. "I guess this means you're really moving out."

"You make it sound like we're married or something."

"You can't image how frustrated I feel, Linda. It's like you've built a wall and I can't get through. There are some things you need to know, some things you need to accomplish. But there's only so much I can tell you before I overstep my bounds. You see I can't interfere with your free will. Giving you unsolicited information can do that. But if you'll ask questions, I can answer most of them, Linda. I wish you'd ask. You have no idea how much I can help you."

"Thanks, Rick. I believe you do sincerely want to help, and the fact of the matter is, you already have. I'm truly grateful. If you really want to talk more about whatever is on you mind, maybe we can go to lunch. We can do it tomorrow if you like."

"Are you going to the Rathskeller tonight?"

"To tell the truth, I'm pretty discouraged. I'm starting to feel desperate. If it seems I'm acting strange, and I guess I am, that's the reason. I'm just plain discouraged and I feel as though Live Oaks is slipping away."

"I understand. I just wish there were something I could do. Let me give you one piece of unsolicited advice, though, and this isn't overstepping my bounds: Don't do anything rash, okay?"

Two hours later, Linda was on the way to the Pritchards' house. Her mind ran down the list of items she'd just purchased at the hardware store: A pick—a small one like mountain climbers use. A small shovel—the one they had bought before was too big. A spade and a flashlight.

Should she have bought a gun? She'd surely feel more comfortable if she had.

For Pete's sake, she wouldn't even know where to buy one.

She turned onto the Pritchard's block, found a place and backed in.

It was twilight. No lights were on in the house. Linda grabbed the sack filled with tools and her overnight bag. She decided to leave her suitcase for another trip.

She held her breath and climbed the steps. Inside, she changed into jeans and a T-shirt. She'd take a basket of laundry to the basement, use that as her cover. If the hole she was going to dig in the crawl space came up dry, she'd dig another later under the azaleas.

She plopped the plastic bag from the hardware store on top of the basket of clothes.

Seconds later, she turned the knob to the cellar door, groped for the light switch and tried not to think about the trip she'd taken down these stairs a few weeks earlier, though it was impossible not to. It was the same dim, twenty-five watt bulb, the same creepy bricks oozing with moisture, that same sickening smell of mold to gag her. Even her skin crawled with the same creepy intensity.

She threw the clothes in the washer and turned it on, hopped over the wall onto the dirt of the crawl space, took out the shovel and began to dig, her stomach an unsettled jumble.

Something about this place—the rafters, the wires, the old coal chute—something made it seem haunted.

She should count her blessings. She hadn't seen any spiders or, heaven forbid, rats. Or ghosts.

Why did she think of ghosts whenever she was here? Because of that demon, of course.

Well, now, how about this? An old wine bottle—Dixie Rose. Probably left by the plumbers when they installed the pipes.

What year would that have been? About 1900? That's went they first had gotten indoor plumbing at Live Oaks. The plumbers had left a stash of empty wine bottles in the basement there.

Take a sip. Solder a pipe. Take a sip, solder. No wonder the pipes at Live Oaks always sprang leaks.

She felt cool breath on her neck. A chill descending.

A ghost?

Whoa. There she went.

Perhaps memories were ghosts, hidden memories you couldn't bring to the surface. If she could only call up that terrible memory. Examine it. It was like Auntie Em was standing in the doorway holding up her hand. "Now, Dorothy, don't look. Don't you dare. If you look, you'll be scared to death."

No kidding.

Well, well. How about this? Another wine bottle.

It's a big job, men. A two-quart job.

If bottles were buried under this dirt it was unlikely anything else was. Anything that post-dated them.

Look at how they were shaped, and the old labels. No doubt about it. These bottles were from another time, a different era. No bodies were buried here. At least not one Linda cared about.

She climbed over the wall and dropped to the floor, the bag of tools in one hand. She would return to her apartment and wait until two in the morning. Then she'd dig in the garden.

Maybe she would set the alarm and try to sleep.

She climbed creaky steps to the entrance hall and remembered that her suitcase was still in the car. Might as well get it now.

The sound of a television drifted from the Pritchards' apartment. She pushed open the front door, descended the steps still gripping the bag of tools. The trees that lined the sidewalk cast black shadows from street lights.

Suddenly she felt eyes on her back and whipped around. A dark form came toward her, a man with arms outstretched. An alarm shrieked in her and she leaped to the side. The form flew past to land on hands and knees. Immediately he scrambled to his feet. Linda swung the bag of tools around her head and let it fly. The sack with shovel, spade, pick and flashlight, crashed into his chest and head, lifting him off the ground.

She ran past him to her car.

An hour later, she sat on Rick's sofa, gazing out the window at canyons of tall buildings that glowed with light. She sipped cognac from a snifter. A key turned in the lock.

Rick stepped into the foyer, an expression of wonder appearing on his face.

"Hello there, Rick. How was the meeting?

He stood motionless.

"Before you come any farther you might want to pick up your jaw. It landed on your chest."

He moved forward. A smile broke onto his face. "What happened, a change of heart?"

"Someone tried to grab me on my way from the Pritchard's house to my car."

"Grab you? Are you all right?"

134

"Never laid a hand on me. I was lucky."

He stopped at the liquor cabinet. "Do you suppose it's connected with the hit and run?"

"I've been thinking about that for the last hour. It's possible, I guess, but I've pretty much decided the two are not connected."

"Just an ordinary mugger, rapist or whatever, prowling the city streets?" Rick shook his head. "Glad he didn't harm you."

"I was really shook up right afterwards, but I'm okay now." She raised her glass. "Thanks for the brandy."

"My pleasure." He poured his own.

"Anyway," she said, "I hope you don't mind if I move back in for a while. I'm still a little jumpy."

Rick raised his drink. "As far as I'm concerned you never moved out."

Fourteen

The following evening, Pedru Ghjuvanni watched the entrance of the parking garage of the granddaughter of Tino Vezzani from the driver's seat of the rented four-door Ford Tempo. Her abduction was turning out to be more difficult than he ever could have imagined. His one opportunity had ended in failure.

He touched the wound on his forehead. A scab had formed.

She had been quicker, more alert than he had expected, had wielded the heavy sack expertly. It very nearly had rendered him unconscious. Not only had the pain been an infuriation, but the episode was a missed opportunity. This upset him, for he had learned that it was rare for her to be alone. Except for that one incident, she was always accompanied by her escort.

The Vezzani woman and her escort approached the entrance to the parking garage of the very tall apartment building.

Pedru's patience was wearing thin. It was time to take a calculated risk, time to do whatever was necessary. Risk was inherent in all opportunity.

Pedru turned the key. The Ford's engine came to life. He stepped on the brake and moved the gearshift lever into drive. The Americans were so incredibly lazy and spoiled they had actually forgotten how to drive cars that required a clutch.

He pulled the Ford close to the rear bumper of the American's car.

Would they notice him? He slid low behind the wheel.

It was as he had expected. They were so absorbed in conversation that neither of them bothered to look around.

The door to the garage opened. The American's car moved forward. Pedru stepped on the accelerator. The garage door closed behind.

He must be careful. This abduction must be carried out quickly, without a flaw. Hesitation could mean disaster. The American looked strong. Pedru must separate them, incapacitate the American, grab Vezzani's granddaughter and flee.

What was this? The American's car was braking. It was turning into a parking place.

Pedru must find one, too.

He mashed the accelerator. Tires screamed, echoing off cavernous walls. He skidded around one turn, then another, and another, searching.

No place—no place to park! Pedru cursed the eyes of the Vezzani granddaughter and her escort for leading him into the bowels of this very tall building. It was a labyrinth of passageways, pipes, pillars, and illuminated exit signs with level after level of parking—blue, green, red, orange, 2A, 3B. How in the name of the Holy Mother was one to find the way?

A parking place at last. He stepped on the brake, he turned the wheel, stepped on the gas, shot forward, screeched to a halt

He pushed open the door. The dull hum of a mechanical device rumbled somewhere below. The burnt scent of electricity reached him. An air conditioning compressor perhaps, or a fan that piped in air. He must be far beneath the ground.

He headed toward a sign that indicated an elevator, looked over his shoulder, turned a circle as he walked. It was not good to be so far from the exit to the street. He could be trapped. Cornered like a beast.

The elevator doors slid open. He stepped in.

This box could be a coffin. The way this operation was unfolding was not to his liking. So many buttons. No way was it possible to know which floor the Vezzani woman was on. He must abort the mission, leave this wretched place.

The doors slid together. He stepped forward and stuck out his hand—too late. They were shut.

Merde.

The elevator started with a jerk.

His car—which level was it on? He scanned the buttons. Red? Green? He looked up at the floor indicator. One numeral after the next flashed red.

P3? P2? P1?

Pedru's eyes moved to the top left corner of the elevator. A camera? Why would there be a camera? Was he being watched? Did this camera lead to a bank of televisions in a central control room as was sometimes seen in American cinema?

He stepped under the camera, into the corner out of its view. By the martyrs of Cap Corse, a security guard may have spotted him already. The guard would see on which floor he got off.

He pushed a button—22.

He must behave as though he belonged here. Surely a handsome fellow such as he would not look out of place.

The doors opened. Pedru stepped into a hallway. He looked both ways with all the causal ease that he could manage. Ah, an exit sign. He would return to the bowels of the basement by the staircase. He would find his car, leave.

He pushed through the door. His eyes came to rest on another television camera, mounted in the stairwell.

He looked down. *Holy Mother of God.* It was like a corkscrew into the center of the earth. Never before had he been so high, except in an airplane. Flight after flight of stairs, descending, descending. They seemed to expand and contract, expand and contract. His knees felt as though they would buckle, as though they were no longer able to support him. He must return to the basement on the elevator.

Pedru turned, pushed against the door.

It held fast.

Why? Why would it be locked?

He hurried down a flight of stairs. The railing felt cold, the risers short. He took two steps at a time until he arrived on the next landing, reached out, grabbed the knob.

Locked!

A hundred curses on the ancestors and the children of the fat American swine. Curses on their paranoia, curses on their untrusting nature.

Pedru backed against the cinder block wall. He inhaled, exhaled, steadied himself.

Above were stairs a far as he could see. Below were stairs into the center of the earth.

He was trapped. Trapped!

Unless he could find an unlocked door.

Pedru ran down another flight.

The door was locked.

Another. Another.

Blessed Virgin, hear my prayer!

He must remain calm. He must think, develop a plan. Yes. He must live up to his reputation for remaining cool in impossible situations. If these cameras were linked to television sets, it would be only a short time before they would come for him.

Beads of perspiration formed on his brow. His palms were moist, his stomach a writhing mass of worms.

He ran down another flight to the next landing, slipped under the staircase, crouched in the shadows. Shivered. Shook himself.

He was cornered like a wild boar in a canyon above the tree line. As the French would say, "In the ass of the bag."

Yes, almost. But not *above* the tree line. A wild boar would be plainly visible in such a situation. Here there was shelter. Here there was a hiding place that would give him the element of surprise.

He reached under his jacket and removed the .45 automatic. He caressed its gunmetal finish, pulled the breech, released it and a cartridge slid into the chamber. He closed his hand around the grip, pressed the safety with his thumb.

This weapon could take off an arm, the entire top half of the head of a three-hundred pound man.

He was ready.

Of course it was true that it would also create an ear-splitting blast in this cavern. It would almost surely wake the dead—every *revenant* from the highest level to the deepest bowels.

He returned the pistol to its holster and removed his new stiletto from the sheath in his boot. It would be more prudent to use the blade, unless he was hopelessly outnumbered.

The click of a lock above, the sound of a door opening.

"Hello!" A man's voice echoed in the stairwell. "Hello! Are you locked out?"

Pedru pressed himself into the corner.

"Hello! Lose your key? I'm here to help!"

Footsteps descended the steps until they reached the landing and stopped. A shadow appeared on the wall—the silhouette of a man in an American policeman's hat. The shadow turned. A pistol came into view. Pedru moved to the opening and darted out. The man's mouth dropped open as Pedru grabbed his wrist and thrust it and the gun against the wall. The pistol fell. Wide, fearful eyes darted from the lost weapon to Pedru, who smiled and nodded as if to say, *I've got you now, you filthy American swine.* Then, with the precision of a skilled surgeon, he plunged the stiletto into the center of an eye.

The man landed on his back. His hat rolled down the steps. One eye pocket filled with thick red liquid as the other eye stared upward, like that of a fish on ice. Arms and legs jerked.

Pedru looked at the name tag on the left side of the man's chest: Bill. He shifted his glance to the knife. The blade was coated with a thin red film.

Pedru knelt and wiped the knife on the man's shirt, unclipped the ring of keys—looked at a television camera as he stood.

Had this little drama been recorded? Perhaps. If so, there was not a minute to lose.

Pedru fumbled with the keys, found one that fit, walked briskly along the hall to the elevator.

Should he attempt to find his car?

A light flashed, a bell rang. The elevator doors opened.

It was not worth the time and risk. He pushed the button for the lobby. The thing to do in this circumstance was to walk out the front door as though he owned the place. Yes, out the front door, into the night. Another car would be easy enough to acquire.

This time he would make sure it was not a Ford Tempo.
And he also would make sure it was one with a clutch.

Fifteen

Linda rolled onto her back and pulled the sheet to her chin. Once again she stared at the ceiling of Rick's living room, at the geometric patterns in the plaster and the swirling shadows created by light that crept in around the drapes. This was the tenth night she had spent on this pull-out sofa. More than a week had passed since someone had tried to run her down. The conversation she'd had earlier that day with Rod Wells played in her mind. She fought to hold back tears.

"Have you set a court date yet, Rod?" she'd asked.

"Next week. Right after the Fourth of July holiday. July Sixth to be exact."

"I see. That doesn't leave much time."

"At the risk of repeating myself, Linda, I think you're better off if you don't find her. This inheritance rightfully belongs to you. That's what your grandfather would have wanted."

"If I were to find her, isn't there a way that I could keep control? And make sure Live Oaks passes to me?"

"Not unless she's willing to sign over power of attorney. Not many people would be willing to do that."

Linda exhaled, turned on her side and jerked the sheet over her shoulder. Every path so far had led a dead end. The Sixth was next Wednesday. Gloria was her only suspect and she seemed such an unlikely candidate. If only time could be put on hold. If only Linda could remember what she had seen in the basement.

Rick believed that every memory, every experience, everything a person had ever seen or experienced, was stored in her subconscious mind. The only problem was to pull it out.

Rick had some strange ideas. Brother. He even believed memories from past lives were there. He'd tried to tell her she was here on earth for a reason, that all this business with her mother and Live Oaks had some greater significance than what appeared on the surface. He'd urged her a second time to make an appointment to be hypnotized. Even had specified a particular parapsychologist.

A parapsychologist? Wasn't the normal kind good enough?

According to Rick it wasn't. He was sure events in an earlier life had something to do with all this. She needed to find out.

How could Rick be taken in by such nonsense? He seemed like such a rational, logical, well-educated individual.

Linda rolled onto her other side and jerked the sheet again.

After all was said and done, though, who really knew for sure? Maybe there was something to the idea of past lives. She felt she'd known Rick before, and she certainly could not have known him in this life.

Soul mates?

What bunk. He was just a good-looking guy. Subconsciously she must wish she'd known him before. Reincarnation or no, she had refused to be hypnotized, and it wasn't because she was afraid of learning about past lives. She was afraid of what she must have seen in this one and would exhaust every possibility before confronting it.

But, hadn't she exhausted them? Hadn't she crashed against another dead end?

Wasn't time about to run out?

Should she do it? Make herself vulnerable?

She was getting desperate, that was sure. Live Oaks was at stake, her family, her roots, her anchor to the world. It was the only course of action left.

She would do it. Rick had a name and a telephone number. She would call first thing tomorrow.

Linda rolled on her back, looked at the geometric patterns and the shadows. It had to be three-thirty in the morning. Time to get some rest. Time to sleep. She'd be worthless tomorrow if she didn't get some sleep. The moment had come to use a technique for getting to sleep that a roommate in college had taught her.

First, she would imagine herself at the top of a staircase with ten steps. As she descended she would become sleepier and sleepier, until at last, when she reached the bottom, she would be fast asleep.

She closed her eyes, told herself to relax. Relax every muscle. Let go. All those troubles and cares—just let go.

First step, sleepy, sleepier . . . second step, beginning to drift away . . . third step, so tired, so comfortable . . . fourth step, peaceful and serene . . .

Her foot touched the last step and she slid onto a billowy, soft, gentle cloud and drifted, floated—weightlessly—into a world of dreams.

She gazed at her feet and saw she was wearing patent leather pumps and white socks. Mrs. Wu offered her a cookie and she grasped it—took a bite.

"What do you say, dear?"

"Thank you, Mrs. Wu."

"You're welcome, Lily. Come again, soon."

Someone held her hand and they walked under the trees. She looked up and saw Maman. She was so tall.

They climbed the stairs and entered the house.

"This way, Lily. We have to get the clothes out of the dryer." Maman spoke to her in French.

"Yes, Maman."

"Careful going down the steps, dear."

"It's dark, Maman." Linda spoke in French as well.

"It's always dark in the basement, dear. Maybe we can ask Tante Annunciate to put in a bigger light bulb the next time she changes it."

"Tante Annunciate says big bulbs cost too much."

"That's what she says, but maybe we can get her to change her mind."

They reached the landing under the twenty-five watt bulb. Two men stepped from the shadows. Linda did not recognize them.

"Papa, Victor, what are you doing here?"

"We've been waiting for you, Nina. There's a debt to pay, and a duty. You're coming with us."

Maman thrust out her hands. "Don't touch me."

Linda stood helpless as the two men grabbed Maman. They tussled. Maman struggled to free herself. She screamed. One of the men clamped a hand over her mouth.

"Stop! Stop! You're hurting Maman, stop!" Linda screamed. One of the men bumped into her and she fell.

Maman broke free and bolted for the steps. "Robbie! Help!"

They grabbed Maman again. One man held her while the other stuffed a rag in her mouth.

Tante Annunciate came down the steps.

One of the men spoke to her in a language Linda did not understand.

"They're hurting Maman. They're hurting Maman," Linda kept shouting between sobs.

Tante Annunciate knelt and took Linda by the shoulders. "Calm down, child, calm down. Your mother will be all right," Tante Annunciate said in French. She picked her up. "Come now. I will take you to your father."

"Maman! Maman! Maman!" Linda flailed her arms, twisted, turned, reached out for her in vain.

"Linda! Linda, wake up!

"Maman! Maman! No! No! Let me go! Let me go!"

"Linda, wake up. You're dreaming. Don't you hear me? Wake up! You're having a nightmare!""

Linda opened her eyes, gasped. Rick's hands clasped her shoulders. He shook her.

Linda threw her arms around him, sobbed uncontrollably.

"Linda, easy. Take it easy. It was a dream. You're okay now." He stroked her.

"She was kidnapped," Linda said between sobs.

"You were crying and screaming like someone was pulling out your fingernails."

Part of it came flooding back. "Mrs. Pritchard—Mrs. Pritchard is my

145

aunt. Tante Annunciate."

"Your aunt?"

"She knew them—the men who took Maman away. Maman knew them. What did she call them? Victor? Papa? That's right, she called one of them Papa. Oh Lord, it was my grandfather."

"Tino Vezzani. Well, well."

"He—he lied to me. He knew all along what had happened. For God's sake, he did it!"

Rick nodded, exhaled. "Boy, did you ever manage to get my pulse working overtime."

Linda had her arms around Rick, his face only inches away. She looked into those kaleidoscope eyes: dilated, dark, welcoming pools. Warm pools inviting her to come in, to enter the place she knew so well. She kissed him. Her body melded into him. So soft, so smooth and warm and sensuous. She pressed her breasts against him, felt a tingling sensation she hadn't felt for a long, long time. It began in her toes and rose up her legs, her thighs, her mid section, all the way to the top of her head. She wanted to stay in his embrace, to pull him all the way into bed and kiss him, kiss his body, be cradled by him, feel those strong arms around her, his body pressed against hers—so safe, so warm, so wonderful.

But this was wrong. She shouldn't. She mustn't.

He belonged to Meg.

She pulled back.

To hell with Meg.

And what about the hurt—the potential hurt? What about safety? What about great joy and the inevitable sorrow?

"I'm sorry," she said. "I'm sorry I frightened you. But most of all, I'm sorry I did that. I don't know what got into me. I'm so embarrassed."

He blushed. "Don't be. I enjoyed it. I mean, any time that feeling comes over you again, don't hesitate."

"I was out of line."

She should level with herself, it had been a heavenly moment and she had enjoyed every millisecond of it. She wanted to do it again. She wanted to do it now. She wanted it to go on and on.

If she were going to recapture it, she'd better get on with it.

Now! Before the chance slips away.

"You weren't out of line at all," Rick said. "Anyway, I'm glad you're all right."

It's slipping away. You're letting it slip away.

"That was really some dream, Rick, you wouldn't believe it. So vivid, real. As though it was happening again."

Linda! All you have on is a skimpy nightshirt!

She pulled up the sheet. "I'm okay now, though. Thanks, Rick, for coming to my rescue."

"Know what, Linda? This is a breakthrough. It was traumatic for you, sure, but think about it. Now you know what happened. You know who was involved."

It was gone. The moment was gone. She had let it slip away.

"You know, Rick, you're right. I had been thinking, trying desperately to remember, but I needed to get back to sleep. And I used an old technique—standing on the top of the stairs and going down. That must have been the connection that dredged it up."

"Whatever you did, it worked."

"I think we should pay my Grandpa a visit, tomorrow. What do you think?"

The next day, Linda pushed through the doors of Vezzani Glass and walked toward the counter. Heads turned. A hush settled over the room. The clerk behind the nearest cash register stopped in mid-transaction.

"Would you please tell Mr. Vezzani that his granddaughter is here to see him?" Linda said.

The clerk's Adam's apple moved up and down. "I . . . I would if I could, Miss. But . . . he, he ain't here."

Linda took another step toward him and placed her knuckles on her hips. "Where can I find him? It's a matter of extreme importance."

"Well, I can't really say, Miss. He's gone away—won't be back until September I've been told."

Linda slid into the front seat of Rick's car and pulled the door shut. "Gone. Vanished. They don't know where he is." She let out a sigh. "They said he won't be back until September."

"You're kidding."

"I don't think the man was lying. Looked too scared—like he was afraid I was going to call the hit men."

"Okay, so he's out of the picture. That leaves Mrs. Pritchard." Rick turned the key.

"I guess so. Brother, does she ever intimidate me."

Rick turned the wheel, mashed the gas. "This time, I'll come with you."

Linda stepped onto the sidewalk in front of the imposing gray stone townhouse. She moved into the shade of a huge oak and scanned the the ornate portico, white marble steps, the stained glass window above the door that held the street number. The butterflies were back, half a dozen or so conducting dive bombing exercises. But there was no time to waste. Today was the first of July. The court date was next Wednesday.

Rick stepped beside her. "Let's go."

They climbed the steps. Linda searched in her pocketbook for the key, found it, inserted it in the lock. It was dark inside and relatively cool. She flipped on the light, looked at familiar cobwebs in the corners of the ceiling, shivered once again at the sight of that cellar door.

She paused at the Pritchard's apartment, took a breath and knocked.

No answer.

She knocked again.

The door opened the width of a latch chain.

"Who's there?"

"Oh, hi, Mr. Pritchard. It's Linda, from upstairs."

The door closed, then slowly opened. Mr. Pritchard stood partially hidden, dressed in a bathrobe and slippers. "Haven't seen you in days. Thought you were off somewhere on vacation or whatever."

"You remember Rick Henderson, don't you, Mr. Pritchard? May we come in?"

"Well, I suppose." He opened the door all the way. "Sorry I'm not dressed. Wasn't expecting anyone."

Linda and Rick followed Mr. Pritchard into a disheveled room that smelled of cat urine. It reminded Linda of a second-hand furniture store that specialize in depression-era oak.

Mr. Pritchard stopped. He seemed befuddled, looked from one chair to the next, then to a love seat. He picked up a stack of mail-order catalogs.

"Down Felix—move. Get out of here you mangy cat. Here, Linda, you and Rick have a seat."

"Is Mrs. Pritchard home?" Linda asked.

"Mrs. Pritchard? Oh, no, no. She's gone—her annual trip to the old country. Won't be back until September."

"The old country?" Rick said.

"Corsica. A beautiful place, I'm told. Never been there myself, actually. Someone has to take care of the house. Hal goes, too, but doesn't stay so long. He'd like to. Sure would. But can't get more than a few weeks off."

"Is that where your wife's brother—Tino Vezzani—went, too?" Linda asked.

Wrinkles appeared in Mr. Pritchard's liver-spotted brow. "Could be I guess. Can't say."

Linda leaned toward him. "There's no reason to beat around the bush, Mr. Pritchard. I'm going to lay it out for you. My mother was Vanina Vezzani, your wife's niece. I'm the little girl who lived upstairs twenty-odd years ago with Nina and my father, Robbie Cheswick."

Mr. Pritchard shifted in his chair. The catalogs slid from his hands. "Oh, no. Now see what I've done."

Rick kneeled and gathered them.

"You knew who I was, didn't you?" Linda said.

He shook his head. "Not right off. Then it came to me, that day in the garden. You were painting the nursery."

"But Mrs. Pritchard knew. She knew the second she saw me. Didn't she?"

Mr. Pritchard frowned, nodded. "Seems likely. Probably why she didn't want me to rent you the apartment."

"Didn't she tell you?" Rick said.

Mr. Pritchard shifted in his seat. "We, we don't talk about the family. Her family. You might say it's a topic of that's off limits."

"What happened to my mother, Mr. Pritchard?"

A twitch shimmied near an eye. He looked at his lap.

Linda said, "Nina's father—Tino. He took her somewhere, didn't he? Your wife was in on it."

Mr. Pritchard sucked in air. "I told you. We don't talk about the family. It's—it's strictly off limits."

"Come now, Mr. Pritchard," Rick said. "You must have some idea what happened to her."

"I'm telling you the truth, darn it. It's the kind of thing she would never talk about. Never. Not even to her own family. They don't even talk among themselves."

"I'm sorry we're putting you on the spot like this, Mr. Pritchard, but it's very important that I find my mother."

He shook his head. "Like to help. Can't."

"You can speculate," Rick said. "You must have thought about it. They took her somewhere. Surely you can guess. Where would they take her? Where, and why?"

Mr. Pritchard looked at Rick, then at Linda. "Like to help you, Miss. You seem nice enough. Certainly keep to yourself. Don't make a bit of racket. But if I speculated—as you say—and if you went and found her—they'd know I told you. Well, I ain't gonna. The last thing I'd do is make these people mad. They get mighty serious when they're mad."

Linda said, "I've lived almost my whole life without a mother, Mr. Pritchard. For years I hated her for abandoning me. Hated her! Last night I found out she was kidnapped. Imagine learning that the horrible things I'd thought about her weren't true. As matter of human decency you've got to tell me whatever you can."

He sighed. "Ain't got to do nothing. Be like signing my own death warrant."

Rick said, "Don't worry, we'll make sure they won't bother you. We'll tell them Victor told us."

Mr. Pritchard blinked. "Victor? How do you know Victor?"

"Victor was with Tino when they took her, wasn't he?" Linda said.

"May have been. But you sure must not know him well. Victor's dead. Killed in one of them vendetta feuds. Ten years ago at least."

"They took her to Corsica, didn't they?" Linda said.

Mr. Pritchard sat in silence.

Rick stood. "Hope you don't mind. I'm going to use the telephone to call the police. I'm going to turn you in for assisting in a kidnapping."

"Turn me in? I didn't kidnap no one. Why would I do that?"

"You're withholding evidence. It's the same thing. Makes you an accomplice." Rick moved toward a telephone on a table by the kitchen doorway.

Mr. Pritchard stood. "Wait just a minute. I didn't have anything to do with it."

Rick picked up the handset. "Tell it to Sergeant Rhinebeck of the Twenty-third Precinct. He's the one working on the case."

Mr. Pritchard moved toward Rick waving his hands, color draining from his face. "Put that down. Put it down, please."

Rick pressed buttons on the phone and extended his arm to keep the old man at bay.

The old man began to hyperventilate. "I'll tell you what I know. Put it down. For God's sake hang up—please."

"I don't know," Rick said. "This seems the better way."

"No, no, no. I'm begging you. I swear I'll tell you everything. Please, please."

Reluctantly it seemed, Rick returned the handset to its cradle. "All right, Mr. Pritchard, but this is against my better judgment. What you say had better be good."

Mr. Pritchard staggered to his chair and flopped down, blowing air between his lips. "What I said about not talking about the family is true. All I know is that they took her to Corsica. At least that's what I assume from what I overheard."

"Why? Why would they take her there?" Linda said.

"I don't know. They wanted her over there I guess. They do what they want. Maybe they didn't like this Robbie fellow. Who knows? That might be it. They don't like me 'cause I'm not one of them. Maybe they didn't like him. I have no idea how they think. All I know is, it was right before one of my wife's visits. One day Nina was here, the next day she was gone."

"But she was married. A grown woman. She had a child," Linda said.

"Look, that's all I know. I heard them talking about taking her to Corsica. And only bits and pieces, at that. Maybe I'm wrong. But I can tell you, if I needed to find her, I'd look in Corsica."

"Okay, so let's assume that's where they took her," Rick said.

"Where in Corsica? It's a big island."

"Wouldn't know. Could be anywhere."

"Where in Corsica is your wife's family from?" Linda asked.

"Soccia. A town called Soccia. I've heard them say that it's in the mountains."

Minutes later, Rick slipped behind the wheel. Linda pulled the car door shut. "I need some time off, Boss. What's the company policy on personal leave after only three weeks on the job?"

Rick looked at her. "A family emergency is a family emergency no matter when it happens. You can take up to five days without getting docked."

"I've got to find her by Wednesday or it will be too late. So, I'm not going to miss much time, no matter what."

"I know you have to go. What worries me, though, is what might happen to you. Obviously, they don't play by the same rules we do."

"Don't worry, Rick. I can take care of myself."

"In practically any other circumstance, I'd agree. But with these people . . . well, I'd be lying if I said I wasn't frightened."

"It's a chance I'm willing to take."

Rick drove in silence, braked for a traffic light. "I'm coming with you. The client's on vacation. The plant's closed. As far as management of the agency is concerned, now will be as good a time as any for me to take a vacation."

"What about Meg?" She said.

He glanced at her from the corner of his eyes. "What do you mean, what about Meg?"

"It's one thing for me to be staying at your apartment. But come with me on a trip to Europe? I wouldn't stand for it if I were Meg."

"You mean, you think Meg and I are—"

"Aren't you?"

"Well, what do you know. Of course. The veil finally has lifted."

"Aren't you?"

"Now that you mention it, I guess we *were*. But I broke it off more than a week ago. The afternoon I had a drink with her."

"Really? You broke it off?"

"Yes. I broke it off."

Rick's eyes were on the road. Linda studied his face.

"Not because of me. You didn't break it off because of me. Did you?"

Rick cut his eyes her way. "You have my permission to draw your own conclusions."

"And now you want to come with me to Corsica?"

"Precisely."

Linda felt a lightness in her chest, a buoyancy, as if a weight had been lifted.

"You've thoroughly considered the fact that it may be dangerous?"

"I could use some excitement."

"Yes, I see. Has been a little boring around here."

"Insipid. Aside from cars trying to run us over."

"Bet they have nice beaches in Corsica."

"All work and no play would make Linda and Rick dull detectives, wouldn't it?"

"I'll call the airlines as soon as we get to your apartment."

Sixteen

Pedru Ghjuvanni handed the ticket agent his passport and credit card. "Corsica—Calvi," he said.

She smiled. "You're the third in a row. That couple just ahead of you is going there as well."

Pedru returned her smile. "I speak only a little English." But he had gotten the gist. "Calvi ess popular. No?"

"*Trés touristique,*" the agent said.

In truth, how little did she know. This was the first of July. Tourists, the slime and scum of Europe, would at this very moment be descending in hordes upon his beloved land. If it were possible, he would build a wall around it with his own hands to keep the rabble out.

Pedru drummed his fingers on the counter and hummed a little tune while the agent fiddled with her computer and ran his credit card through a machine.

It was fortunate he had been following the granddaughter of Tino Vezzani when she and her American escort had come to the airport with their suitcases. Of course, it was unlikely that she could have left the country without him knowing. Except for the Saturday he had lost track of them for the entire day, he had had her under surveillance almost every hour since he first had spotted her more than a week ago in the place of business of Tino Vezzani.

It was fortunate that she now was on her way to the land of her ancestors, and that he, Pedru Ghjuvanni, would be accompanying her and her escort. Of course, he would keep his distance until they were on Corsican soil. He would keep his distance until the time came to make his move.

It was fortunate for several reasons, but perhaps most of all because the American police no doubt eventually would discover the rented car in the basement parking garage of the very tall apartment building. With passport and credit card records it would be a simple matter to trace the car to Pedru. There probably also were television pictures of him inside the building, perhaps even pictures of him disposing of the guard. If the car were discovered, if the connection were made, his passport photograph would be circulated. United States and French immigration officials would be put on the alert.

The incident was less than eighteen hours old. Surely, the rented car would not yet have aroused suspicion.

The ticket agent handed Pedru his passport, credit card, and ticket. "Everything is in order, Mr. Ghjuvanni," she said in French. "Boarding will begin in half an hour, gate twenty-four."

Pedru smiled and nodded. "Thank you very much."

His smile had been genuine. The Vezzani woman was returning to her homeland and so was he. It was not often things worked out so well. As near to perfect as could be hoped for. Corsica was the fitting place for her execution. It was extremely fitting that her blood should soak into the soil from which it first had sprung many, many generations in the past.

Ashes to ashes, dust to dust. And sacred dust at that.

Pedru spotted the Vezzani granddaughter. Incredible how American she looked. Her scarf, however, was French. He had seen one like it in the duty free shop at Orly. Hermes was the brand. More evidence the Vezzani clan had not the proper reverence for the Isle of Beauty. It was most apt that their blood should consecrate it. Not only were they cutthroats and thieves, their patriarch lived most of the time in the lurid land of America. It was said that the children and grand children were sent to the continent for school and university studies. It had been said by those in a position to know that among themselves they spoke the language of France. Imagine. The tongue of fascist pigs. In so doing, they forsook their roots and joined ranks with the colonists.

Annihilation was the just and proper reward for a family of Corsica that was guilty of such blatant desecration and implied collaboration.

The redheaded woman, beautiful though she was, would be next. Pedru would do his duty. He would do it well, and slowly.

Yes. Things were working out much better than he possibly could have hoped.

Pedru smiled as he settled into his seat. It seemed somehow ironic and perhaps too good to be true that doing one's duty, doing what one must, should provide a man with such a prize.

Seventeen

It was quiet on the Baltimore-to-Paris flight. The movie was over and most of the reading lights were out. Linda twisted and turned in a vain attempt to find a comfortable position. Only two hours remained before the plane was to land at three in the morning stateside, nine o'clock Paris time. She was looking forward to using her French again. No wonder the language had been so easy for her. She had been fluent as a child.

She gazed out the window. The moon shone above clouds, puffs of white cotton floating in midnight blue. The hum of the engines was soothing. Yet those engines were all that was between her and the ocean fifty-thousand feet below. Fifty-thousand feet. Almost ten miles. A long, long way to fall.

She had come a long, long way from the basement of a house in Baltimore to an estate on the James River east of Richmond, she thought as she rested her head against the plastic molding that surrounded the window. Now she was on her way to Corsica to discover where the other half of her had come from, and to answer the question that had nagged at her for as long as she could remember:

Why her mother had left.

At least now she knew that it had not been her mother's will.

But why hadn't Maman returned? She was a grown woman. Certainly a grown woman could, and would, return for her child.

And what about the answers to other questions?

Who had tried to run them down? Had the smashed fender of Gloria's car merely been a coincidence? It seemed unlikely. But why would Gloria want them dead?

If not Gloria, then who? Who wanted them dead? *Her* dead?

Uncle William, of course.

Would he stoop to murder? Had Uncle William had her tailed and in the process found out she was on her mother's trail, that Linda actually might locate her? If that were the case, would he—how did they say it in old movies?—would he put out a contract on her? And, if that didn't work, would he put one out on Maman?

It did not seem likely. Uncle William seemed more a jerk than a villain. But sometimes people surprised you. Deceived you. She'd best keep up her guard.

Deception. People could deceived you, of course. But wasn't it ironic that you also could deceive yourself? All her life she had fought against the tendency. She always had believed that her inclination toward self-deception was the result of her having been abandoned. Her fragile three-year-old ego could not face rejection by her mother, could not face that her father had left her in preference for fighting a dirty little war others were trying desperately to avoid. The icing on the cake was that her grandmother, the only one in a position to be close to her, to give her love, that Minnie thought her to be descended from a gutter snipe.

Even so, she managed to fool herself a good deal of the time. But not tonight. Not at this moment. Not at fifty-thousand feet. A period existed in each twenty-four hours when self-deception was impossible: Now, the endless span between midnight and morning. She had been through it before, had lain awake for hours while one revelation after another had come forth, bringing with it a tingling of fear, or remorse, or regret, or emptiness, or longing. Whatever the circumstance, whatever the feeling, she had experienced it at the very center of her being. Had cried. Had felt pain. Had felt the loneliness.

Rick had told her it was good to meditate, good to get in touch with the higher self, the part of each person that knows all, the part that is incapable of self-deception.

If getting in touch were good, why did it hurt, she'd asked.

Life is difficult, he'd said. One cannot go through life and accomplish what one came here to accomplish, one cannot unfold as one is meant to, one cannot grow and avoid suffering in the process, because suffering is an essential ingredient. We learn from both agony and bliss.

Perhaps Rick was right. She had suffered, but she had unfolded, too. She had grown. Matured. She certainly was not the little girl who had been in the car with her dad on the way to meet her grandmother for the first time. More important, she was not the person who had had that crush on Brad.

She rolled over, snuggled against the cushion and looked at Rick. His eyes were closed, his face bathed in soft, fluorescent light. Shadows outlined his chiseled features. One had formed in the indentation of the dimple on his cheek. A surge of emotion welled, rolled over her like a breaker against the shore. Thank God Rick was not Brad, was nothing like that selfish, egocentric brute. Taking, never giving back. Rick was kind. He was genuinely concerned about her and about her well-being. He expected nothing in return

She wanted to give her all to him.

Give her all?

It was true. Here, at fifty-thousand feet, in the endless span, she might as well face it. It was too late *not* to become involved. She had crossed the Rubicon. It was too late to avoid great joy that surely would mean great sorrow. Rick was part of her life. She had allowed herself to be ever so gently coaxed closer and closer. She had allowed herself to be hooked. Now she was in the boat. Twisting and flapping. But in the boat, squarely in the position of vulnerability she had fought so desperately to avoid. If she lost him now she surely would go through what she had gone through when her father had died, when her mother had disappeared, when Brad had turned out to be . . . Brad.

Rick. Dear Rick. It was ironic that she had clung so tightly to Live Oaks, thinking Live Oaks would be the ultimate loss. In so doing she had acquired something greater to lose, something that was even more precious.

Dear God. What should she do?

Stop fooling herself. Put an end to it. No reason now to hold back.

Or was there?

Rick opened drowsy eyes and smiled, then closed them and snuggled his pillow.

What would their next night together bring? They surely would share a room. It might well be a room with only one bed. No pull-out sofa.

Could she handle it? What about sex? What about that awful, degrading—

But wait. The kiss she and Rick had shared when she had awakened from the dream—was that a taste of what it would be like? If so, perhaps she could handle it. Make the most of it. If she was going to be vulnerable, if the sorrow part of the equation was inevitable, then at least the joy, the ecstasy, the up-side should be worth the pain.

Maybe it would be. *If* she had the courage.

The plane landed in Paris and they disembarked. Linda felt as though she were submerged in water. Her surroundings took on an odd, dreamlike quality. Things seem fuzzy around the edges, lights were too bright, noises overly loud. A buzzing of fluorescent bulbs echoed in her ears. She gave her head a shake, patted her cheek, opened her eyes wide as she placed a foot on the moving sidewalk that led to the baggage claim of Charles de Gaulle International Airport. She was glad to rest her shoulder bag on a hand rail that moved with her. Projectors recessed in the ceiling clicked and whirred, flashing advertisements onto spheres for Remy Martin, Chanel, Dubonnet and other French products.

"A bank is up ahead," Rick said. "You go ahead to the baggage claim. I'll stop and change some money."

Linda fished in her purse, handed Rick three one-hundred dollar bills. "This'll get me started. Don't think we should change it all here, do you?"

"No, you're right. Exchange rates at airports and train stations usually aren't so hot."

Minutes later, the long, flat blast of a horn startled her. The baggage carousel began to turn and an amber warning light flashed. Linda's eyes locked for an instant on those of a man who quickly turned away. Short, wiry. Where had she seen him? Those dark eyes, greasy jet-black hair, the heavy five o'clock shadow? His nose had been flattened, probably broken and not set properly. He wore a charcoal-gray suit with slacks that flared slightly. No cuffs.

Could it have been at the airport in Baltimore?

Maybe. Probably a French businessman.

Rick appeared. "See our bags yet?"

"The bags? Sorry, my mind wandered."

"There's one." He snatched it.

Customs was almost non-existent. Linda and Rick walked through a door under a green sign that said, "Nothing to Declare." Rick looked first one way, then the other.

"The bus to Orly is this way," Linda said.

"There's a newsstand. I'd like to get a paper."

Rick searched a rack. Linda spotted a guidebook on Corsica, picked it up. Rick bought a copy of the *International Herald-Tribune.*

They climbed on board and took seats. A huge diamond caught Linda's eye. It was on the ring finger of an aristocratic-looking lady who sat across the aisle.

Three burly men with tattoos and mustaches stared at Linda. She looked away.

"Ever get the feeling we're surrounded by international diamond smugglers and Muslim terrorists?" She said softly.

Rick opened his paper. "My knees are shaking. We could be hijacked to Libya."

Linda opened the guidebook.

"Speaking of terrorism. Take a look at this." Rick pointed to an article. "Corsican Tourist Trade—Bombs."

He scanned the article. "Whoa. I don't like the looks of this. More than six hundred vacation homes owned by people from the continent have been leveled by explosives since the first of the year." He ran a finger down the column. "Apparently, a faction in Corsica wants to keep all foreigners out—particularly the French. They consider them colonists. Want to rid the island of French colonial rule. Tourist trade's off twenty-five percent as a result."

"How interesting. We're on our way to a war zone. Well, you said you wanted action."

"Look on the bright side," Rick said. "We shouldn't have any trouble getting seated at stylish restaurants. Especially stylish *French* restaurants. Although on second thought, I wonder if they have a McDonald's there, since it's the French they're after."

"You said they wanted to keep *all* foreigners out."

"Guess that does include us. Pity, isn't it?" Rick turned the page.

Linda stared at the first page of the guidebook.

By the time they had been on board Air Inter flight 561 to Calvi long enough to settle in, she had learned that Corsica was known by the local citizenry as the "Isle of Beauty," that the average temperature in summer was twenty-three degrees Celsius, which she calculated to be the low seventies, that eighty percent of the rain each year fell between November and April, that there were mountains with snow on them year-round, magnificent beaches, and that tourism was the fastest-growing industry.

No doubt that last statement would be deleted in future editions.

A flight attendant pushing a refreshment cart stopped at her side.

"Something to drink?" she said in French.

"Jus d'orange, s'il vous plait," Linda said.

Rick pulled a ten franc note from the breast pocket of his shirt. "Beer for me, thanks."

Linda felt a wrinkle form in her brow.

Rick Shrugged. "It may be six o'clock in the morning in Baltimore, but it's noon here."

Linda took a sip and put the cup on the fold-down tray. She picked up the guidebook. "This says that Christopher Columbus was born in Calvi. You can even visit the ruin of the house where he supposedly grew up."

"Christopher Columbus was Italian."

"I suppose you remember that from a previous life?"

"Let's see, 1492. Actually, no. I was ensconced somewhere in the Pacific northwest at the time. Into totem poles. It was perpetually damp.

No rain dances needed there, as I recall."

"Well, according to this, he was Genoese. At that time Corsica was part of the city-state of Genoa. Amazing. Last week I'd never heard of Corsica." Linda closed her eyes and yawned. Suddenly she felt very, very tired. "Yes, and now I'm on my way there to learn about my roots." She yawned again.

"And to meet your mother," Rick said as she dozed off.

She was spinning, turning, soaring high up into the sky, when she heard Rick calling to her.

"Linda, look. Down there."

She opened her eyes. "What? What is it?"

"Out the window."

She leaned over. Below, in the distance, rugged mountains jutted from dark blue sea, patches of snow in crevices near the peaks. White, puffy clouds floated nearby, encircling some. The image came to her of Wendy Darling and Peter Pan on their approach to Never Land. Far below Captain Hook's pirate ship was anchored in a blue lagoon.

A bump jolted Linda. Then she heard a thump. The plane banked.

She looked out as they glided past an old, walled city at the edge of the sea; swooped over a horseshoe-shaped harbor dotted with sailboats and wind surfers. A lone speed boat skimmed along. It pulled a skier spewing a white cock's tail. He cut across the wake, jumping the troughs, on a single slalom ski.

Suddenly, they were headed between mountains. A bell sounded. The seat belt warning light flashed on. The flight attendant's voice crackled over the speaker, first in French, then in English: "Ladies and gentlemen, the captain has turned on the fasten-seat-belt sign in preparation for landing—"

For an uneasy minute mountains loomed on all sides, but the plane soon touched down and taxied to a concrete, block-like building. Two men in royal blue coveralls, mustaches and berets, pushed a staircase on wheels toward the plane.

Linda and Rick stepped out of the cabin into bright sunshine, descended the metal steps and walked to the terminal along with eighty or ninety other passengers. Linda gazed at the bright, blue sky. She breathed in clean, dry air and the scent of salt water. A gentle breeze caressed her cheek.

"Marvelous," she said.

"Tricky to fly into." Rick turned a complete circle as he walked. "Mountains on three sides."

They entered the building and followed signs to the baggage claim.

"I've been wondering," Rick said as they approached the carousel. "How are we going to find your mother? It wouldn't be smart to go barreling into that little town, asking a lot of questions."

Linda spotted one of the bags. "You're right. I don't want to embarrass her. People here, her friends and neighbors, they probably don't know I exist."

Phil carried their bags outdoors. Ahead was a parking lot and on the left an open air cafe with gleaming white tables and chairs. Red and yellow umbrellas advertised a drink called Suze. People behind dark glasses leaned back and sipped, their faces angled toward the sun. A beat up white Peugeot taxi in need of a wash pulled up. Rick opened the rear door and Linda slid in. "Grand Hotel," she said with the French pronunciation.

The driver flipped down the arm of the meter and mashed the accelerator.

Linda leaned forward. "I understand business does not go well this year," she said in French.

"Bahf—can't complain," the driver said. "You're English, no?"

"American."

He glanced over his shoulder. "Americans, really? Haven't seen Americans since I was a boy."

The car bounced along a winding, dusty road, air billowing in through open windows. Linda breathed in the spicy smell of the maquis.

"Americans don't come here?" she said.

"Not since the war, and that was very long ago. Ah, but I remember well. The Americans drove out the *Boche*."

"The *Boche*?"

"Germans." He nodded to the left. "The Americans had a base over there. They flew their P-51s to Italy and France. . . . Oh yes, the Americans licked the Germans, all right. The Italians, too." He grabbed the steering wheel as though he were flying an airplane, his thumbs

164

on cannon triggers. "Rat-ta-tat-tat! I like the Americans."

Linda chuckled. This man seemed friendly enough—which she hadn't expected after the article in the *Herald-Tribune.*

"My family on my mother's side is Corsican," she said. "This is my first visit."

The driver glanced at her in the rearview mirror. He said something she didn't understand.

"Pardon?" she said.

"No, no, pardon me, Madame. I spoke to you in the language of Corsica."

"You have your own language?"

His blow furrowed. "I am surprised you do not know, Madame, if your family is from Corsica."

"Only on my mother's side. In truth I do not know much about them."

"The name of your mother's family—what is it?"

"Vezzani. Their name is Vezzani."

Rick gave her a quizzical look.

"Ah-ha," the driver said. "Vezzani. They come from Soccia." He pronounced the word, "Zocha," the double c making the sound of ch and the i silent. "They are very well known." He slapped the steering wheel. "Yes, yes, I see now. Tino Vezzani lives in America. He is your uncle, perhaps?"

Grandfather, she thought. But perhaps it was best to put some distance between herself and him.

"My uncle—yes. But I do not know him well. I met him just one time."

"But Madame, Corsican families are close. Even in America it must be so."

"Well, you see, my father's side is of English derivation, and we lived very far away. The Vezzani family lives in Baltimore in Maryland, and I grew up near Richmond in Virginia. Different cities, different states."

"I see. In America the distances are great, no?"

"Very, very great."

Rick leaned close and spoke softly into her ear. "What are you and this guy talking about?"

165

"Tell you later."

"This town—Soccia," she said to the driver. "Is it nice?"

"Very lovely. It is in the mountains—high up. Some distance east, and perhaps a little south of Calvi."

The driver braked for a traffic light. Linda noticed they were no longer on a country road. Buildings lined the way ahead and on the right was a gasoline station—Elf.

"Sometime perhaps you could take us there—to Soccia," she said. "I would like to see it."

The driver stepped on the accelerator. "It is a long way. Four hours, more or less, by car."

"Four hours? It did not look that far on a map."

"The roads in Corsica, Madame, perhaps they are not like the roads in America."

"We could start early in the morning."

"For the day, I would have to charge five hundred francs."

Linda mentally divided by the exchange rate. "Let us think about it."

They drove in silence. The man looked over his shoulder, then back at the road.

"You know, Madame, I have been thinking. It is none of my business I assure you, but perhaps you are unaware. There is some difficulty between the Vezzani and the Ghjuvanni clans." He shrugged. "I myself am non-aligned, and would prefer to keep it that way."

"Difficulty? I do not understand."

"It is not for me to talk about politics. I tell you for your own good. Do not quote me. I will deny it."

They were now on a narrow city street. Sidewalks overflowed with pedestrians. A motor scooter pulled in front of them. The driver blew his horn and cursed, raised his fist. "Tourists! They do not know how to drive."

He edged to the side to allow a delivery truck to pass.

"When you said there was difficulty," Linda said. "When you said that you did not want to get involved. Did you mean you are unwilling to take us to Soccia?"

The driver tilted his head as if to catch a thought. "It means I will have to charge one thousand francs. It is also a form of friendly advice. Watch out whom you tell you are of the family of Vezzani."

The driver turned the wheel. The cab stopped with a jerk. "Your hotel, Madame." He hopped out of the car and headed to the trunk.

Rick opened the door. "I can't wait to hear what you've been talking about."

Linda followed. "Yes. It has been interesting."

The driver stood by the luggage, his hand out. "Twenty-seven francs, monsieur."

"Where will we find you if we decide to take that trip?" Linda said.

He pointed. "The cab stand across from the post office. Over there on the way to the beach."

Eighteen

The desk clerk fumbled with the key. Linda had seen no bellhops. He pushed the door open and picked up the bags.

Linda's eyes locked on the bed—a double. The only one. Her knees felt weak.

On one wall was a simple chest of drawers. Against another, a sink and bidet. Across from the foot of the bed was a window shrouded by drapes. The clerk drew them aside and light came pouring in.

He pushed open French windows, turned and bowed from the waist. "Monsieur—dam, you will be comfortable here. Ah yes, the toilet and the douche—that way, down the hall. You will see."

Rick handed him some coins and he left.

"Better not lie down," Rick said. "If we do we'll fall asleep. That will really throw us off."

Linda went to the window and breathed in. The aroma of fresh bread was mixed with a hint of garlic and the scent of salty air. Below was a courtyard surrounded by whitewashed walls. Palm trees sprouted from tree wells in the terra cotta tile. People sat at tables covered in blue and white tablecloths, eating and talking.

168

"Let's have lunch, then hit the beach." She lifted her suitcase onto a stand at the foot of the bed. "First priority, though, is a shower."

It was only a short distance down the hall. She carefully nudged the door open to a tiled shower room. The scene from *Psycho* flashed in her mind—quick cuts followed by blood running into the drain.

She forced away the thought, closed the door and bolted it, adjusted the hot and cold knobs, stood under the warm water, letting it flow over her.

Why had that hideous scene come to her?

She was jumpy. Nervous. She was in a foreign country where feuds between families still existed. My God, she'd just learned her family was engaged in one, she thought, as the warm water beat against her neck, ran across her shoulders and down her back. It was difficult to imagine such things still happened. Could Corsicans be so different?

On her return to the room the sound of a door closing startled her.

Eyes on her back. Where?

The feeling was undeniable. Someone had been watching.

She darted into the room, closed the door. Rick was sprawled on the bed, his mouth open, asleep. He looked so childlike. And he'd just said that they would be hopelessly off schedule if they slept.

She slid onto the bed, and looked at him from four inches away. Should she? She had, after all, crossed the Rubicon.

No guts, no glory.

She tied her robe tight around her, then kissed him in the ear.

He smiled, opened his eyes drowsily, ran his hand along the curve of her body.

"Hummm. . . . " He brought his hand to the small of her back and pulled her to him. The stubble of whiskers scratched her cheek, an unfamiliar sensation stirred. The knot returned and she began to stiffen.

"Shower's free, now, Romeo."

He breathed in. "Hummm . . . you smell so . . . fresh."

She patted his face, gently rubbed the backs of her fingers against the stubble.

"Yes, well, it seems as though I haven't had my daily dose of Dial." He sat. "Sorry to interrupt this, but I think I'll take that shower."

She put on a kiwi and mustard two-piece bathing suit while he was gone and inspected herself in the mirror over the sink. The colors were perfect. They coordinated nicely with her auburn hair and creamy skin. The only problem was that the suit seemed more revealing now than it had in the store. She hadn't noticed then, her breasts were a bit too large for the cut.

Too late now. That shop was thirty-five hundred miles due west.

She dug in her suitcase and found the olive green wrap-around dress she had brought for a cover up. The bathing suit would have to do. Besides, it would probably turn out to be modest compared to what French women would have on.

Later, when they walked out the front door of the hotel, Linda noticed for the first time that the hotel was on a busy, though narrow street. Shops along each side were flush to the sidewalk. She and Rick waited several minutes for a break in the stream of motor bikes and cars, then crossed. Rick gazed into the window of a wine store. She stopped at a bakery and admired scrumptious looking pastries and sweets. Restaurants with menus tacked up outside were interspersed among shoe stores, clothing and dry goods outlets, many of which spilled onto the sidewalk where racks and tables were piled with wares. Crowds seemed to gather in these spots. The mood was festive. Almost everyone dressed in light pullovers and wore shorts or bathing suits. Most conversed in French, but she also heard German and Italian. One or two spoke English with British accents. It was apparent they were in Calvi to enjoy the sun, the glorious weather and the beach.

Linda had spent some time in London and in Paris. She knew how dreary and cold those cities could be.

Rick stopped in front of a newsstand and pointed to a paper with a masthead that said, *Corse-Matin.*

"Does that say what I think it does?"

"Murder in Calvi," Linda said.

Below the headline was a photo of a body that lay in the street in a pool of blood. Gendarmes in flat-topped hats stood by, rifles at the ready.

Rick handed a couple of coins to a girl and stashed the paper under his arm.

"We'll decipher this later," he said.

Linda turned into an opening between buildings where a stone stairway led downhill. They took it to a plaza with more shops and an outdoor restaurant.

Eyes on her back.

Where?

Rick came beside.

"I have a feeling," she said softly. "I think we're being followed."

"Followed?" Rick looked behind. "You must be imagining."

Linda took another narrow stairway between buildings to another busy street full of motor scooters, three-wheel delivery trucks, a throng of pedestrians. Ahead she could see the white masts of sailboats. Hundreds of them were docked at a network of piers protected by a jetty. Far in the distance, across the water, purple-tinted mountains rose up to meet blue sky. She stopped to take in the scene and to feel the warmth of the sun on her face. A breeze caressed her skin.

Rick pointed to a strip of sand across the water that ringed the crescent-shaped harbor. "That must be the beach."

Linda raised a hand to shade her eyes. "I see umbrellas." She also could make out buildings where white sand met green foliage. "Let's try to find a place over there to eat."

They moved along and came to a row of outdoor cafes on the waterfront.

"How about one of these?" Rick said.

Eyes on her back.

Where?

People sat at tables, sipping drinks and enjoying the sun. Linda scanned their faces. A handsome man with tanned skin and blond hair smiled at her.

"I'd rather try the beach."

They reached the sand and Linda decided remove her sandals. She noticed three young women in bikinis stretched out on blankets a few feet away.

"My, my," Rick said. "Wasn't prepared for this."

Linda looked more closely. The tops of their bikinis were missing. Six bare breasts as tan as the rest of them pointed skyward.

Rick took Linda's arm as they walked and said, "I wasn't sure before but now I am. I'm going to like it here."

The two of them walked along the water's edge. Linda let the gentle surf roll over her feet. It wasn't like the ocean. Baby waves only inches high lapped at the shore.

She gazed at the mountains in the distance, marveled that snow was on top of some. A statuesque woman walked past, bare breasted.

"They're beautiful," she said. "The mountains. The mountains over there, across the water."

As the beach became more and more populated, Linda realized she was the only female within miles wearing a top. Even women well into their seventies went bare chested. And she had thought the skimpy thing she had on was daring.

An all-girl volley ball game came into view. Linda cut her eyes toward Rick. His seemed to linger on the contestants.

"Careful not to strain your neck," she said through her teeth.

He looked at Linda, smiled and shrugged.

"It appears that Corsica is not as backward as we thought," she said.

"Oh, I don't think this says all that much about Corsica. Except for the hotel clerk and the cab driver, we haven't seen any real, live Corsicans. These folks are French or German. A few Italians. One or two English. Now and then a Swede. Dutch. Speaking of Swedes—"

"I get the point. Let's eat, okay?"

"Eat? Who needs food? As long as one is in the flesh, why not spend a little time admiring it?"

"Over there." She pointed to a block-like building surrounded by a patio with tables, chairs and beach umbrellas. She headed for it.

Two flags were flying, one the black, red, yellow of Germany, the other she'd never seen before. On a white background was the silhouette of what appeared to be a black man's profile, a white bandanna around his head.

Linda sat. "Unusual flag, isn't it? Wonder what it stands for."

Rick shrugged.

"It is the flag of Corsica, Madame." A man had appeared with menus. He was dressed in a black stretch bathing suit and a flowered shirt open to his navel. "This is your first visit to the Isle of Beauty?"

Rick nodded.

He bowed slightly from the waist. "I hope you will enjoy your stay."

"Thank you," Linda said. "By the way, I must compliment you on your English."

"You are very kind. But we have many visitors from the British Isles—you see. Allow me to introduce myself." He brought the heels of his bare feet together and made another slight bow. "I am Jean-Baptiste de Bavella, and this is my humble restaurant."

Rick stood and offered his hand. "I'm Rick Henderson and this is Linda Cheswick. We're from Baltimore."

"Baltimore?"

"The United States," Linda said.

"Ah, the *United States*. That is interesting. I am honored that you came so far to be in my country when you have so many fine beaches from which to choose. Malibu!" He kissed his finger tips. "I saw it in a film."

"Yes, well, Malibu is some distance from Baltimore," Rick said.

"Tell me," Linda said. "Why do you fly the German flag?"

Jean-Baptiste looked at it out of the corner of his eyes, then leaned close. "It is—how do you say? Poo-bliss-ee-tay?"

"Publicity? Advertising?"

"Yes. That is it," he said softly. "To make the Germans feel more welcome. I can use all the business I can get."

"I read business is off this year," Rick said.

Jean-Baptiste rolled his eyes and shook his head. "Those crazy people who blow up houses. One of these days they will pick the wrong one."

"So, not everyone is against the tourist trade?" Linda said.

"A small number I assure you. Very small. But very noisy. For me, tourism, it is—how do you say? My livelihood?"

Rick unfolded the newspaper and pointed to the photograph. "I see that someone here was gunned down last night."

Jean-Baptiste put two fingers to his temple and twisted them. "Such craziness. A vendetta murder, the third—hopefully the last—in a series. It does not have to do with tourists, believe me. You are safe. Very safe."

"Why do you say the *last* in a series?" Rick asked.

"Read the story for yourself, Monsieur. There were three birds tacked to the door. Their throats were cut. This was the third killing." He shrugged.

Rick looked at the page.

Jean-Baptiste brought his hands together in a silent clap. "Now. What can I get you to drink?"

"White wine," Linda said.

"Beer. A big one."

Rick's eyes returned to the paper. His lips moved as he deciphered the French. "Ghjuvanni," he said. "The man murdered was named Ghjuvanni. Didn't you tell me the cab driver said your family and one named Ghjuvanni were having a feud?"

The butterflies were back. "Ghjuvanni was the name all right."

She had that feeling again of someone watching. Where? Linda turned. A man diverted his glance, raised a newspaper.

"Over there, Rick. That man with the newspaper. I saw him in the baggage claim at Charles de Gaulle."

"Charles de Gaulle *airport?* In the baggage claim? Can't be. That was before we went through customs."

"He must be following us."

"Think about it, Linda. He'd have to have been following us since Baltimore."

Jean-Baptiste stopped at the man's table and they exchanged some words.

Yes. She recognized the flattened nose, the slicked-back hair.

"Maybe Uncle William is having us followed. That would explain it. It might also explain the car trying to run me down."

"Hadn't thought of that." Rick looked toward the man. "I can't see him. The paper's hiding his face."

A moment later, Jean-Baptiste arrived at their table and arranged their drinks.

"That gentleman over there," Linda said. "You were just talking to him. Is he an American?"

Jean-Baptiste glanced at him, then back at Linda. "No, Mademoiselle. He is Corsican."

"*Corsican?* How do you know?"

"He spoke to me in the language of Corsica. Now—" He brought his hands together. "May I get you something to eat?"

"Just a few minutes, please," Rick said. "I need some time with the menu."

Jean-Baptiste nodded and left.

Linda said, "I know I saw that man at Charles de Gaulle, Rick. I'm certain of it. But William wouldn't hire a Corsican. Why would he? How *could* he? It doesn't make any sense. You don't suppose it could have anything to do with the Ghjuvanni-Vezzani feud, do you?"

"Why would a Ghjuvanni follow you here from Baltimore? Anyway, how would he know you're related? How would he even know you're a Vezzani?" Rick shook his head. "Impossible."

"What, then?"

Rick's brow wrinkled, then released. He leaned toward her. "Here's what happened. Old Mr. Pritchard spilled the beans about our visit. He tipped off your grandfather. Your grandfather put someone on our tail."

Linda felt her eyebrows lift. "Very good. That's really very good to figure it out so quickly. Intuition?"

"Not this time. Basic mental computer."

"So, now that we know, what are we going do about it?"

"Do?"

"About this guy tailing us?" she said.

"Try to lose him, I guess. You don't think he'd try to hurt us, do you? I mean, your grandfather's a gangster—sure. Has Ghjuvannis knocked off right and left. Tacks up birds or whatever—cuts their throats. But, you're a Vezzani. He isn't going to knock off his own flesh and blood."

"Maybe not. But he could kidnap us, like he did my mother."

"For what purpose? The Vezzani family may not be happy about our visit, I agree. Especially if your mother is still alive—remarried, for example—and people don't know she has an American daughter. But why kidnap us?"

Linda picked up the menu. "I guess you're right. Maybe he was sent to keep an eye on us and that's all. But let's be careful. And, let's try to lose him as soon as we get the chance."

Rick glanced at the newspaper. "I was beginning to like this place, but now I'm not so sure." He folded it. "I suggest we find our friend the cab driver and line him up for tomorrow morning. Let's go to Soccia as fast as possible, find your mother, and get the hell out of here."

By the time they were finished lunch no question remained in Linda's mind about whether the dark stranger was tailing them. He never lowered the newspaper and he never turned a page.

Rick paid the bill and they stood to leave.

Linda said, "Let's walk that way—to the other side of those beach umbrellas—and see what our shadow does,"

"After that, let's go for a swim. It's about time you took off that wrap. You're going topless, right? Can't wait to see how you put all the other women to shame."

"Yeah, right. And I can't wait to see you do a back flip triple somersault off the lifeguard stand into a bucket of water."

Linda reached an umbrella, stopped and crouched behind it.

The stranger paid his bill.

"Let's jog back," she said. "Maybe we can lose him."

"Jog? Let's sprint. Last one to the cabstand is a topless go-go dancer." Rick started running, Linda close behind.

She stayed within a few feet of Rick. He ran to the water's edge, weaved between sunbathers and children building sand castles. She dodged a frisbee, looked over her shoulder. No stranger.

Linda settled into a steady stride. How marvelous this place was with its white sand, blue sky and sea. Mountains all around. Across the water, the old walled section of the city of Calvi stood like a fortress as it had for a thousand years. According to the tour book, Carthaginian ships once had brought warriors to conquer. Now there was an invasion of French and Italian yachts, and topless tourists. The old French saying was true, the more things changed, the more they stayed the same.

It struck Linda that this place, this paradise, was the home of ancestors she knew nothing about. She knew about the ancestors who had journeyed to Virginia from England more than two hundred years ago. She knew about the ancestors who had inhabited Live Oaks. She knew them intimately and considered them her friends. But this side, the Corsican side that had called this island home for a thousand years or more, they were her family, too. She wanted to know them. To walk with them along this beach. To climb the mountains with them, to experience a sunset, to inhale the odor of the maquis and the salty air of the Mediterranean. She wanted to feel their blood running through her veins, to experience their pain and their passion.

Rick reached the hard surface of the parking area by the entrance to the beach and stopped running. Linda pulled up and looked behind as she slipped on her sandals.

"Lost him," she said.

"I have a feeling he'll be back. Let's go strike a deal with that cab driver."

Linda took the lead this time. She followed a walkway past an ice cream stand and a train station and arrived at a square shaded by olive trees. People sat on benches talking, eating, relaxing. The old Peugeot was twenty yards ahead.

The driver squinted and looked up at her. His arm rested on the the window opening.

"Good day, again," he said in French.

"Good day, again." She cleared her throat. "After some discussion, we have decided to ask you to take us to Soccia tomorrow morning."

"I have given my full consideration to your recent offer, Madame." The driver licked his lips. "After a careful reading of today's *Corse-Matin*, however, I must confess that I am unavailable to drive you there."

"But you said that you would. A thousand francs, remember?"

"I remember well, Madame, but I do not wish to become involved. After recent events the Ghjuvanni family will be seeking revenge. I would not like to find myself between a Ghjuvanni and a Vezzani. You represent one half of the equation."

She looked at Rick. "He says he won't take us."

"Why not?"

She turned to the driver. "We will pay you *two thousand* francs." She held up a finger and a thumb, the French way to make two. "Anyway, you have nothing to worry about. No one knows I'm Tino Vezzani's granddaughter."

"*Granddaughter?* You said you were his *niece.*" He shook his head. "I would not do it for two thousand. Not five thousand. No amount would be enough. My advice for you is to take the next boat to Nice."

"But, but—please. I must go. I have a very important reason."

He stared at her, still squinting. "It is folly, Madame. But if you must, why don't you rent a car? There is Hertz across the plaza."

"I suppose we could."

He shook his head. "I hope for your sake it is a very, *very* important reason. The boat to Nice leaves at five o'clock. They say it is very pleasant there this time of year."

"I see. Well. Thank you, and good day."

She turned and started to walk. Rick came beside.

"What did he say?"

"Unfortunately, he read this morning's newspaper. He says the Ghjuvanni clan will be looking for revenge."

"You told him no one knows we're here, right?"

"Yes, of course. Even so, he suggested that we get on the first boat to Nice."

"Not a bad idea."

"Oh, Rick. You know I didn't come all this way to—"

"Just kidding. So now what?"

"He said there's a Hertz car rental office over there."

They reserved a car for early the next morning; then took a walk by the docks.

"Look at that," said Rick.

He pointed to a ship. It was completely white and seemed to glisten in the sun. Across the stern in dark blue letters were written the words, *Comte de Nice.*

"That must be the boat to Nice the cab driver was talking about," Linda said. "*Comte de Nice.* The Count of Nice."

"Looks like the Love Boat to me." Rick gave her a little poke.

"Yeah, right. Maybe we should think about taking it, after all."

"As I said earlier—not a bad idea."

"Maybe later. We'll find my mother, then all three of us will go."

"Oh great," Rick said. "Can't wait."

"It's time to do some sight-seeing, don't you think? Only problem is, my feet hurt."

Rick and Linda returned to the hotel so she could put on different shoes. She led the way up the stairs.

The hallway was shrouded in shadows, but as she approached she thought she saw something on the door. Something odd.

The butterflies took flight; her heart thumped. A circle had been painted in red with a line through it. Beneath the circle was a word in black: "Soccia."

Rick rubbed his chin. "Looks like the Ghostbusters sign. 'No ghosts?' 'No U-turn?' 'No Soccia!' Our shadow is warning us not to go there." He shrugged. "Not surprising, really."

All the sons and daughters of the One Life who have
evolved in this universe will return as universe
builders. We shall be morning stars who sing
together for joy as we begin to work together in
cooperation with the Logos in His new task in
the new Universe in a realm of new ideals
and new conceptions of reality.

W. E. Butler
(1898-1978)

Nineteen

Linda leaned against the stone wall, propped her chin on her hands and gazed at the old port city a hundred feet below. Lights from cafes and restaurants on the land side and from sailboats in the harbor glowed and twinkled white, red and yellow. The moon's reflection glimmered and danced on jet black ripples. She breathed in salty air, exhaled slowly. "I wonder what it was like seven or eight hundred years ago when it was built."

"Not very different," Rick said softly. "Probably not as populated. Torches and lanterns instead of electric lights."

She felt a warm sea breeze against her cheeks and rustling through her hair. "To think Columbus may have grown up here, may have walked these streets, may have stood right here against this wall. It seems incredible."

"Harbor Place wasn't even a campground for the Indians," Rick said. "This world has come a long way in a short time."

"I want to get to know this place, Rick. I want to get in touch with it and understand the people."

"It would be interesting, educational, to understand how Corsicans think. To contrast that with the Waspy part of your background. Perhaps you would find they weren't really so different underneath the cultural veneer. Simply egocentric and xenophobic like most of humanity."

"It's funny," Linda said. "There's always been part of me I've kept hidden. Even from myself. I think that's it, the Corsican part, the passionate, Mediterranean part. I've been afraid to recognize it, to bring it into the open, afraid where it might lead me. When you feel things strongly the way this part of me wants to feel, it's got to hurt sometimes. You can't avoid it."

Rick nodded. "Most people, wherever they live, wherever they grew up, have shadows under the surface, demons they've created that they would like to ignore. They deny them because they're frightening, but they'll come out one way or the other and really will do harm, unless a person comes to grips with them first. Brings them into the open. Examines them. Accepts them, and in so doing, tames them. It's not easy but it's the only way to grow. Otherwise an individual becomes a bundle of neuroses."

A man in dark clothes walked past and darted down a staircase.

Linda shook her head. "Thought for a second our chaperone was back."

Rick leaned against the wall and looked up at the *Citadelle*. "He's had a workout if he tailed us all afternoon."

"Let's go down to one of those cafes by the harbor. I'm ready to sit for a while."

Rick fell in step bedside her. "Anyway, if he's back on our tail, he's been discreet about it."

"Maybe he's really our bodyguard. Maybe my grandfather wants to make sure the Ghjuvannis don't nab us and that's why he arranged a shadow."

"Maybe." Rick did not seem convinced. "But, if that's the case, why doesn't he just say so?"

They found themselves on a street lined with outdoor cafes that ran along the harbor.

Linda stopped. "Let's sit here, okay?"

She scanned the faces as they weaved to a vacant table. Everyone looked windblown and healthy.

Rick sat, blew through his lips. "My aching feet thank you for suggesting this."

"Do you think Columbus was really born here?"

"You mean, maybe the tour book is just some Corsican fantasy? Possibly it is, but this was part of Genoa."

She followed his gaze to the walled city that towered up at the entrance to the harbor. "It isn't difficult to imagine him up there, looking out from the highest point, watching ships crawl over the horizon. The air's so clear."

"Strange to think about, isn't it? Imagine. Everyone thinks the world is flat, is absolutely convinced, and you've had a peek at a photograph that was sent back from the moon." He shook his head. "I know that feeling well."

Linda was about to ask Rick what on earth he was talking about when a waiter stopped at their table. Instead, she ordered white wine, then chuckled as Rick gestured and stammered French words that meant "big" and "beer." The waiter nodded and left.

Rick looked handsome in this light, his sandy blond hair like windblown straw. It fell across his forehead. A glow radiated from his skin, pinkish-amber from the sun. The dark, wide pupils of his kaleidoscope eyes drew her. She gazed into them without speaking. Finally she said, "Where's the world going—what do you predict?"

"Funny you should ask. The truth is, I think we don't have a lot of time left for things to remain the way they are. Big changes are coming and very few people are ready. For example, you're not ready."

"What on earth are you talking about, Rick?"

"You really want to know? Free will, remember?"

"Of course I do."

"Good. I've alluded to it before but now I'll give it to you straight. Every person on earth, is here for a reason, and that reason is to grow through experiences that are possible only while we exist in physical form. That's why each person should do his utmost to live life to its full potential. We're here to evolve, and the way we evolve is by feeling with our emotions what we already know to be true abstractly. This rounds out and fills up our souls. A time is coming when those who are ready will move to a different reality, one that is far superior to this one. The rest of humanity will be left behind. Some will be recycled and start over. Some will never make it, will be lost souls forever."

"Sounds like the apocalypse."

"Does, doesn't it?"

"Oh, Rick, you don't really believe—"

"Afraid I do. It's what I meant about being sympathetic with how Columbus must have felt. Knowing something while others are convinced otherwise."

"Rick, how could you know? How could anyone?"

The waiter returned and placed a glass of wine in front of Linda and a huge beer mug in front of Rick. It must have held two liters.

"Took me literally," Rick said.

She held her glass in a toast. "To the future of mankind."

He lifted his mug, took a sip, wiped foam with the back of his hand.

"Have you ever thought, Linda, about the fact that we each come into this life with a case of amnesia?"

"We're back to the subject of past lives, are we?"

"Past lives, and our existence between lives."

"If I've lived many times, then I'm not really who I think I am, am I?" she said.

"No, you're not."

"Who am I then, Rick?'

"We each are spirit, nonlocal in time and space. Spirit that is having an in-body experience. You might compare us to radio or television waves. We're everywhere at once, totally intertwined with all the other radio and television waves. Our bodies are the equivalent of radio or television sets which are tuned to our particular frequency. They aren't us. We mistakenly believe we're the receiver but we're not. We're the transmission. And we're in these bodies to experience who we are. You see, you are who you are, but you simply don't remember. If you did your experiences would be anticlimactic at best and defeat the whole purpose."

"Uh-huh, I see. Well, I guess I do. And I don't realize this because I was born with amnesia?"

He leaned close, holding her captive with kaleidoscope eyes. "Yes. The amnesia serves a purpose. It insures we have free will, that we won't be influenced by knowing what the lessons are and how we're supposed to react. It levels the playing field, allows each person to create himself anew. Free will forces us to have faith or we won't succeed. We have to work at learning why we're here and when we have to work at something, the lesson is one we own. In other times, in other epochs, it was a good system because the basic assumption was that we are here for a reason. That life was a test. Now, in this scientific age, the prevailing view is that the world and all creation is a giant accident. Millions of monkeys with typewriters banging out *War and Peace*. Life's a bitch, then you die. Well, life's a bitch all right, but there's a reason for it. Once you realize that, accept it in your heart, it changes your outlook. You're in position to make progress." He looked into his beer for a moment, then back at her. "I want *you* to make progress, Linda. You can't imagine how much I do. If you don't, well—"

"Why *am* I here, Rick? Specifically, that is."

He drew a breath. "I can't tell you, Linda. It's part of the deal. You have to find out on your own so you can learn what you have to learn by experiencing firsthand what you need to. Then you'll realize who you are. You see, Linda, you must *create yourself*. I can't help you. If I told you specifically, the experience you're here to have wouldn't happen. It would be like knowing the end of an Alfred Hitchcock movie beforehand. The experience just wouldn't be there for you."

Linda studied his face. Could he be serious? "Sometimes I do feel as though I've known you for a long, long time. As though perhaps we've shared other lives."

"We have. Many of them."

"By the way, who is Alfred Hitchcock?"

Rick's eyebrows lifted. "Oh, I see. Missed him in this life, is that it?"

"When did he live?"

"Forties, Fifties. We caught all his flicks the last time around."

"Was it a good life, Rick? Fun? Romantic?"

"All of the above. You know something, Linda. I want to go on sharing lives with you."

"And if I don't make progress, you'll move on and I won't, is that what you believe?"

He nodded. "You got it." He glanced skyward. "I didn't help her, Otto. She figured it out."

"And I have to find out the specifics on my own?"

"Now perhaps it won't be so difficult."

185

She sipped, looked into the wine. "Frankly, I don't know what I believe." She raised her eyes to meet his. "Are you sure you're not a raving lunatic?"

He took her hands. "Yeah, I'm crazy. Crazy the way Christopher Columbus was."

She studied his face. "The sensation that I've known you before is eerie."

"Now we're making progress." He paused. "In all my many lives, Linda, I've never met a woman like you."

"No kidding? What's so different about me?"

"Your soul. I see it in your beautiful green eyes. It needs to heal, of course. By that I mean there's a piece of it you still need to create. But practically everyone alive today has a soul that needs to heal. Why else would they be here?"

"How will I know when I've accomplished this healing?"

"You'll know. Trust me. It'll be clear to you when it happens."

The knot had returned. She could feel it in the pit of her stomach, growing. Maybe Rick was nuts. Maybe she was. But it was time to give her Corsican blood a chance. It was time to follow her instincts and to find out who she was.

"You know, Rick, perhaps it wouldn't be so bad to share the rest of my lives with you."

He chuckled. "Did I mention that in this life, this end of the twentieth century life, not only do you have beautiful big green eyes, you have a really great pair of legs?"

She felt her face relax in a smile. "If you're trying to butter me up, flattery will get you pretty far. Keep at it."

"Let's see. You're fearless and you're loyal—two qualities I admire. You're prepared to take on anyone or anything, no matter what danger is involved, for a cause you believe in. Though your present cause is somewhat misguided. Even so, one doesn't find qualities like that in a woman except maybe once in a millennium or so."

"Believe me, I've got my share of flaws."

"Ah-ha. Now you're getting somewhere. Once you recognize them, you're in position to do something about them. That's how a person creates himself."

"I suppose. Someday, when I know you better, I'll tell you about a

186

few."

"No need. How many lives have we been together now?"

"You know about my flaws already? Down to my propensity for burning toast?"

"I know the big one you haven't yet discovered. It's the reason that I'm here. But that doesn't mean I don't want to get to know Linda Cheswick better. The you of this life. Your present incarnation is, shall we say, interesting."

"I suppose that's why you came on this trip."

He seemed to consider. "Actually, I always wanted to see a beautiful Mediterranean isle at the end of the twentieth century with a fearless and loyal, long-legged, green-eyed beauty. Hey, why not? How could anyone beat that?"

A song of love drifted on the balmy air. She looked into his eyes. "Now, my companion and love of many lives duration, a serious question. What do you predict for you and me in this particular one?"

"I have high hopes, high long range hopes, that is. You're distracted now. You've had a lot to deal with. This thing about your mother and Live Oaks. A new job. A new place to live. Finding out you have a reason for being here on earth that you also have to work through. Now you'll be trying to figure that out on top of everything. Of course, all of it is intertwined." He nodded. "It'll take a while to untangle it." He sipped his beer. "Nevertheless, I have high hopes for you and me."

Linda fingered her wine glass. "That's all? High hopes?"

"Okay, if you must know, I'm crazy about you. I have been for a long, long time. The problem is, I can't tell you everything. Probably I've said more than I should. Aside from interfering with free will, I might scare you off. Maybe I have already. You may have concluded that I'm totally insane. Plenty of people would."

The knot grew to the size of a grapefruit. "Yes, but somehow, even though I know you're bonkers, it doesn't seem to matter. You see, I've been giving a lot of thought to how I feel, and I've decided to stop fooling myself."

"Oh, good. You're going to bring some shadow or other into the light. Creation time. Let's have a look."

"It's the one I keep hidden by telling myself I don't want to get involved. That I have to get this thing with my mother behind me."

She looked past him to the harbor and the sailboats flooded with light. Her gaze moved from an Italian flag at the stern of one to the French Tricolor on another. It came to rest on the profile of the black man with the white bandanna. "The truth is I do want to get involved. Not with just anyone. With you. My problem is, I'm frightened of rejection." She looked into his eyes, then at the table. "I guess I've come to the conclusion that we can't avoid what life has in store. We can try, we can flail against events, but we'll only cause ourselves more anguish. The approach I'm going take from now on is to live life, to go for it, and when things go wrong, I'll just have to suffer, but it won't be because I was trying to avoid it."

"That a girl. You're making progress faster than I thought."

An American song floated on the night air.

"Listen," she said.

"Coca-cola, dungarees, rock 'n roll." Rick took another sip. "Still, it doesn't mean they think the way we do. You need to delve into that. Look at things from their perspective. Hope you're listening—doubt you are."

"Know something? I'm glad I came . . . and I'm glad you're here."

Rick pulled coins from his pocket, placed them on a tray. "We've had something to eat and a nightcap. I've bared my soul and so have you." He stood and stretched. "It's time to turn in, don't you think?"

The image of one double bed flashed in her mind. The butterflies took flight as she slipped her arm though his. They walked along a narrow street.

"Rick. There's something else."

"Yes?"

"I'm not sure where to begin."

"Just dive in."

"I guess what I want to say is that I'm not very experienced, but I'll do my best. Okay?"

He squeezed her hand.

"You see, I've never really been serious with anyone."

"Not in this life?"

"No, not in this life. Wait, I take that back. Once almost, but I—even so, I'm sort of a novice."

"Now I understand." He pulled her close. "It wouldn't be smart to

188

take chances, is that it?"

"That's part of it, yes."

The hotel came into view.

"I hope you won't think that I'm presumptuous, but I was a boy scout. Even though I only made it to second class and that was in a different incarnation, I have the motto committed to memory."

She gave him a little punch as they entered the front door. "Is it normal for me not to feel angry?"

"Quite normal. I'd even say it's encouraging."

They climbed the steps. Rick pushed open the door to the room. She walked to the open window.

"Feel the breeze," she said.

Below, people sat at tables. Candles flickered inside glass goblets. A male voice crooned a Latin ballad to a melody played on a steel guitar.

"I suppose it could be more romantic—although for the life of me, I don't know how."

She turned and opened her arms. He came to her. Her lips met his, so soft and warm. A kind of magnetism melded her to him. A tingling spread throughout. She gasped. He kissed her neck, drew back and put his nose to hers, his kaleidoscope eyes an inch away.

In an instant her dress was off her shoulders. It dropped to the floor. He unhooked the top of her bathing suit and she shook free.

"Okay, Romeo," she said softly. "You know about equal rights."

He stepped back. In a second, his shirt was over his head, his bathing trunks on the floor.

She surveyed his body—strong, hard. Her gaze came to rest on the tuft of blond hair in the middle of his chest.

He moved to her. "No rush, we'll take it slow." He kissed her, kissed her all over, caressed her skin. It was like a gentle breeze, a heavenly breeze, a puffy white cloud that carried her away. Slowly, gently, she returned his caresses, and his kisses. She smoothed the tuft of hair on his chest. Her lips found his—so soft, moist, full of life.

He pulled her to him. She felt his strength, his energy, the firmness of his body, the power of his embrace.

Their lips separated. "Oh, Rick, I've never felt like this."

She was diving now into a pool of warm welcoming water, deeper, deeper, losing herself in that strange, wonderful pool. His mouth, his lips were instruments of pleasure that produced beautiful music and made her tingle all over, tingle and spin, spin around and around in a whirlpool, deeper and deeper into bliss. She was lost in a fantasy, in unimaginable ecstasy. Soaring, dipping, turning, flying higher and higher, up up up, then swooping down, down, down. Then up again, down again, up up, higher and higher each time, each time more intense than the one before. Nothing could stop her, nothing would stop her. This was ecstasy, this was what really feeling was all about, this was what she'd been missing and it was better than anything she had ever imagined. If only this rhapsody would last forever, but it couldn't, nothing this wonderful could last, but she would try to make it so, to draw it out, until—she couldn't, but she must, it must, must, must—

An incredible surge engulfed her. It started in her toes and moved up, all the way up, until it encompassed her entire body, rushing from the inside out in thrilling, joyful upheaval that went on and on and on until at last, it began to fade. Slowly, slowly.

She collapsed on his chest, out of breath, content, her heart thumping as though she'd just run a hundred yard dash.

Twenty

The red Fiat rumbled out of Calvi with Rick behind the wheel and Linda riding shotgun. She checked her seat belt, leaned forward and pulled down the sun visor. As she'd hoped, a vanity mirror was there.

Her appearance fit her mood. Although she'd been careful to use sun block, her skin had taken on a rich, warm glow and her auburn hair sparkled with new highlights. She felt pretty and desirable, even sexy, dressed in khaki linen culottes, matching jacket and sun blaze tank top.

Rick downshifted into second. They rounded a corner, passed a sign in the shape of an arrow that indicated they were headed toward Ajaccio. He pointed a finger upward. "Why not see what you can do with the sun roof."

Linda flipped a latch and shoved. The vinyl slid open accordion style. In rushed dry air that felt cool against her skin. Above, white, puffy clouds floated in bright burning blue sky. The sun warmed her skin.

"Amazing that it works." Rick cut his eyes her way. "You know what Fiat stands for—"

191

"No. What?"

"Fix It Again, Tony."

She chuckled. "Not to worry. We can always ask our shadow for a ride."

Rick glanced into the rearview mirror. "Where is he, anyway?"

Linda felt her brow wrinkle. "What do you suppose that graffiti on our door was all about?"

"Makes me nervous, I have to admit."

Linda leaned back and rested her head, gazed at the dazzling sky, inhaled the scent of wild rosemary and thyme. "It'll all be over this afternoon. We'll hop on that boat to Nice—take our cabdriver friend's advice."

"If our shadow decides to show himself, I may just slam on brakes and demand he take us to your mother. It's time to cut the bull."

Linda glanced toward Rick. A solitary butterfly took flight. "Speaking of bull, or the lack there of, there's something I want to know. How do you feel toward me this morning? You know, respect wise?"

A smile transformed his face. "Linda, my dear, it's not as though we met last night at the cafe on the wharf. We've spent lifetimes together. Last night didn't change a thing. Not for me. Hey, I might even let you persuade me to indulge in a repeat performance, possibly as early as this evening."

"Is that a promise, boss?"

"Not unless you promise never to call me boss again."

The road wound along the coast. Linda gazed at the royal blue sea on one side, purple mountains on the other. The memory of lying in Rick's arms soothed her, but the recollection of ecstasy sent her pulse into double-time. A warm surge was triggered by images of what they had done.

As the time passed it seemed odd at first, but after a while normal, that she did not find it necessary to fill every moment with conversation. She was comfortable, totally at ease. Whether she spoke, or whether he spoke, was of little consequence. A bond had formed. Perhaps it had always been there as Rick seemed determined to believe. It was unspoken, did not require asking, did not require checking. This bond seemed to be an unquestioned knowing that he felt about her as she did of him.

Near the outskirts of a town called Les Calanche, Rick turned the car away from the coast and they climbed a winding road into the hills. Linda gazed out an open window at cork and olive trees, and breathed in the heavily scented odor of the maquis, the underbrush comprised of anise and dozens of other herbs and spices that grew wild. The narrow road wound and meandered its way up the sides of mountains and into fertile valleys. After a while they arrived at a fork and followed Route 40.

Linda opened a map and traced the road with her finger. "Shouldn't be long now. Soccia's practically on the horizon." She glanced at Rick who seemed preoccupied with the rearview mirror. "Something back there?"

"A dark blue Jaguar. He's been on our tail for a while. Now he's gaining on us fast."

Linda turned. The car was within twenty yards, accelerating. "Maybe he wants to pass. Give him room. He's driving like a maniac."

Rick edged the Fiat toward the shoulder. Linda watched in disbelief as the blue Jaguar hurled forward and crashed into the rear.

"Good Lord!"

She was pushed into her seat, then flung forward. The safety belt snapped against her chest.

Rick slammed the gearshift into second and stepped on the gas. "It's him—our shadow. I can see him in the mirror."

"What in the world? Oh God, Rick, he's trying to kill us! Here he comes again! Look out!" Rick thrust the lever into third without taking his foot off the accelerator. The Fiat lunged.

Linda felt another bump but not as hard.

Rick turned the wheel, the tires squealed. The Fiat swayed one way, then the other. "He's coming along side."

"Look out, Rick—Oh my God."

They skidded into a curve on the left side of the road. Linda grabbed the window opening as she was thrown toward Rick. The car fishtailed. Rick cut the wheel into the skid. The car straightened up and dove onto a downhill stretch. Rick kept the accelerator on the floor, pulled the lever into fourth.

The Fiat accelerated—faster, faster. Brush, trees, fence posts whizzed by. Linda saw another curve coming—they would be into it in seconds.

"Rick, slow down!"

He down-shifted into third, took his foot off the gas, let out the clutch. The motor screamed. He turned the wheel. Linda was slammed against the door. Tires squealed and moaned. Rick mashed the gas again and slammed into fourth.

A straight stretch lay ahead. Linda looked behind. Fifty yards or more were between them and the Jaguar but it was gaining.

"Here he comes."

"Never did see a Fiat that could outrun a Jaguar," Rick said.

A hand with a gun in it emerged from the passenger's side of the Jaguar. A puff of smoke appeared, followed by the crack of a high caliber pistol.

Tires screamed. Linda was thrown toward Rick. Her seat belt strained. Rick down-shifted, let out the clutch, turned the wheel. The Fiat skidded, leveled out, accelerated on another straightaway. Linda glanced behind. The gun emerged again, followed by another puff, a crack and a thud. Another puff, crack. The Fiat fishtailed. A violent flapping noise filled Linda's ears. The car began to wobble.

"A tire," Rick said.

The car turned sideways and continued through three-hundred-sixty degrees. Linda experienced a terrifying sense of weightlessness as though she were on the rapid descent of an elevator—then a glancing blow. Another. A bone-jarring crash.

The next thing she was aware of was a burning sensation across her thighs. She opened her eyes, struggled to orient herself. The world was askew. She felt nauseated and dizzy. Gradually, her surroundings came into focus. She was hanging upside down by her seat belt. The car had landed on the roof.

She looked at Rick. He was pinned against the seat by the steering wheel, his eyes closed, a grimace on his face.

"Rick, are you all right?"

No answer.

She touched him, gave him a little shake.

"Are you okay?"

No answer.

Dear God, he's unconscious. Please let him be all right.

She pushed one hand against the roof and searched for the buckle of her seat belt with the other. She released the clasp and dropped.

She twisted and shoved the handle of the door. It wouldn't budge. She turned until her feet were against the door, held the handle down and pushed with everything she could muster. The door popped open with a groan of metal rubbing against metal.

She was in a grove of trees. The car must have glanced off several before it slammed into this one. The front end was buckled, folded like an accordion. Rick's side had taken the brunt.

Oh God, Rick, please, please . . .

She reached for the door handle on his side and pulled.

It was jammed.

She stepped back. The car had hit the tree off center. The door was wedged tight. She would have to get him out on the passenger's side. No time to waste.

She circled the car, crawled in, found his wrist.

Please, Please let there be a pulse. Oh dear God.

"Mademoiselle Vezzani?" It was a male voice.

Linda dropped Rick's wrist. "Who's there?"

More words came that she didn't understand. She backed out.

The dark stranger stood above her, his hands on his hips.

Her entire body flushed. "You, you murderous thug, you caused this!" She raised up, lunged, flailed her fists. "He's injured—it's your fault! He may be dead! You did this!"

He backed up, pulled a gun from a holster under his jacket. "I do not speak English."

She stopped. "You slimy piece of . . . "

"I do not speak English."

No doubt about his identity. It was the same ugly mug. The same flattened nose. The same greasy black hair. The same five o'clock shadow. She wanted to kill him, to pull out his fingernails one at a time, to watch him plead for mercy.

"Who are you and why have you been following me?" she asked in French. "Why did you chase us, shoot at us?"

"You do not speak Corsican?"

"Why should I speak Corsican? Who are you, anyway?"

"My name is Pedru Ghjuvanni. You are my captive. You should speak the language of Corsica because you are the granddaughter of Tino Vezzani."

"What do you mean I'm your captive?"

Pedru stepped aside and gestured with a flourish. "And this is my cousin, Santu Ghjuvanni. He is a very impatient young man. I am afraid it was he who shot the tire of your car. I told him it would not be necessary, but he did so, anyway."

Linda looked at a skinny youth of eighteen or nineteen who stood behind Pedru. He needed a healthy dose of Clearasil.

"What do you mean I'm your captive?"

"Indeed, that is the situation. You will come with us." Pedru motioned with the gun. "We are most honored. You will be our guest."

"But my friend is in there, unconscious. He may be terribly hurt. We can't leave him here—don't you understand?"

"Go. Ahead of me, behind Santu."

Linda walked. "But my friend. We can't leave him. For God's sake, please, please. We must get help. He could die. You can't, you just can't. Please."

"Do not worry for your friend. Perhaps the two of you will be rejoined in paradise."

"What do you mean? What are you planning to do with me?"

"You are a Vezzani, the granddaughter of Tino Vezzani. Your grandfather, your cousins, your brothers have brought great pain upon my family. Pain will be visited upon them as a result. Your death will cause that pain."

"You must be crazy. You mean you're going to murder me for revenge in this vendetta feud? Why, that's the most ridiculous thing I've ever heard. I have nothing to do with it."

"I would not talk so much if I were you," Pedru said. "You would not want to make me angry, and your chatter and your accusations make me angry. What you are about to experience will be difficult enough, believe me."

Linda bent over and touched rocks to keep from falling as they climbed a steep embankment to the road. Should she grab one and fling it at Pedru?

What about Rick? She must do something. They were leaving him. He might have internal injuries. He could bleed to death. But the man had a gun, and it was pointed at her back. If she died, she would be no help at all.

Santu held the door of the dark blue Jaguar.

"Get in," Pedru said. "I will ride in back with you. Santu will drive."

The black opening of the barrel of the gun filled her vision as Pedru climbed in. A salty flow of saliva gushed into her mouth. She swallowed hard, tried to close her throat.

"I do not believe Tino Vezzani or any member of the Vezzani family will care one way or the other if you murder me," she said.

"Santu, I do not want you to go any faster than fifty kilometers an hour," Pedru said. "I do not want to be pulled over by a gendarme, you understand?"

"Yes, cousin." Santu turned the key and pulled the shift knob.

"And now, Mademoiselle Vezzani, let us settle back and enjoy the view. It must be pleasant for you here. No matter how many times you visit Corsica, you must feel great joy each time that you return."

Linda felt dizzy. Patches of black appeared before her eyes, then flecks of white and gold.

What about Rick?

She must not allow herself to faint. She must survive. Escape. The only way she could help Rick was to escape. She must gather her wits. Center herself.

"My name is not Vezzani, it is Cheswick. Linda Cheswick. And this is the first time I've ever been to Corsica. You've got the wrong person, don't you understand?"

Pedru stared at her. "You are the granddaughter of Tino Vezzani. There can be no mistake. I heard you tell others this yourself."

That was where she had seen him—*in the glass shop.*

"Yes, it is true, I am his granddaughter. But, I don't really *know* him. I met him only one time—once—the time you saw me in the glass shop in Baltimore. I swear it. I have never even met anyone else from the Vezzani family. Don't you understand?"

Pedru frowned. "I understand. I understand that you are trying to save your skin."

"No, no—you don't. You think you have someone they will care about. You are looking for revenge, correct? It won't *be* revenge. They will probably be happy to be rid of me. I am the daughter of a daughter of Tino Vezzani who ran away from home twenty years ago. You will be doing them a favor."

Pedru shook his head. "Such a story. I don't believe it."

Rick was back there and he was going to die. She felt her lip quiver. "But it is true. You must believe me."

He stared at her with dark eyes. She glanced at the gun resting on his knee. No way was he going to believe her. No way could she convince him. But she must keep talking. The only chance was to convince him somehow that he was making a terrible mistake. She must save Rick. She must.

"You tried to run me down in Baltimore, didn't you? That would have gotten it over quickly but you missed. Why didn't you just shoot me back at the wreck? You are going to a lot of trouble to take me with you."

"I tried to grab you on a sidewalk once. I still have a scar to show for that." He touched his forehead. "And I tried to enter your apartment building in Baltimore, yes. But you are mistaken. I did not try to run over you. Such a demise would be too quick. The quality of the revenge is in proportion to the suffering."

"No? A car almost ran me down. It *must* have been you."

"Not I, Mademoiselle. No. That would be too easy. I seek payment in kind. You have been chosen. You will suffer. Of this you can be sure."

His words came like a knife thrust into her abdomen and slowly turned. "Is that why you scribbled on the door of our hotel—the sign telling us not to come to Soccia? I am the mouse. You are the cat. Is that it? A game?"

Pedru stared at her. "I do not know what you are talking about, Mademoiselle. I did not scribble anything on your door, or on any door. Why would I? I have been very careful not to give you any warning. I have succeeded. Your are my captive. You will suffer. You can be sure of it." His eyebrows lifted and he nodded.

Twenty-One

Fifteen or twenty minutes after Linda had been kidnapped, the car sped through a village called Santa Regina. Twenty or thirty minutes after that, it entered the town of Corte, passed through the center square, turned and came to a stop at an iron gate that hung between two stone pillars.

Santu flipped down the visor, pressed a button on a remote control. The gates swung open. They entered a cobbled courtyard surrounded by a high wall and came to a stop in front of a gray, imposing mansion.

"Welcome to the ancestral home of Ghjuvanni," Pedru said.

Santu opened the door. Pedru got out without turning his back to Linda. He pointed the gun at her. "Come."

Linda stepped out and looked up. High turrets at each end of the house were connected by a steeply pitched roof. Alternating light and dark tiles created a herringbone pattern.

She took a step. Her knees wobbled, almost gave way. She must force herself to persevere.

"Impressive," she said.

"More so than the home of the family of Vezzani. You will have to agree to that."

"The truth is, I wouldn't know," she said. "I have told you several times, but each time you refuse to listen. I have absolutely no knowledge of the Vezzani family. I have never seen the ancestral home." *Dear God,* she thought, *please let a motorist see the Fiat in the grove of trees.*

Santu opened the front door of the mansion. Pedru nudged Linda with the gun. Unsteadily she stepped forward.

"Look at me. Do I dress like a Corsican woman? I do not know the Corsican language. I have no knowledge of the Vezzani family home. All this because I am Linda Cheswick from Richmond in the state of Virginia. I am American, not Corsican. You must realize you are making a terrible mistake."

Pedru pushed shut the door. The sound of the lock when it clicked reminded Linda of the cell door closing in an old prison movie.

Pedru brought his heels together, bowed as if he were a host welcoming her. "You are most spirited. This is to be admired. But throughout this protestation, you have not denied that you are the granddaughter of Tino Vezzani." He gestured. "This way."

She walked before him along a dimly lit hallway. "But I told you. I met him only one time."

"Even if it is so, it does not matter. Tino Vezzani will have his nose tweaked when he finds your naked and lifeless body on his threshold. Perhaps we will nail it upside down to the door and cut your throat. Yes. The only problem is, the hammering may wake him in the middle of the night. It is a problem that deserves careful consideration."

The man was insane. Her only hope, Rick's only hope, lay in escape. How?

Linda stopped at the entrance to a salon, perhaps thirty by forty feet. The floor was gray flagstone, the ceiling thirty feet up with exposed beams. They were enormous and dark, almost black with age and soot, no doubt from the huge fireplace at one end. A balcony with stairs on each side traversed the other.

Pedru pointed down a hallway. "Let us continue."

She must persist. She must not give up, not give in, not accept this fate, this, this horrible, surrealistic doom. "Tino Vezzani will think you are a fool! I mean nothing to him, *nothing!* Don't you see? If you murder me, he will think you have gone mad. Raving mad. He will laugh. Yes, *laugh.* He will think you are a lunatic!"

Pedru stopped in mid stride and turned. Slowly, deliberately, he placed the pistol in the holster under his coat. He took hold of her lapels. His lips curled to reveal nicotine-stained teeth and he jerked her close. She could count the stubble, smell foul breath, feel spittle as he spoke in crisp clear tones. "It is clear that the women of Vezzani do not know their place. You talk much too much, *putain.* If I were you I would do everything within my power to refrain from further utterances. Your loose tongue is increasing my desire to watch you suffer. I advise you to save your voice to scream with. You will have plenty of opportunity."

He released one lapel, pushed open a door and shoved her. She stumbled, fell, stuck out her hands to break her fall, looked up as the door slammed shut.

A key turned in the lock.

She pulled her knees to her chest, buried her face and cried. Sobbed. She rolled onto her side.

What had she done to deserve this?

Oh, God. Dear God.

And Rick? What about Rick? Was he dead? If not, had they left him to die? Was he bleeding internally? Would he wake up and wonder where she had gone, only to pass out, never to wake again?

Or, dare she hope? Would somebody find him?

Oh please, please, God, let somebody find him.

She wiped her eyes, placed her chin on her knees. Tears continued to flow.

What was she going to do?

Oh God, what?

If Rick were dead, maybe it would be better if she died, too.

But wait. What had he said about her not being able to move on to the next reality? Would she be left behind? Would they never be together?

How could this be happening? Was there some unwritten law that said whenever you had someone who made you happy, that someone would be snatched away? Was this some cruel repeat of

Brad?

She must calm herself. She must keep a cool head, she must think. Think. Think. He wasn't dead. At least she didn't *know* that he was dead. She could not give up, would not give up. Not as long as there was hope. Not as long as there was life left in her body.

And Live Oaks. She still had Live Oaks to worry about. By God, she wasn't going to let that lazy, good-for-nothing uncle of hers ruin it. Live Oaks was something to live for.

Uncle William. Of course. Uncle William had been behind the failed hit-and-run. Pedru had no reason to lie to her. Why would he lie?

And the graffiti? Had Uncle William or his henchman followed her all this way?

The rotten bastard. Whatever, however, she must not let him get away with it.

Linda lifted her head to study her surroundings. Plaster, white-washed walls. An irregular stone floor. Exposed beam ceiling, cracked plaster. A simple wooded table, gray with age. Two handmade chairs, primitive—the only furniture. One small window high up, one by two feet—the only source of light. Bars over it.

It seemed like a cell, but had probably been a pantry. Or maybe a servant's room. Either way, it was not used for anything now, unless it was some kind of office.

An interrogation room?

Think, Linda, think. Get hold of yourself. You've got to escape.

She stood, went to the table, sat on a chair. No drawer, no paper, nothing to write with. No evidence it was used on a regular basis.

Pedru had stashed her in a spare room, a cell all right, to await execution.

Execution? No, no, no!

And torture. How would he torture her. He said he would. Rape? Oh, God, would rape be part of it?

Christ, no.

Would they use a whip?

What evil could their twisted minds devise? Vivisection?

Lord, hear my prayer.

There must be some way out.

The window?

She stood on the chair, could just reach the opening with her outstretched arms.

The table—of course.

She shoved it against the wall, lifted a chair on top, climbed all the way up. The window was large enough for her to squeeze through, but there was glass in it and bars on the other side of that. Outside was a garden or a courtyard. Fruit trees, gravel walkways, stone benches. Surrounded by a wall.

The molding and the glass seemed very old. Crumbling grout was all that held it together. She stuck a finger in a crack and pulled. A chunk dislodged.

Removing this glass would not be difficult. But the bars?

They did not appear to be embedded in the stone. In fact, they weren't separate bars at all. All one piece! Yes. All one piece! A grate. So, get the glass out, push out the grate. Break apart one of the chairs if necessary. Slam it against the wall. Use a piece of it like a crowbar.

She pulled out chunk after chunk of grout, glanced back and forth between the outside, her work, and the door that Pedru had slammed.

How much noise would the grate make when it fell on gravel walkway?

Hold onto it, and pull it back inside. Yes. And once she was outside, how much time before they spotted her? Was there a gate? Would it be locked? She might have to scale the wall.

Look, over there. Bougainvillea climbed up one side. Good as a ladder. Shame it was daylight. She would have a better chance at night.

What time was it? Almost one o'clock. Pedru was probably having lunch, the demented thug. He wasn't in a hurry. He'd take his time. Have desert. A glass of brandy. Then he'd come for her.

Oh, God.

This was her chance, maybe her only chance. She would have to make a dash for it. Pray they didn't see her. She must get back to Rick. She must.

The glass was loose. She could stick her fingernail in the crack and lift. One more piece of grout—yes. It was free!

A noise, oh no. *No!*

A key turning in the lock. *Put the glass back in place, climb down!*

She brought the chair with her and sat as the door swung open. A pretty girl in her late teens, petite, came in carrying a tray with food on it. She wore a black bonnet and a black dress, the hemline at the middle of her calf. Black leather buttons ran down the front. She lifted her head and looked at Linda with doleful eyes. "My name is Columba," she said in French. "I have persuaded them to allow me to bring you lunch."

She placed the tray on the table and arranged the food. "Men. They are such barbarians. The men of my family are included in this assessment. I am ashamed for them, especially."

A potential ally? "You are aware they plan to murder me?"

The girl lifted her head. Her eyes seemed sunken. Lines had formed prematurely. "There is hope. It may not come to that. By the blessed Virgin, I pray that it will not." She crossed herself.

"Hope? Why?"

Columba backed against the wall, placed her palms flat against it. "At this moment they are having lunch. My grandfather and my uncles. They are discussing what course of action to take."

"There are options?"

"Albertu says you should be ransomed. Pedru argues for punishment and death." Columba crossed herself again. "My grandfather will decide. The women are not allowed to have opinions."

"Punishment? Why—for what? I do not understand."

"You are the granddaughter of Tino Vezzani. He is responsible for the deaths of three of my uncles and much more. He has brought much sadness upon the house of Ghjuvanni."

Linda shook her head. "If they decide to ransom me, he won't give them a sou. I don't even know the man. I only met him once. It appears that I am as good as dead."

"He is also my grandfather."

"Who? Tino Vezzani? How can that be?"

"My mother is a daughter of his. Through an arrangement that was made to end the ancient feud between the Ghjuvanni and the Vezzani families, she was betrothed, then married, to the oldest son of Bernardu Ghjuvanni—the family patriarch—also my grandfather."

"But it didn't stop the feud."

204

"No, the marriage was not good. My mother is very . . . different. She and her husband cohabited only for a few weeks, then lived separately. In different rooms. I was the only offspring. Now my father is dead."

Columba crossed herself.

"Killed by a Vezzani?"

Columba nodded.

Linda glanced above Columba's head to the window. The glass was still in place. "We're cousins, then."

"I knew the minute that I saw you. I saw the resemblance—the Vezzani features, the Vezzani *look* in your face."

"And you do not wish to see me killed?"

"Of course not. I would do anything if it could be avoided."

"Then help me escape."

"If I could." Columba shook her head. "It is impossible."

"That window, what is on the other side?"

"The garden."

"I believe I can crawl through the window."

"There is a wall."

"I can climb over it."

"But now—in the middle of the day . . . no, the rooms, most of them face the garden. You will be seen instantly." She seemed to consider. "Perhaps it is possible, but in the middle of the night."

A male voice, "Columba?"

Santu stood in the doorway. "Grandfather says to come, immediately. He does not want you talking to the Vezzani woman."

Columba started toward the door, then turned her back to Santu. She mouthed the word, "Tonight."

Linda held her breath. The door closed, and she exhaled.

Tonight? What if they decided to murder her this afternoon? And Rick. He could be dead by then—if he wasn't already.

Dear Rick. Oh Lord, please.

She looked at the window. Should she try it now? Make a dash for it?

If all the rooms faced the garden they would catch her halfway up the bougainvillea. Then they would put her in a different room where it would be impossible to escape, might even post a guard to make

205

doubly sure. That would prevent Columba from being in position to help.

She could not help Rick if she could not get to him. She could not help if she were locked in a room.

She must wait. If the elder Ghjuvanni was as vengeful as seem likely, he would probably decide to stretch things out, to let his enemy, Tino, know about her capture and then let him wait and worry about what they were doing to her.

Little did they know that Tino didn't care.

Yes. She should wait. Time also would be required if they were going to try to ransom her. It might take several days.

Unless Tino shot back an answer, "No."

Would he do that? Would he say, go ahead and kill this young woman. She is my flesh and blood, perhaps, but I do not care if she exists. I do not care what you do to her.

He had offered her money. He'd held up a wad and said that money was not important to him, that he had plenty. Take it, he'd said. It was hers if she wanted it.

She needed his generosity now. She needed him to give that money to these crazy Ghjuvannis in exchange for her life.

Waiting was the wisest course.

In the meantime, she would finish getting the window ready for her escape.

Twenty-Two

Pedru Ghjuvanni pushed a leaf of lettuce to the corner of his plate and put down his fork. He was satiated. Both the rabbit in Dijon mustard sauce and the wild boar, which had been marinated in red wine for three full days, had been delectable, and he had eaten heartily. After almost two weeks of bland American cooking he had forgotten how thoroughly satisfying food could be. As a result, he had eaten more than his usual amount. A full stomach would make him sleepy and sluggish. It was not a feeling that he relished.

He reached for the bottle of Corsican rosé and poured himself half a glass. "The boar was excellent, Grandfather. You are to be congratulated."

Grandfather glanced at him over the half moon glasses balanced on his nose. A hand with a fork stopped midway to his mouth. His gray mustache twitched. "It was not I who prepared the boar, Pedru."

Pedru raised his glass in the gesture of a toast. "But it was you who killed the boar, Grandfather. You shot a most delicious one."

"And the rabbit," said Albertu. "Not a bad catch either—would you not say?"

207

Pedru took a sip of wine. He smacked his lips. Albertu was such an ass. No doubt he felt compelled to remind everyone that he had actually shot and killed something.

"It was a good one, Albertu. Young and succulent. But I am surprised that you did not spare it, considering you are philosophically opposed to killing."

The effeminate way in which Albertu dabbed the napkin to his lips caused Pedru to wonder whether his cousin was in fact a homosexual. Was it possible that his wife and children simply were decoys?

"There is a difference, Pedru, between killing an animal to eat, and killing a human being for the pleasure of it."

"For the pleasure of it?" Pedru said. "Is she not a Vezzani? Did not the Lord say an eye for an eye, a tooth for a tooth? Does not the Vezzani clan owe us much more than an eye, much more than a tooth? Much, much more?"

"And you will undertake this task yourself, Pedru?" Albertu said.

"It is my unpleasant and humble duty. A duty to the house of Ghjuvanni."

"Indeed," Albertu said. "You are truly a sadist, Pedru. Totally perverted. Totally sick. There must be an end to the killing. An end. The cycle must be broken. You speak of the Bible, but you forget to mention that our savior Jesus Christ directed us turn the other cheek."

Pedru leaned toward Albertu and pointed his finger. "*You* are the one who is sick, Albertu. Do not accuse me of perversions when it is *you* who is perverted."

Grandfather slapped the table. "Stop this, stop it now. It is for me to decide what course of action is best."

Columba entered the room with a tray of cheese, walked directly to her Grandfather and held it.

He served himself. "You saw the Vezzani woman, Columba?"

"Yes, Grandfather."

He waved the tray away. "What did you think of her?"

Columba glanced at him cautiously. "She is not like a Corsican woman, Grandfather."

She offered the tray to Pedru.

"Not like a Corsican? What do you mean?"

"Her clothes are of bright colors. She wears no gray or black. Her skirt is short, her hair is short." Columba sighed. "I suppose one might say that she resembles a tourist from the continent."

"*See*," Pedru said. "There can be no doubt. She deserves to die. Her behavior also is unconscionable. Her mouth is constantly in motion, and all the words that spew forth from it are French. It is a fact that I found most shocking. She does not speak the language of Corsica." He shook his head.

Grandfather picked up a piece bread and tore it in two. He smeared on soft cheese. "It is true that the family of Vezzani has become more French than Corsican. It is an outrage, but then, everything about the family of Vezzani is outrageous." He took a bite, and chewed. "I have not heard what you think, Santu. What do you think we should do with the Vezzani woman?"

"Me, Grandfather?"

"You are now a man, Santu. And you have seen the Vezzani woman. What do you think should be done?"

Santu cut his eyes to Albertu, then Pedru. They came to rest on the cheese tray being offered to him by Columba.

He shook his head—waved it away. "It seems to me, Grandfather, that Uncle Pedru is right. The Vezzani family owes the house of Ghjuvanni a great debt. The score is far from even, not even close to even. To ransom the woman as Albertu suggests would mean that the only payment extracted from the Vezzani slime would be in the form of money. Money is not enough. How can *money* pay for the lives of my uncles and my brothers?"

Grandfather nodded. He brought a glass of wine to his lips, took what was left in it. He placed the glass on the table as if care were required to insure that it did not fall over.

"You are a thoughtful young man, Santu," Grandfather said. "Someday you will be a leader of the Ghjuvanni clan—as Pedru and as Albertu now are leaders of the Ghjuvanni clan. I agree with you. What you and Pedru say is true. No amount of money can pay for the blood of the house of Ghjuvanni which has been spilled by the scourge of the family of Vezzani."

Pedru smiled and took another sip. The old goat did have some sense left. For a while he had not been sure. Now it looked as though Pedru's wishes would prevail. Not only would the Vezzani *putain* be made to grovel at his feet, Grandfather would no doubt select him, Pedru, heir to the seat of power at the head of the family of Ghjuvanni. The time to choose a successor was near, and his Grandfather was certain to choose someone with whom he saw eye to eye.

"On the other hand, I agree with Albertu," Grandfather continued. "Perhaps it is Albertu, in fact, who brings a voice of reason that is needed to quell the madness that has surrounded our family and the family of Vezzani for many, many years. Somehow, sometime, some way, the killing must be brought to an end. Something must be done or there will be no more house of Ghjuvanni. No more family of Vezzani. We will all be dead."

The old man shook his head. "It is a dilemma of the first degree. To give in and to give up, to fail to even the score, is dishonorable, and honor is at the very core of the heart of every Corsican. Certainly it is the basic standard by which the Ghjuvanni family has lived for centuries. Yet not to offer the olive branch, to persist and to proceed with the vendetta could mean suicide."

Grandfather lifted his empty glass two centimeters and held it while Pedru filled it halfway to the top.

The old man brought the glass to the light of the window. He turned it slowly, then drank it all in one swallow.

"I must think," he said. "I must take everything, all ramifications, into consideration. Let us move to the library for brandy. Afterward, I will tell you of my decision."

We see inner reality only through an "aha!"
experience, a sudden insight into our own being.
There is no way to describe inner reality directly;
we can only hope to lead people
into a perception of it.

John A. Sanford
The Kingdom Within

Twenty-Three

It took only an hour to jiggle and shake loose the grate from its place inside the stone frame of the window. Linda held onto it when it popped out. Then carefully replaced it.

She backed away, studied it.

Good. It would not arouse suspicion but could be removed in a couple of seconds.

Next, she returned the glass to its place and climbed down.

Waiting was all that was left.

She sat on the floor and rested her back against the wall, closed her eyes. She could feel blood pulsating rhythmically in her temples, a tingling on her skin. She shifted. It was impossible to get comfortable, impossible to allow her muscles to relax. Her entire body was coiled in anticipation. The door might fling open at any moment to reveal Pedru with his pistol, a whip or some other instrument of torture. She could picture him laughing, showing her the leather straps he would to use to tie her.

She must push him out of her mind, direct her thoughts to something else. Perhaps to Rick. Yes, to Rick and their night together in

Calvi. She never would have been able to guess how wonderful a romantic interlude could be. Some women probably never had, never would experience anything close to it. If she died now, at least she would have had this. As with Juliet in Shakespeare's tragedy, her life had been complete the moment she lay in her lover's arms.

Complete? Not according to Rick. He had said she was here to learn, that she must find out something for herself if she were to move to the next level of existence. They would be separated for all eternity if she failed.

Could it be?

If so, what? What was she supposed to learn?

The vision flashed in her mind of Rick pinned between the steering wheel and the seat.

She leaned forward and pulled her knees to her chest with hands that trembled. Her heart began to pound. Her body flushed. A tingle lingered, burning hot. The image of Pedru's face with his flattened nose flashed before her. If only she could reach out and claw his skin to bloody shreds.

Was Rick dead?

Oh, God, no. Please, no.

She must not think about it. Nothing could be done to help him now. No way could she find out what had happened. All she could do was wait. And wait. And wait.

Darkness came, and with it Linda felt a sense of relief that started small and grew as the hours inched by. She was not out of danger, not by a long way. But surely if they were going to murder her or torture her today, the ordeal would have begun.

She sat on the floor with her back against the cool stone wall. Never had she experienced such total silence. No sound interrupted it, not even an occasional serenade from a cicada.

Moonlight shone through the small window. The shadows from the bars created a patchwork design on the beams of the ceiling. This reminded her of the pattern made by the morning light when it passed though the window in Minnie's room and landed on her bed. It had done so that morning, the last time she had seen Minnie alive.

But that had been sunlight. This was moonlight. Moonlight.

She had lain awake and studied the designs the moonlight had made on the ceiling of Rick's apartment. She had stared at that ceiling for hours, too. The last time had been three nights ago. Was it possible? It seemed more like years, ages. Eternity.

Eternity? The totality of time without beginning or end. How could there be anything without beginning or end?

She had come into being in the womb. Her beginning had been the moment Robbie Cheswick's sperm and Nina Vezzani's egg had come together. If a different spermatozoa had reached the egg, she would not have been. Someone else would be sitting here. She simply would not exist.

But Rick had said she was not this body. She was spirit. Nonlocal. Everywhere at once.

Like eternity? No beginning? No end?

He'd said she was totally intertwined with all other spirit. Like radio and television waves were intertwined. One frequency along a band of frequencies. Even here in Corsica, this room was full of radio and television transmissions, all intertwined.

So she was spirit that was intertwined with other spirit. With other spirits? Other people? All one? All was one.

Hear, oh Israel, the Lord thy God, the Lord is one.

Eternity? God?

Her body was a receiver like a television set.

She was the *transmission*.

Was that what she was here to learn? That all was one?

Rick had said a time was coming when some would move to a new reality, and others . . .

Was it like school? If you didn't pass geometry you had to do the eighth grade over? She'd have to do this grade over? Pedru would walk through that door and rape her and kill her. Then she'd have to do this grade over? It didn't make sense.

No, he'd said it wasn't school. Not exactly. He'd said our souls know all there is to know but on a kind of intellectual level. Abstractly was the word he'd used. Yet to be complete, to heal or create ourselves, we must experience what we know. We must feel the attendant emotions. Only on the physical plane was this possible. That was the reason she was here, to take to heart the final experience that would allow her to move on.

What could that possibly be?

What had Rick said? *Get into the heads of Corsicans and see how they think.* They're probably egocentric and xenophobic like the rest of humanity.

Yes, of course. They were indeed. Pedru wanted to kill her because she was a Vezzani, which she hadn't even known until a few days before. But the spirit of Pedru and her spirit were intertwined. They were one. All was one. The two of them just looked separate because they had different receivers. TV sets tuned to different channels. An illusion of being separate.

The Montagus and the Capulets had been one, too, but were having a feud. Romeo and Juliet couldn't get married because of it. Both died as a result.

Linda's mother and her father were the same. The Cheswicks were English, the Vezzani's were Corsican, but in spirit they all were one. Yet they had disliked and distrusted each other. Were xenophobic. Yes. And yet they all were one. *That was it!* She could *feel* it, just as he'd said she would. The house of Ghjuvanni, the family of Vezzani. *All one.* But they would be held back. They wouldn't make the grade. They'd be recycled. No one could make the grade until they understood that *all was one.*

What else? What else didn't she understand?

Rick had said she was fearless and loyal and willing to take on anything for a cause she believed in. He admired that, even though the cause was misguided.

What had he meant?

Her cause was to save Live Oaks from the developers. She would be willing to lie down in front of a bulldozer.

Why? Why would she be willing to lie down?

She loved the land, the house. It was her family. She wanted to keep Live Oaks for herself. To keep it for her children. But the Indians had said she couldn't. She couldn't keep it for herself. No one could own the land. *She belonged to the land,* the land did not belong to her.

Of course. If she were spirit having an in-body experience, how could she own anything? Spirit didn't own anything, it just *was.* The land itself was a manifestation of spirit, a projection of the one ground of being of which she was a part.

Hear, oh Israel, the Lord thy God, the Lord is one.

All-that-is was one. Owning the land, owning anything was an illusion. Even her ancestors. They were spirit. They were not Live Oaks. Like them, when her body was destroyed she would return to spirit and the land would remain. It all seemed so clear now. It was *impossible* to own it. She could *feel* this reality. The inner vision no longer was an abstraction.

A sound brought Linda upright. A key turned slowly in the lock. She stood, checked her watch—pressed the button on the dial for light. It was three-twenty-five in the morning.

The door opened. Columba pressed a finger to her lips. "I do not know what they would do if they found me here."

"I have prepared the window," Linda said softly. "I can have the glass and the bars out in an instant."

"Yes, remove them. It must look as though you have escaped on your own. But it will not be necessary for you to pass through the window."

"Not necessary?" Linda placed the chair on the table and climbed.

"I will lead you through the house," Columba said. "It will be better. You might be hurt if you jump, or someone might hear you drop to the ground, see you scale the wall."

Linda placed her feet carefully and breathed as silently as possible as Columba led the way first along one hallway, then another. They descended steps, stopped at a door, pushed it open silently, stepped outside into a colonnade. The night air was cool and dry. Stars blanketed the sky, even though the moon was almost full. Light from it cast black shadows on the walkway.

Columba stopped at a door, took a key from her pocket and turned it in a lock. Linda followed her into a gardener's shed.

"Be careful. It is very dark." Columba moved through the shadows to another door, inserted the key, pushed it open. She reached for something. "This was my cousin's. He is no longer here, so it will not be missed." She rolled a motor scooter through the opening.

Linda followed her. They were outside the wall, on a street.

"Start it by turning this switch and kicking this pedal," Columba said. "But do not do so until you are well away. It is downhill the full distance to the center of town. Coast until you arrive there."

"This is wonderful—magnificent. I had no idea. I thought I would have to walk. I don't know how to thank you."

"This is the throttle." Columba turned it. "Here is the clutch. The gears are operated with your foot. Down all the way for forward." She stepped on a lever, pulled up with her toe. "Up, in this position for neutral. . . . Oh, and I have something else."

She slid her hand inside her dress and produced a small, nickel-plated pistol. She gave it to Linda handle-first. "It fires seven rounds."

Linda closed her hand around the grip, felt her finger on the trigger. "You've thought of everything." She put it in the pocket of her jacket. "How can I ever thank you?"

"There is no need. I do what I must, what you would do for me. Men, Corsican men for certain have no sense of decency. To survive, women must help one another. It is the only way, my cousin." Columba took Linda's hand, squeezed. "My wish is that I could come with you to freedom in America."

"Then do. Come with me."

"I must tell you that I am tempted. I am sick to death of my life here. Women are nothing. We must do as we are told. Our opinions not only are never considered, we are not even asked. It is as though the men think we are less than human."

"Climb on. Come with me. I will help you begin a new life where attitudes are different."

Columba shook her head. "If it were not for my mother, perhaps. But, she needs me. I must stay."

Linda looked at Columba in the silver glow of moonlight. What a pretty girl, and what a sad, sad existence she must lead in a society so primitive that women were little more than property. Chattel. It would be a long time before Corsicans realized the unity of life.

But Linda could not help her. Not now. It was time to go before someone discovered them.

Linda said, "I want to go back toward—what was the name of the town? Santa Regina? Can you tell me which way?"

"Follow the road downhill to the center of town. There will be signs."

217

Linda straddled the scooter, pushed off, drifted silently downhill, past a sign that said, *Toutes Directiones*. After coasting several hundred yards, she reached the circle, turned the switch, slipped the scooter into gear and let out the clutch. The motor hummed, sputtered, purred to life. She flipped a button on the handle bars. The headlight flashed on. Not that she needed it. The moon was bright and so were the stars. But on-coming cars, should she pass any at this time of night, might not see her if she did not have a light on.

Was it wise to go back to the scene of the crash? Or should she go to the police?

No. Definitely not. The police in this town were no doubt in the pocket of the Ghjuvanni family.

She leaned into a curve, sped down one hill, up another. How clear the air was and how cool.

She found herself on a straight stretch, rotated the throttle wide open. The motor instantly responded, revved to a higher pitch.

She glanced at the speedometer mounted near the center of the handlebars. Fifty-five, sixty. That translated to about thirty-five miles an hour. Not bad. She should arrive by daybreak.

The sky became the pinkish blue of morning, clear and cloudless. A ray of sun flashed over the horizon and rippled across a green, fertile valley scented with rosemary in bloom. Linda rotated the throttle away from her. The scooter slowed to twenty-five kilometers an hour. The spot where she and Rick had left the road was somewhere along this stretch. She stained to see ahead, twisted to look behind. Which curve had it been?

There, those rocks. She had climbed over them with Pedru's gun pointed at her back.

She brought the scooter to a stop, lowered the kick stand, pulled back on the handlebars.

The car would be in the middle of the grove of trees.

She started down the bank, slid but kept her balance as loose gravel slipped under her.

She reached level ground and jogged.

She could see the trees clearly now. The Fiat wasn't there.

She stepped up her pace, ran to the spot.

This, this was the tree. It had to be. The bark was missing where the car had rammed into it.

She spun around and studied the way to the road. Near the top of the embankment, could those be tire marks? She hadn't noticed them before.

She ran, scrambled up the incline.

There could be no doubt. There were tire marks, much wider than the Fiat would have made.

She suddenly felt giddy, lightheaded. It were as though an enormous weight were lifted from her. He'd been found. Rick had been found.

A jolt of realization: had it been in time? Had he been alive?

Air escaped from her. The crash had happened eighteen hours ago. How long before he was discovered?

She must find him, go to him now.

She ran to the scooter, flipped the switch, kicked the starter. The motor sputtered, then purred—blue smoke swirled from the exhaust.

She pushed off, opened the throttle, leaned into a curve.

A sign came into view: *Calvi 105.*

A hundred and five kilometers to Calvi? That was over sixty miles. It would take hours.

She should call ahead. She should telephone Hertz—by now they certainly would know what had happened.

But where? Where was a telephone?

Mountains, maquis, olive trees and winding road were all that lay ahead. Behind was more of the same, except . . . wait. She had been looking at the map.

What had she said just before Rick had spotted Pedru's Jaguar in the rearview mirror?

"Soccia is practically on the horizon."

Linda eased back on the throttle, applied the brake, edged to the right. Then she leaned hard to the left, made a complete turn, brought the scooter upright and rotated the throttle wide open. She would call from Soccia. Wherever there was a post office in France, there also were telephones.

Soccia. She would complete the journey she and Rick had started. And what a journey it had been. Whatever happened from this moment on, her life would never be the same. Now she understood what it had been about. Why she had been born to Robbie and Nina Cheswick. Why she was here on earth. She had learned that all life was one in spirit. Yes. And that a person could own nothing in the material world. Whatever one thought she owned had simply been borrowed for a while.

Dear Rick. He had been right. If he had told her these things in just so many words, she wouldn't have experienced the emotion, that click of the light switch as it was flipped on. The amnesia about why she was here made sense. Because of it, this knowledge would be a part of her for all time. At least now, whether Rick was dead or alive, she could take comfort in the realization that they would be together eventually. She had experienced what she had needed to experience and would move to the next plane of existence.

Dear Lord God. Not eventually, though. Please.

She felt the wind in her hair. To Soccia—as fast as this thing would go. To the post office.

In fact who needed a post office? She would call from the home of the family of Vezzani.

After twenty minutes a sign appeared announcing the town of Soccia only three kilometers ahead. Her heart began to pound. She was almost there.

Moments later she reached the crest of a hill and glanced in the rearview mirror. A dark blue Jaguar was two hundred yards behind.

Damn, damn, damn. They had discovered that she was missing. And it hadn't take an MIT graduate to think of looking for her on the road to Soccia.

She shot over the crest of another hill and around a curve, leaning low, throttle open. She gasped. A village in the distance seemed to cling to the side of a mountain. Blue sky and white, puffy clouds formed a backdrop for terra cotta roofs and stucco walls that glistened in the sun.

At the crest of the next hill she spotted the Jag again. It had closed half the distance.

She breezed past an old man dressed in blue peasant garb who led a donkey loaded down with wood. She passed a sign that announced the town limits of Soccia, sped past an old woman on a bicycle who wore gray and black with a bonnet, past a dusty Renault delivery truck with rust holes in the fenders. Houses flashed by on each side, then a church.

She was in the center of the town now. There had to be a police station or a post office, somewhere she would be safe.

Where?

She sped by a small plaza with trees and benches. A group of old men played *la petanque*. Should she stop and plead with them to help? Would they? Could they?

It was doubtful. She needed the police. Where were they?

Across the street she saw umbrellas, tables, chairs on the sidewalk. A cafe. Not a police station, but it was something. There would be a telephone.

Move Linda.

Would Pedru walk into a cafe in broad daylight and kidnap her?

Probably.

In the hometown of his mortal enemies, the family of Vezzani?

Maybe not.

She dismounted and glanced through plate glass window. Men sat at formica-topped tables, playing checkers, drinking coffee. Corn paper cigarettes dangled from their lips.

She rushed inside, inhaled the odors of stale tobacco and last night's Pastis. She hurried across the room, leaned against the bar, practically embraced it.

"Excuse me," she said in French.

The bartender had his head down, arranging bottles. He looked up. A wry smile appeared on his face.

"The usual?"

Hal Junior?

"My American cousin. Fancy seeing you here. On the Fourth of July, too." He twisted the end of his bushy mustache. "White wine, isn't it?"

"*You?*"

"Me."

"What are *you* doing *here?*"

He chuckled. "That's what I should be asking you. You're in Soccia, the family hometown. This is the family business, Little Lily. How did you get loose?"

"I don't believe it."

He spoke in Corsican to a young man who stood by the cash register. The young man picked up a telephone and dialed.

Hal Junior cocked his thumb. "Just told Robertu here to call grandpa and tell him to relax. You wiggled loose on your own."

"This is incredible."

"You just wouldn't heed the little warnings I gave you, would you?" Hal Junior shook his head. "Vezzani women always were hard-headed."

"Warnings? What warnings?"

"The sign on your door in Calvi. The close call with the car in Baltimore."

"*You?*"

"Me."

"You bastard."

"Calm down. It was for your own good. A bit unorthodox, but if you had paid attention, you and everyone else would be lot better off."

"What do you mean?"

"I mean, coming to Soccia was a dangerous thing for you to do. In fact, I'd say you found that out."

"And the car? The attempted hit and run?"

"It was only to scare you. I had no intention of hurting anyone. I just wanted you to stop asking all those questions."

"I don't believe it. Why didn't you just tell me, face to face?"

"Didn't want to have to get into it, to explain everything."

"Explain everything? Explain everything about my mother, for instance?"

"About your mother in particular. I didn't want to have to explain how Grandpa married her off to a Ghjuvanni, and how that little maneuver backfired on the family. Big time. I want you to know I had nothing to do with it. I was in Vietnam at the time."

"Married her off? How could he marry her off? She was *already* married."

"Grandpa never approved of Robbie—refused to recognize the marriage. He was a damn WASP." Hal Junior shrugged. "He didn't approve of my father either, so don't feel like the Lone Ranger. Having

222

that in common was the main reason my mother let your mother live in our house."

"This is incredible. Where is she? Where *is* my mother?"

"Where the Ghjuvannis are. In Corte, I guess."

Corte? *Columba!*

Columba was her *sister?*

Suddenly, an explosion shook the building. Plate glass shattered, followed by an earsplitting *bang! bang! bang! kaboom!*

Hal Junior ducked out of sight. Linda spun around. Men dove to the floor in slow motion. She turned. A spider web of cracks appeared in the mirror behind the spot where Hal Junior just had stood. A long sliver fell toward her. She stepped out of the way, and it shattered into a million tiny shards.

Through a jagged hole in the storefront window she saw a dark blue Jaguar speed away. Linda was the only one in the cafe left standing, the only sound a ticking clock. One by one the men lifted their heads. One by one, they got to their feet. One by one they brushed themselves off and began to speak. A murmur filled the room.

Linda stood on tiptoes and leaned over the bar. Hal Junior peered up at her, his face a scowl. He scrambled to his feet.

"Those Ghjuvanni bastards."

"They're in a dark blue Jaguar," Linda said. "I saw them pull away. Pedru and Santu."

Hal Junior spoke to Robertu in Corsican, who pulled a rifle from under the bar. The two of them ran out the door.

Linda followed.

Robertu got behind the wheel of a dusty green Mercedes. Hal Junior took the passenger's side.

She shouted, "Wait!" and climbed in back.

Tires squealed.

"That way, toward Corte," she said.

Robertu ran through the gears with the accelerator pressed to the floor. They whizzed past donkeys, bicycles, delivery trucks, but the dark blue Jag was so far ahead they lost sight of it. Linda doubted that they would catch up. She began to relax, and to think.

"There's something I want to know. The close call in Baltimore, did you use Gloria's car?"

Hal Junior glanced at her. "Yeah. I borrowed it for the evening. Not the first time she let me use it. Really pissed off my mom when Gloria presented her with a bill. Gave me hell, I can assure you."

They sped around a tractor pulling a wagon and up a hill. Linda felt an uncomfortable lift in her stomach as the Mercedes cleared the crest and plunged down the other side. She thought she caught a glimpse of the blue Jaguar a couple of hills ahead. Maybe they would catch up.

The car picked up speed on the downhill slope, slammed into a curve and skidded sideways toward a truck hauling livestock. The driver laid on the horn. Linda closed her eyes and prayed.

The horn changed pitch.

Thank God.

They skidded around one curve after another, almost crashed or left the road a dozen times. Linda wished to heaven she had not followed her impulse to come along, but she could do nothing now except hang on and pray.

Before long the Mercedes was within twenty yards of the Jaguar, closing fast. The Jag took a curve to the right. A pistol emerged from the passenger window.

A puff of smoke. A crack.

The electric window slid down on Hal Junior's side of the Mercedes. Air rushed in. He pushed the barrel of the rifle into the wind. His arms, shoulders, his head followed. He aimed, fired. A hole appeared in the rear windshield of the Jag.

He fired again.

The Jag slammed into another right hand curve. The pistol came out of the passenger window. A series of puffs and cracks followed in rapid succession until what sounded like the smack of a baseball into a catcher's mitt jolted Linda. The windshield of the Mercedes shattered as she dove to the floor.

She felt a violent rumble and heard a bump, bump, bump, bump. They were spinning.

She felt a jarring thud, saw stars. Blackness closed in until there was nothing.

Then there was light. Piercing red light.

A sharp, loud noise. Another.

Someone was talking. Talking.

Talking to her?

Was she dead? Was this what it was like? Funny. She didn't remember it being this way. Didn't someone, a guide or an old friend, come for you?

She could see something—something round and blurry. Two black holes. Black holes a few inches apart.

A face?

Yes, it was a face—distorted, out of focus—but a face. Someone was standing over her, leaning close.

She blinked, tried to bring the image into focus. A grin. Yellow teeth. Rotten breath, stubble.

"Wake up *putain*. Now is not the time to sleep." He shook her, slapped her. "We have a room waiting for you in Corte. This time you will not escape."

He pulled her from the Mercedes into the sunlight. She leaned against him, caught herself, blinked.

"The others?" she said. "Where are they?"

"Dead. Oh, they were still breathing when we arrived, but now they have bullets through their brains. You are less fortunate." Pedru nodded toward the Jaguar. " Move."

He opened the back door, took her arm, shoved her in. The black barrel of his gun loomed large as he climbed in after her.

"You are very resourceful, for a woman." He smiled. "You even stole the little motor scooter. Quite clever. We underestimated you. It will not happen again."

He said something in Corsican to Santu, who turned the key and started off.

Pedru chuckled. "What a wonderful day. What good fortune. Two Vezzani men dead, their cafe in shambles, and the granddaughter of Tino Vezzani in our hands." He slapped his knee. "Grandfather cannot deny my wishes now." He lowered the gun, leaned toward her, put his free hand on her thigh and rubbed. "We will have some fun, you and I, before you depart this earth." He puckered his lips, made kissing noises.

Linda slid her hand into the pocket of her jacket. The small nickel-plated pistol Columba had given her was where she'd left it.

She felt her finger on the trigger.

Should she? All she had to do was point and squeeze.

But, *kill* a man?

Good God, Linda, he intends to rape and kill you. He told you himself. Pull the trigger, for the love of Pete.

Could she? Did she have the guts?

She was half Corsican, wasn't she? She had the passionate blood of this island coursing through her veins. Didn't she?

Yes, but she was spirit, he was spirit. Behind the veil they were one.

Uh-huh. And if you don't do something quick, your spirit will be out one more body to inhabit. Kaput. No more receiver for your frequency.

She pulled the trigger three times.

His body jerked. His eyes grew wide as he raised his gun. She reached out, pushed it to the side. It discharged with a deafening crack. The car swerved. Linda felt air rush in through the window behind her head as Pedru twisted, writhed. His gun dropped to the floor.

She leaned toward the front seat, pressed the muzzle of her pistol to the back of Santu's neck and picked up Pedru's gun with her free hand. "Stop the car. Pull over to the side and give me the keys. It's time for you to get out and walk, you little creep."

As you grow in consciousness toward the higher levels,
you no longer identify the essence of you with your
body, your worldly status, your programming, or
your rational mind-stuff. You deeply experience
your essence as being pure Conscious-awareness
that just watches the drama of your life as it is
acted out on the myriad stages of the world.

Ken Keyes, Jr.
Handbook to Higher Consciousness

Twenty-Four

It was afternoon before Linda was able to sit at a telephone and make the calls needed to track down Rick. She almost could not believe her ears.

"Rick, is it *really* you?"

"Linda! You can't know how wonderful it is to hear your voice. I've been worried sick."

"*You've* been worried?"

"Of course. I had no idea what happened. Where did they take you? Are you okay?"

"I'm okay, Rick. But it's a long, complicated story. One that can wait until we're together. Just let me say that no matter what happens now, I believe we will be together for the rest of our lives, including those on the next plane. The question is, how are *you?*"

"Bruised. Black and blue from the neck down. But the doctor says there are no internal injuries, nothing serious he can find. He's going to let me out of here tomorrow."

"I should be there, maybe by noon, if everything goes according to plan."

"Did you find your mother?"

She hesitated. "I found out *where* she is, but I haven't seen her yet. I'm going to try tonight. If all goes well, I'll be back in Calvi by tomorrow. Around lunchtime."

"Great. I should be out of the hospital by then."

"Meet me at the hotel?"

"You bet."

"And the *Comte de Nice*, what time does it sail?"

"Now you're talking—sails at five o'clock sharp. I'll reserve a first class cabin. A few days on the Riviera will do wonders for these bruises."

"I could be held up. If I don't make it to Calvi before four o'clock, meet me at the boat. Okay?"

"I'll be there with a magnum of champagne. Iced. And your luggage as well as mine."

Linda replaced the handset of the old black telephone. She stood and went to the room they had given her, laid down on the bed and stared at the ceiling. She was exhausted and closed her eyes. She must block out the horror of the morning, sleep. She needed to be in top form to do what she must do when evening came.

And sleep she did. When Linda awoke, her body was rested and she was able to think clearly. No doubt remained that what she had decided earlier was the right course.

She dressed and went down the stairs. She entered a room with a twenty-foot ceiling and a fireplace big enough to roast a wild boar. The floor was stone, the furniture dark, heavy wood. The carpets were worn, threadbare orientals in deep red and brick. Candles blazed atop stands on and around two closed caskets, one of which contained the body of Hal Junior and the other, Robertu Vezzani.

Mrs. Pritchard, dressed totally in black and wearing a small round hat and a veil that covered her face, sat in a chair moaning softly. Linda touched her gently on the shoulder. "Thank you, Tante Annunciate. Thank you for the telephone and for the use of the car, the clothes—"

Mrs. Pritchard took her hand and cupped it. "We have mistreated you, my dear." Her voice trembled. "I begged Tino not to force your mother to marry the Ghjuvanni heir so many years ago. But what do we women ever have to say? The men never listen." She released Linda's hand. "When you returned I was afraid, afraid of what you would do if you discovered . . . ah, but now my worse fears have come to pass and it is not your fault. It is the men. They will never learn."

"It is time for me to go."

Mrs. Pritchard looked up, seemed to regard Linda for the first time. "The clothes of mourning." She shook her head. "They are all too common in this sunny land of ours."

Linda nodded. She could not see Mrs. Pritchard's face through the gauze of her dark veil, but she could imagine that tears streamed from her eyes.

The old woman said, "I am sorry that you will not be here for the wake."

"My apologies. But I have a pressing matter to attend to, as we discussed."

Linda left by the front door, walked past a group of mourners who were coming up the lane. She reached the small Renault and turned to look at the mansion. Pedru had been correct. It was not as impressive as the ancestral home of Ghjuvanni. But it was impressive nonetheless: massive stone walls, a peaked roof of black slate, French doors that opened onto balconies.

She opened the car door, hiked up the long black dress and climbed behind the wheel.

She gave the mansion a last look. Not as impressive perhaps as that of Ghjuvanni, but not far from it. Perhaps even comparable to the ancestral home of Cheswick.

She rotated the key and pressed the starter button. The engine turned over once, twice—came to life.

It was difficult to comprehend the depth of irony, almost impossible to fathom, that the head of each side of her family had so strongly disapproved of the other. The matriarch of the aristocratic family of Cheswick, and the patriarch of the proud and noble family of Vezzani. In their zeal they had succeeded in destroying their own children. Now the very existences of the families they loved so dearly were in peril. They had remained enemies to the end, enemies who had never even met. Enemies who felt their way of life was the right way, the only way worth living. Yet both had come into this life from the same

230

place and would so return. They would return to the unseen realm behind the physical world, the true home of all members of humanity. For one family or race or nationality to try to destroy another was utter tragedy and sheer folly, one limb of an oak attempting to cut off the other branches. Unless they woke up and stopped, the entire tree would be destroyed.

She pushed in the clutch and slipped the shift lever into first. She must get going. It would take over an hour to reach her destination.

Linda parked the Renault in a long line of parked cars and got out. Her heart began to pound when she caught sight of the imposing mansion rising up behind the stone wall. She adjusted her hat and her veil. It was warm and this outfit covered practically every inch of her, but the discomfort was well worth it. No one would recognize her.

She felt an impulse to move ahead, but held back, waited, hovered by the gate until a small group of mourners came her way. She fell in, walked in their company between stately stone pillars, across the cobbled courtyard to the massive wooden door. A man stepped back so they could enter. In the large room down the hallway, Linda caught a glimpse of the open coffin. She followed the others toward it.

One by one, they filed past. Dozens of candles in golden candelabra cast a yellow-orange glow. Even so, Pedru's face looked pasty white. Pale hands were folded across his chest. Black hairs were visible on the backs of his fingers and around his wrists. Reflections of flames sparkled and danced on greasy, jet black hair.

She told herself that he was a pathological killer, a killer who had deserved to die. Why, then, did she feel sorrow and regret?

She fought to hold back tears, slipped a hand with a handkerchief underneath her veil. He had deserved exactly what he got. It had been the only way she could have avoided a horrible and humiliating death. Yet, he had been a human being and she had taken his life. She would always have to live with that.

She stepped forward, closer to the head of the coffin. Those in front paid last respects, crossed themselves, moved on. It was Linda's turn. She stared at his pallid skin, at the flattened nose, at the five o'clock shadow he wore even in death, felt a salty taste in her mouth and the sudden impulse to vomit.

Dear Lord Jesus, forgive me for what I've done . . . and for not feeling worse about it than I do.

She turned away and scanned the room. It was filled with veiled women in black and men in dark suits. They sat on folding chairs. Her mother would be among them, but where? Which one? How would Linda know her?

Her eyes stopped on a young woman. Columba?

Judging by the slim build, it must be. No other woman in the room was so petite. Linda took the adjacent seat.

Groans, moans, the soft sobbing of women provided constant background noise. Now and then, someone would cry out in anguish, but very little conversation took place among the mourners. Linda sat in silence for a long time. Finally, she decided to risk it. Softly she said, "Columba? Is that you?"

"Yes?"

"Do not be alarmed. Sit quietly. It is Linda."

"What are you doing here? They will *kill* you."

"Your mother's name is Vanina, correct?"

"Yes, but—"

"I must see her. Which one is she?"

Columba was silent. Then, "She is not here."

"Not here? But she lives in this house. Will she come later? Will she be at the funeral in the morning?"

Silence. Then, "She does not leave her room. Ever. She refuses."

Linda let this thought sink in. "Where is it?" she said. "Which room is hers?"

"You cannot go there. Certainly not now. Anyway, she will not see you. She sees no one except me."

A hundred thoughts and feelings ran through Linda's mind: the dread of being caught, the uneasiness of having her mother so near but not knowing where, the curiosity to know more about her half-sister, the wondering what she would do when she came face to face with her mother. She tried to sort them, to stop each one in its tracks and analyze it in an attempt to calm her cluttered mind, but this effort only intensified the anxiety she felt. She tried to shut down her thoughts and to find the quiet place at the center of her being. She breathed in and out, focused on her breathing, felt her pulse settle into a slow, regular rhythm. This helped, though occasionally the moans and the cries of anguish of the people in the room broke through and demanded her attention.

She opened her eyes and watched the candles flicker. She studied Pedru's profile, his flattened nose, and she thought: *This is my only chance. This is it. I've got to go for it.* "Please do not react to what I am about to say, Columba," Linda said softly. "Sit in silence. Will you promise me?"

"Yes."

Linda took a breath. "I am her daughter. You are my sister, my half-sister. She was married in Baltimore four years before she was brought here to marry your father. I must see her. It is extremely important. Not idle curiosity."

Columba did not speak for thirty seconds, which seemed much longer. An eternity.

At last she said, "What is your father's name?"

"Robert Cheswick. People called him Robbie. He is dead."

"And did they call you Little Lily?"

"Yes."

"It is as I suspected. She says she sees him, and you. She talks to both of you—often."

"Talks to us? I do not understand."

"They say that she is crazy. Perhaps it is so."

"Will you help me? Will you help me see her?"

Columba seemed to be thinking. Finally she said, "It can do no harm. Perhaps seeing you, seeing you grown, an adult, perhaps it will help her understand the lie she lives."

"How shall we do it?" Linda said. "Can we slip away?"

"Not now. When the others leave to take Pedru to the cemetery, we will stay behind."

Linda sat in silence. It was going to be a long night but it would be worth it. Uncle William might be in for a whopper of a surprise after all. He and his lawyers were due in court day after tomorrow.

Eventually, in spite of the nap she'd taken, Linda nodded off.

She was jarred awake by the shuffling sounds of chairs as they scrapped against the floor, and the murmur of people softly talking.

The funeral had begun.

The pall bearers lifted the coffin. One of them was Santu.

They carried it along the hallway toward the front door. Mourners fell in behind, two by two. Linda and Columba held back, brought up the rear. Before they reached the hallway, Columba turned and motioned for Linda to follow. They climbed the stairs, reached a landing, turned down one hallway, then another. Finally, they came to a large, rough hewn wooden door. Columba pulled off her veil and hat. Linda did the same.

Columba knocked. *"Maman?"*

"Yes, Columba?" The words were French.

"May I come in? I have someone with me, Maman. It is—" Columba looked at Linda, waited.

"It is Lily, Maman," Linda said. "Little Lily."

The door swung open. The blank spot in Linda's memory where her mother should have been filled up and out like a time lapse motion picture of a flower unfolding. Maman was dressed in the style of Corsica but she was still slim and perky. Yet she was older, much older. Her jet black hair was streaked with white. Her face was lined. Crow's feet sprayed from the corners of her dark brown eyes.

Maman smiled one of her kind, loving smiles. "Little Lily, where have you been? Playing in the garden again?"

"I've, I've been looking for you," Linda said.

"Now, now. I've been here all the time. You know that."

Linda glanced at Columba, who gave a little shrug.

Maman walked toward French doors that opened to a balcony. Linda followed.

Her mother leaned against a banister. "Your father will be home soon, Lily. Better pick up your toys."

What was going on? "Maman, you haven't seen me in more than twenty years. I'm Linda. I'm a grown woman. I don't have toys."

"Don't speak nonsense, darling. You'll be grown soon enough."

Maman seemed to enjoy the bright sunshine. She angled her face toward it, closed her eyes, inhaled. She opened them and her face lit up. "Why, Mr. Pritchard has planted azaleas over Stuffy's grave."

"Stuffy? Who is Stuffy?"

"Your cat, darling." Maman turned to Linda, a question in her face.

234

"You haven't forgotten Stuffy, have you?"

Did Maman think she was in Baltimore? The Baltimore of twenty years ago? Stuffy, a cat, was buried under the azaleas?

Wait—her cat was buried under the azaleas? Was that why the view from the bedroom window affected her so?

"Maman, this is Corsica, not Baltimore. I'm not a little girl, I'm a grown woman."

A puzzled look. "What are you saying, dear?"

"Don't you remember? Your father and Victor . . . they made you come to Corsica. They made you marry—" Linda looked at Columba for help.

"Paulu. My father's name was Paulu."

Maman stared at Linda with a blank look on her face. "But what about your father, dear?"

"He died, he died in Vietnam." Linda winced. "Sorry to blurt it out like that. I guess you didn't know."

"Vietnam? Where? Is that in Indochina? He told me of his time in Indochina."

"You seem confused, Maman," Linda said.

Maman laughed. "Lily—so precocious. You do put on such airs."

Linda glanced at Columba, who wore a look of resignation. There had to be some way to get through.

"Maman," Linda said. "What happened in the basement? The basement of Tante Annunciate's house?"

Maman frowned. "I do not like the basement."

"That's where they came for you, isn't it? Papa and Victor. They grabbed you, took you away with them."

The color drained from Maman's face. She turned toward the garden, leaned against the banister, pointed to a Mediterranean laurel. "The rhododendron soon will be in bloom."

"Do they treat you well here, Maman? Do you like it here? Or, would you rather come with me to the United States?"

Maman rotated her head until her eyes met Linda's. Her expression became stern. "They leave me alone, thank God. It is all that I ask of them and they do it. They leave me well enough alone."

"There's a word, Maman. There's a word for your condition. It's called denial. *Denial.* Denial of *reality.* But there's no reason for you to

235

hold on to reality, is there? As long as you're completely out of touch, as long as you're off in your own little world, they leave you alone—and that's exactly, precisely, what you want. Isn't it?"

"Your father comes here, you know, here to this very place. He comes to visit me."

"I don't believe you're really as nuts as you appear, Maman. There's no reason to pretend with me. I'm not one of them. I came here to see if I could help."

Maman's nostrils flared. "How dare you speak to me with such insolence? Who do you think you are? The life I've lead is not a life that I have chosen, but I've done the best with it under the circumstances. At least I escaped from the beast they paired me with." She folded her arms across her chest.

Linda grappled for words that wouldn't come.

Then Maman's expression softened, her eyes grew round, and a tear rolled down her cheek. She dropped her head to her chest, fell to her knees and began to sob. "Oh Lily, Little Lily, why should you understand? I loved my life in Baltimore, I loved you and I loved your father. I was devastated when they brought me here. Thoroughly, utterly devastated."

Linda moved to her, put her hand on her shoulder. "Please, Maman, I only want to help. Please let me."

She looked up with eyes that grew narrow. "Do you mean it?"

"Of course, I mean it."

Maman's eyes took on a pleading look. "Did you also mean it when you said that you would take me to America?"

"Of course—absolutely. But we will have to leave immediately, while they're still at the cemetery."

"And Columba? Would you bring Columba?"

"Of course I will bring Columba."

Her mother stood. Her face lit with joy. Suddenly, wrinkles appeared in her brow, and her mouth turned downward. She shook her head. "A dream. A fantasy. I have hoped so long, dreamed so long of leaving here, leaving this prison. These four walls. It has been my obsession. So much so that I do leave here in my mind. I go to the only other place I know." She stared at the garden. "And now, now you come. You find me here. For a moment it seemed possible." Maman

236

turned to Columba. "It did seem possible for a moment, didn't it?" She turned until her eyes met Linda's. "But it is *not* possible. How would we *live*? *Where* would we live?" She shook her head. "It is cruel but it is as you say. It is reality."

Linda smiled. "Believe me, it is possible. It is absolutely possible. There will be enough, no, there will be *plenty* for you to live on and a beautiful place for you to live if you choose. All I ask is one small favor in return. I do not believe you will consider it to be too much for me to ask." Linda looked at her watch. "It will take some time to explain the details and we must hurry. But you can believe me. What I am telling you is *true.*"

Linda down-shifted into third and steered the Renault around a curve that hugged the jagged coast. She pressed the accelerator to the floor. The little car struggled up a grade until the crest was reached.

She had been worried that they would find Maman and Columba missing and come after them, though Columba had assured her they would not be missed. No one ever came to see Maman, in fact purposefully avoided doing so, and it would be assumed that Columba was in the room with her, the two of them consoling one another in the grief they must feel for the loss of a father and husband.

Nevertheless Linda felt elation when she glanced in the rearview mirror. It were as though a weight had lifted. Whatever they had or had not done, it appeared that no Ghjuvannis had followed them to Calvi. The city was not far ahead and there had been no sign of anyone in pursuit. She could now breathe freely.

She took in the beauty of her surroundings and it occurred to her that the summer sky in Virginia was never as clear or blue. She breathed in salty air mixed with spice from the maquis and gazed at the razor-sharp horizon.

"Corsica is a beautiful country," Linda said.

Maman was in the front passenger's seat. Columba sat in back.

Maman said, "It is true that Corsicans are very proud of the beauty of this island. But when I look at the sea, I see prison walls."

"It is like the prison island of the count of Monte Cristo," Columba said.

"You both will be free. In the United States, you both will be free to live whatever life you choose."

"I am not sure I will know how to begin," Maman said. "For me, it will be overwhelming."

"Alas," Columba said. "When you have never known freedom, you cannot run to it with open arms."

"Spend some time at Live Oaks. Spend some time getting used to the idea of freedom."

Maman smiled and shook her head. "It is ironic, is it not, that I will be the owner? Robbie was unable to take me there because of his mother. She was the owner then. Yes, I find it to be very ironic."

Linda nodded. Indeed it was.

She drove straight ahead for another quarter of a mile, then brought the car to a stop at a traffic light.

The light turned green. She felt a flutter. She was going to see Rick.

Her pulse quickened as she maneuvered along a street crowded with pedestrians, motorbikes, and cars. She edged onto the sidewalk to pass by a delivery truck and brought the Renault to a halt in front of the Grand Hotel, tugged on the hand brake, searched the crowd.

His tousled mop of straw-colored hair stood out. He rose from a bench, one hand aloft. A smile lit his face. His eyes sparkled. She was out of the car. Horns blared as she darted across the street, rushed to him, threw her arms around him. Her heart pounded. "I didn't know—how could I? How could I know how thrilling this would be?"

"Linda, Linda . . . easy . . . easy . . . easy, my love, easy on the ribs."

She pulled back, laughed. She was giddy, dizzy, incredibly lightheaded. She looked at him through eyes blurry with tears. "Oh, Rick, I'm sorry . . . sorry . . . I forgot, forgot for a moment about your bruises."

His face came to her and they kissed. Her body melted into his. Their beings merged. She was totally unbounded, at one with the eternal, completely lost in bliss.

On and on the kiss continued until at last she came up for air. His face, those eyes filled her vision. She wiped her cheek with the back of her hand. Found it drenched with tears of joy. "Am I acting like a jerk? Too sappy? I'm sorry, I really am, but it's just—"

"For everything there is a season," he said. "Now's a good one for sappy."

Something caught her attention and she turned. Columba and Maman were watching with wide grins. "Oh, dear, where are my manners? Rick, here are a couple of people I'd like you to meet."

Linda wanted to place a call to the United States immediately but couldn't because of the six-hour difference in time. Instead, they all had lunch at an outdoor cafe by the harbor. Afterward, Linda did place a call to Rod Wells of the law firm of Carter Wells Randolph & Studwick.

"Linda, how are you? *Where* are you?"

"I'm in Calvi, Corsica, Rod, and I've got good news—bad news for Uncle William. I found her."

"You *found* your mother?"

"That's right. She's with me now. We're going over to Nice for a few days and then back to the States. She's anxious to claim her inheritance."

"Well, I'll be. You aren't kidding, are you? I never thought you'd actually pull it off."

"Do I need to put something in writing and fax it to you, Rod? Do you need it notarized? I've located an attorney's office here in Cavi. I'll be happy to sign a statement or whatever, have it notarized and fax it to you."

There was a short pause as if he were thinking. "That won't be necessary, Linda. After all, I am your family lawyer and I do of course believe you. Your word is good enough."

"Thanks, Rod. Guess you'll have to cancel that court date. Tomorrow, isn't it?"

"Man oh man. I'm not looking forward to breaking this news to William."

"Oh Rod, there is one more thing. When you're putting all the papers together?"

"Yes?"

"My mother isn't comfortable when it comes to legal matters, business dealings and the like. She wants me to handle all that sort of thing. She asked me to have papers drawn up giving me full power of attorney on her behalf."

"Well, well. Now isn't that interesting? It looks as though things are working out just fine for you, Linda."

"You can say that again, Rod."

"Have a great time in Nice, Linda. And don't worry about a thing. Everything will be in order when you get here."

"Thanks, Rod. I'll be in touch."

Linda hung up, opened the door of the booth and stepped into the bright sunshine. She put her arm though Rick's.

As they walked, her gaze swept across the dark blue water of the harbor to the bright white sand of the beach. It slipped past green trees to purple mountains in the distance. This was truly a beautiful land and she could understand the passion that the Corsican people felt for it. She recognized that same passion in herself for the place she had been raised. But she knew now she was no more Corsican than she was English. The opposing sides had come together in the drama of this life to show her that she was neither and both at the same time. It had been an unforgettable experience. She was all. She was herself. She was spirit, spirit that had manifested as Linda Cheswick. Spirit that belonged to a land called earth.

Live Oaks represented earth in this life of hers. In this life, Live Oaks was home. There would be times of course when she would live apart from it. She might go for long stretches when her only contact would be for a few days. Even so, Live Oaks was and would remain the place from which she sprang. It would always be the one spot that she called home. Eventually the deed would say that it was hers, but she would know that the deed would not tell the truth. The truth was just the opposite.

Linda and Rick stopped. She gazed at the old walled city of Calvi. This would be the last time she would see it. But somehow, it didn't seem to matter. She was glad she had come here, glad she had gotten in touch with what had been out of reach. Glad to have experienced the lesson of this life. Now it was time to move on.

Columba and Maman walked to her. She and Rick joined with them and together they climbed the gangplank to the *Comte de Nice.*